D0408146

Skeleton at the Feast

Patricia Hall

Skeleton at the Feast

9/15/21

don't dels

didn't

go past

Ch 1

St. Martin's Minotaur
New York

www.minotaurbooks.com

ISBN 0-312-28208-7

First published in Great Britain by
Busby and Allison, Ltd.

First St. Martin's Minotaur Edition: January 2002

10 9 8 7 6 5 4 3 2 1

Chapter One

Michael Thackeray stood at the narrow window and gazed down at the deepening shadows in the quadrangle below and knew that he should not have come. It was not simply the fact that he had been hustled away from Bradfield for other people's convenience. It was not even the fact that Superintendant Jack Longley had lied without the slightest sign of embarrassment when he assured him that the course in Oxford would be good for his career. They both knew that very little would be good for his career with an inquest and an internal inquiry into the death of one of his officers hanging over his head. The deep unease he felt at returning by chance to his old college in Oxford went much deeper than that.

It had hit him full in the face, a particularly vicious squall from the past, as soon as he had turned into the arched stone gateway and signed in at the gloomy porter's lodge. The young man in a dark suit who had allotted him his room and handed him his keys could not possibly have known him. He had probably imagined the chill in his eyes, and guessed that even if it was real, it was no more than an automatic response to the wariness in his own. But its unwelcome matched his mood precisely.

In twenty years, it had never once crossed his mind to come back to Friddies, and as the ancient stone walls engulfed him and he made his way up the bleak and narrow staircase – not his own as a student but no different – to the set of rooms two flights up, and dropped his suitcase onto the narrow bed, he knew that his instincts had been right. The churning of his emotions doubled him up. He had hated the place then, and this inadvertent return would raise ghosts he would rather remained laid.

He had taken off his jacket and tie and flung open the narrow window in the hope of fresh air to take the taste of bile from his mouth. But the late summer Sunday evening was heavy and very still, the leaves of the ancient oak, which cast a dense black shade over the sparse grass of the quad, were motionless and a wisp of Oxford mist drifted between him and the dimly lit entrance to the chapel, where lights still glowed from the tall latticed windows. Thackeray started slightly as the first of the city's clocks began to strike eight, a clear note at first, soon joined hastily by others, deeper and more sonorous, sounding as if they did not wish to be left behind.

"Bloody bells," Thackeray muttered, recalling sleepless nights spent on tenterhooks waiting for the relentless chimes. "Fat chance of dreams, as I remember."

He smiled grimly and stepped back from the window alcove.

"Well, I suppose I'd better get on with it," he muttered to himself wondering if this was the first sign of the madness which, he recalled, had afflicted an alarming number of his contemporaries in this place, teachers and taught alike.

He pulled on a dark sweater over his shirt and glanced at the course programme. Supper on this first night, he read, was to be an informal affair in the buttery. The start of the university term was still a good four weeks away and there would be no undergraduates about. It seemed as if the course members, from police forces all over the country and abroad, recruited to learn about new approaches to crime, would have the facilities of St Frideswides pretty much to themselves. He was about to leave the chilly room, with its bare walls, empty bookcases and forsaken desk, when he was startled by a sharp double knock on the inner of the two oak doors which protected him from the rest of the college. Surprised, because as far as he was aware only the young porter knew that he had arrived, he opened the door and found himself face-to-face with the one part of his past that was not entirely unwelcome.

"I thought it must be you when I saw the name on the list of participants," said Hugh Greenaway, recently appointed master of St Frideswide's. "I asked them to let me know when you arrived." He held out a hand, which Thackeray shook warmly.

"Good God," Thackeray said. "I never expected to see you. I thought commercial ventures like this would be way beneath you."

"Which just goes to show how little you know about Oxford colleges these days," Greenaway said, with a wry smile.

"Congratulations, anyway," Thackeray said. "You've come a long way since we used to argue about the English Civil War."

"And you?" Greenaway asked. "I try to follow the careers of all the people I've tutored."

"That's a long story," Thackeray said evasively, though he knew that the cool grey eyes which had dissected not just his essays but, it had sometimes felt, his soul all those years ago, would not be fooled.

"Tell me over dinner," Greenaway said. "I thought you would rather eat with me than bother with the sort of buffet they're likely to lay on in the buttery."

"I'm flattered," Thackeray said. "There are far more eminent coppers than me on this course."

"But none so interesting, I think," Greenaway said. He glanced at Thackeray's sweater. He was wearing a dark suit and bright blue and gold silk tie. "No need to dress up. My housekeeper's left a meal for us at the Lodgings. Sounds a much grander place than it is, in fact. Looks elegant but it's as old and cold and draughty as most of these mediaeval slums. I rattle around in it like a pea in a drum." There had been a wife and family, Thackeray recalled, but evidently no longer.

"I'm amazed they elected you master if you feel like that," he said, recalling his slight sense of surprise when he had seen the announcement of the appointment earlier in the year. Greenaway, as a young history tutor, had always had an irreverent streak, which had slightly shocked the nervous young under-graduate from Yorkshire at their weekly sessions.

"Ah, well, thereby hangs a tale," Greenaway said. "Come on, I've got a bottle of decent claret decanted. I'll tell you all about it over a glass." Thackeray opened his mouth and then thought better of what he had been about to say and shrugged lightly. Greenaway's presence rekindled an old affection but the gulf of twenty years lay between them and he knew that it would not be possible to bridge it easily – even if he chose to try. He did not think that Hugh Greenaway would count him as one of the college's great successes.

Professor Hugh Greenaway, a mere two weeks into his appointment as Master of St Frideswide's College, now in its five hundred and ninety-ninth year, sprawled in his chair, jacket off and tie loosened, and watched his guest intently across his brandy glass. He was a small wiry man, dwarfed by Thackeray's height and bulk, his hair greying and fine lines around the eyes and mouth. But the eyes were as knowing and sharp as Thackeray remembered them, and there was still a humorous twist to the mouth, though he seemed to laugh less often than he used to.

They had lingered over a cold meal at the extensive mahogany dining table where the master had raised no more than an ironic eyebrow when Thackeray had refused wine.

"Occupational hazard?" he had asked gently, but had not pressed for the answer Thackeray did not wish to offer.

The talk over the meal had been general. Greenaway could still be amusing when he chose and so far he had chosen. A quick and ironic résumé of his academic career told his guest that he had remained ten years after Thackeray had graduated at Friddies. He had then moved on, in frustration at Oxford's traditional torpor, even when beseiged by England's 1980s' lust for loot at home and conquest in the South Atlantic, to a chair in New England. There he had lost a wife to a colleague but found the energy to produce the series of elegantly written and surprisingly popular books on the Stuarts and the English Civil War, which had consolidated his name academically.

"You still regard Oliver Cromwell as a national disaster, then?" Thackeray asked when they had settled into comfortable chairs in the drawing room, which was marginally warmer than the dining room. He had read Greenaway's reviews, if not his books.

"Think what anguish we'd have avoided in Ireland if James II had remained on the throne," Greenaway said. "I thought you were a Catholic? You must appreciate that."

"Was a Catholic, but always with an un-Irish suspicion of divine rights of any kind," Thackeray said shortly. "I guess I'm more my father's son than my mother's. Anyway, I gave all that up."

"And a lot else besides?" Greenaway surmised, and he suddenly looked his age, which, Thackeray guessed, must be nearer sixty than fifty. He wondered why he had come back from Massachusetts to take on a job which he did not seem to relish. He did not answer Greenaway's question. He had been aware throughout their meal that the master had been subtly fleshing out the events of the last twenty years of his own life without ever using anything so crude as a direct question. But he had the feeling as they settled over coffee that the direct questions were to come, though even with his long experience of the black arts of interrogation, he could not guess where his charming host was leading him.

The master sniffed his brandy appreciatively and then put his glass down on the coffee table in front of him.

"Of course, I've invited you here under false pretences," he said briskly. "I wouldn't expect a policeman of your seniority and experience not to have realised that by now."

"I'm here on a course," Thackeray said evenly. "I have a lot of problems back in Bradfield. My boss thought it was a good chance for me to get away for a bit."

"I know. I took the liberty of speaking to your chief constable after I noticed your name on the list of participants. We were at Cambridge together."

Thackeray's lips tightened.

"I thought you disliked that sort of networking," he said sharply. Greenaway acknowledged the criticism with a rueful smile.

"You were always far too sharp for a boy who had so many disadvantages in this place, I recall. Not much changes. I can only guess at the problems which have left you as a chief inspector when I would have expected you to have gone much further. I didn't invade your privacy by asking the chief constable about that."

"So why is a mere chief inspector being treated to a meal with the Master of St Frideswide's when I've no doubt you could have summoned the Home Secretary to dinner with a fair chance of his accepting?" Thackeray asked, with an edge of anger in his voice. "It's obviously not just for old time's sake."

"I'd be sorry if you thought it was not that too," Greenaway said. "But I did have an ulterior motive. I have a problem, which I thought you might be able to help me with. Not something I can take up officially with the police. But something I would like your professional advice on."

Thackeray leaned back in his chair and tried to relax. Just for a moment he had felt that old incoherent self-consciousness which had been his abiding emotion during his years at Frideswide's. Only on the rugby pitch and, imperceptibly in tutorials as Greenaway drew him out, had he felt able to break free of the defensive shell in which he had taken refuge as soon as he had realised how different he was, in background, in accent, in interests, from the almost completely and aggressively male, public school society to which he had gained admittance through what he still regarded as some gothic celestial joke.

St Frideswide's had been one of the most reluctant of the Oxford colleges to admit boys from state schools, and Thackeray guessed it was his sporting ability more than his admitted facility in examinations that had gained him admission a couple of years before the college had also grudgingly accepted its first tiny group of women students. With his broad northern vowels, his gauche manners and his complete ignorance of the world of southern boarding schools, he had felt just as alien as the women who had clustered for safety at a single table in a corner of the junior common room and walked the quads in pairs for self-protection in his final year.

And now Greenaway, who had been his salvation, wanted his help. And there was no doubt in either of their minds that Thackeray owed him and that dues were being called in.

"If I can help, I will," he said, without enthusiasm, consoling himself with the thought that if the course proved less interesting than he anticipated, Greenaway's ulterior motive might assist with the very necessary distraction he needed.

"I know it sounds absurd, but I'm missing one of my fellows," Greenaway said, spreading his hands wide in exaggerated despair. "An eminent scientist, tutor in chemistry, top man in his research field, apparently went walkabout months ago and has never been seen since."

"Have the local police made inquiries?" Thackeray asked cautiously.

"My equally eminent colleague Magnus Partridge says not. He was in charge of the college after my predecessor's unfortunately fatal final heart attack and throughout the typically leisurely appointment process which followed . . ."

"I remember Dr Partridge," Thackeray said, and his tone left little doubt that he would rather not remember the tutor in mediaeval literature.

"Yes, I expect you do," Greenaway said, with a slightly impish smile. "He was never the most popular fellow with the

11

undergraduates. He's senior tutor now but you'll be pleased to hear that he has generally been on the losing side of college arguments over the years – ever since I helped persuade them to admit women, in the teeth of his fanatical opposition."

"Did he not expect to become master?"

Greenaway's smile broadened into a grin, which was certainly not without malice.

"Oh, undoubtedly, yes," he said. "Particularly as he'd almost run the place during my predecessor's long decline. Fortunately, my colleagues were so determined to deny him that consummation that they came to Boston in the depths of a bitter New England winter and practically begged me on bended knee to return. Your Oliver Cromwell would have got on well with Magnus, I always think, so I suppose you could call my being here a sort of Restoration. Let singing and dancing be unconfined, so to speak. Though I'm not sure British academics or undergraduates can afford that sort of thing any more. And it's probably in breach of the college statutes. Most things are."

"And the man who's gone missing?" Thackeray asked, fascinated in spite of himself by the inevitable intrigue and jealousies of a closed community.

"His wife reported him missing, but there'd been some problems there, it seemed, some sub-Clintonesque drama in the senior common room apparently, so the police marked it down as a missing person, an abandoned wife, and did very little about it."

"And you think I could find out more?" Thackeray asked, sceptically. "I have to say it's a very long shot. Most people who want to disappear do so very effectively, and I'd guess an Oxford academic would devise a better plan than most. I'm only in Oxford for two weeks . . ."

"I know, I know," Greenaway said, draining his brandy and leaning back in his chair slightly wearily. "I just find it very irritating that the man should be able to walk out, not just on his wife and family but on a whole clutch of research students he was supposed to be supervising. There are actually draft chapters of kids' theses missing. Young idiots who gave him their computer discs and didn't keep back-up copies. And . . ."

He hesitated for a moment, controlling his evident anger and giving Thackeray a slightly sly sideways glance.

"You'll remember him of course. He was here as a post-graduate when you were an undergraduate. You must have played rugby with him . . ."

"Harrison," Thackeray said explosively. "One of the rugger buggers. I remember Mark Harrison." What he remembered was the heart-stopping thud and thump of muddy bodies in a ruck in which it was not always obvious whether kicks were coming from friend or foe.

"Playing rugby was one of the things which made it worth being here for me," he said. "But most of that team were bastards – racist, sexist, homophobic snobs, though I didn't know the words then. The sixties hadn't made much of an impact on my Arnedale comprehensive."

"They were still letting some of them in on their sporting ability then, when they thought I wouldn't notice," Greenaway said. "That's why we had such a high proportion of public school oafs. It was a disgrace. It's better now, believe me." He looked at Thackeray with a slightly sideways smile.

"I must admit, when I first met you I thought you were from the same mould – albeit with your northern vowels and that bloody great chip on your scrum half's shoulders. You've no idea what a relief it was to discover I was tutoring a rugger bugger who also had a brain."

"Aye, well, I was tough enough to survive the Harrisons of this world," Thackeray said, recalling the remembered satis-faction of settling scores with a well-aimed boot when the opportunity offered. "The people I was really sorry for were the girls you let in for that final year of mine. They had a rotten time."

13

"We really have made some progress since then," Greenaway said soberly. "After that young woman died. What was her name?"

"Elizabeth Selby," Thackeray said, so quickly that he knew he had given himself away.

"You knew her well?"

"Well enough." Thackeray tried to sound more non-committal than he felt.

"Was she a girlfriend? I never could decide."

"No, she wasn't," Thackeray said. "But those bastards killed her."

"Surely a tragic accident," Greenaway said quickly. "I was abroad at a conference when it happened but there was a thorough investigation."

"A tragic death, sure," Thackeray said. "But not an accident. And there was a thorough cover-up. You must know that. The inquest was a farce. Liz Selby's death was one of the things that made me decide to join the police. The whole thing stank to high heaven and I swore I'd not watch that again without being in a position to do something about it."

"Good God," Greenaway said. "I'd no idea that was why . . . You didn't come back for graduation did you? I remember now."

"I hadn't the stomach for it after what had happened that term," Thackeray said.

"So I was right to think you might be tempted to find Mark Harrison and persuade him to come back and face his responsibilities?"

"I just might," Thackeray conceded reluctantly, recognising how effectively he had been manipulated. "But not for old time's sake."

14

Chapter Two

Detective Sergeant Kevin Mower sat by Kelly James's hospital bed feeling sick and exhausted. The girl was barely conscious, her face bruised and swollen out of all recognition, her head wrapped in bandages like a mummy, a drip pulsing hypnotically into a vein in her arm. Her injuries, the hospital had assured the police, were not life threatening, but as she drifted in and out of either sleep or unconsciousness, the soporific combination of shock and sedatives meant that Mower's trip to the hospital to talk to her had been a waste of time.

He shrugged, ran a hand across his short cropped hair and got up to go. His eyes were like pools on which the light reflected back nothing but darkness. Like half of Bradfield CID, he had been dragged out of his lethargic Sunday morning tumble of duvet and tabloids by news that a young girl had been found half dead on waste ground near the deserted, litter-strewn, morning-after-the-night-before town centre.

"Let us know when she's fit to talk, will you?" he asked the nurse who was bustling about at the other end of the ward.

"Her parents are in the relatives room if you want to talk to them," the nurse said over her shoulder. "Lorraine James and Carl Hegerty. But I don't think they have the remotest idea where she was last night or who she was with. Makes you sick, doesn't it? Thirteen years old, would you believe?"

Mower had no difficulty in believing. Bradfield's pub and club scene, which had burgeoned over the last couple of years, constantly threw up a stream of twelve-year-olds in trouble at weekends, most of them girls in micro-skirts made up to look at least eighteen so they could sweet-talk their way past anyone's door policy. Usually they turned up in custody, drunk and hysterical, or in casualty, drunk and semi-conscious. Occasionally, it was worse. Kelly James was much worse.

Her mother, in jeans and a short denim jacket over a low-cut top and looking barely old enough to go to the pub herself, was sitting in the relatives room alone when Mower arrived. Her eyes met Mower's defiantly from under the black slash of mascara and a curtain of tousled blonde hair.

"He's gone out for a fag, her dad," she said.

"She's going to be all right," Mower said. "She was lucky."

"Lucky?" Lorraine James said. "Call that lucky? He raped her, didn't he?" She twisted her hands, with their chewed fingernails, together in her lap.

"We won't know that for sure until we can talk to Kelly," Mower said. "But the doctor thinks it's certain she had sex – willingly or not. And that's illegal at her age. Have you any idea who she was with last night?"

"She went off with Tracey and Cath, our Brenda's two, didn't she? I thought they'd be OK together. Look after each other, like." Under the streaked make-up her face was haggard and Mower could see bruising on her arm. She hurriedly pulled down the sleeve of her jacket when she caught his glance.

"And how old are Tracey and Cath?" Mower asked.

"Fourteen." The answer came back defiantly and Mower guessed that she too had been allowed the freedom of the streets at that sort of age. The family came from the Heights, the estate of flats which loomed over the western side of the town and whose demolition was eagerly awaited by its residents and even more fervently by its close neighbours.

"Does she have a boyfriend?" he asked, trying to keep his voice as neutral as it should be.

"Just lads from t'school she hangs round with. Nowt serious, like," her mother said.

"Names and addresses?" he said, taking out his notebook. "I'll need to talk to Tracey and Cath and anyone else she was with. What time were you expecting her home?"

Lorraine glanced away, wiping her mouth with a trembling hand and removing most of the lipstick.

"We weren't, really, like. We didn't tell her a time because we were going out ourselves, down t'Zodiac Club. We got in about two and went straight to bed. We were a bit pissed, to be honest. I never looked in her room. I just thought she were asleep, didn't I? It weren't till t'bobbies came round this morning that I realised she weren't there. We'd slept in, hadn't we? Sunday morning."

Mower took a deep breath to stave off another wave of nausea and made a meticulous note of the information he needed before he got up to go.

"We'll need to talk to Kelly as soon as she wakes up properly," he said. "Hopefully, she'll be able to remember what happened."

"Right," Kelly's mother said. She looked sideways at Mower as he opened the door.

"You don't think she'll get AIDS, do you?" she whispered. "You never know who does that sort of thing, do you?"

"She's a damn sight more likely to get pregnant," Mower said, and there was little sympathy in his eyes. "Did it never strike you that thirteen's a bit young to be swanning around the town on a Saturday night?"

He shut the door without waiting for an answer and strode swiftly out of the infirmary and across the town hall square where groups of Asian men in traditional dress were sitting gossiping under the cherry trees in the slanting rays of the afternoon sun. Mower had never felt much affection for this hilly little Yorkshire town, with its gothic Victorian centre, its narrow steep streets and sprawling suburbs and estates. He had come here several years before to get away from troubles of his own making in London, only to find now that he was being pursued by even fiercer demons than a disgruntled senior officer at Paddington Green with whose wife he had found some temporary and inadvisable amusement.

He strode into the main CID office at police headquarters, hung his jacket carefully on the back of his chair, loosened his tie and flung himself down at his desk, knowing that the eyes of the handful of colleagues in the room were folllowing his every move.

"What are people doing letting kids that age out on the streets at night?" he asked no-one in particular. "The hospital says her blood alcohol level was through the roof. She was wearing a mini-skirt up to her knickers and a top down to her belly-button. And then her parents are surprised when she gets raped."

"So it's her fault, is it, sarge?" said DC Val Ridley, blonde, contained and evidently angry.

"Oh, don't come all feminist with me, Val," Mower snapped. "If grown up women want to take chances, that's up to them. But this one's a child. She should have been tucked up in bed with her Barbie dolls instead of prancing about looking like one.

"This would happen just when the boss has buggered off to the dreaming spires and his replacement's not due till Tuesday. Anyway, the super's told us to get on with it and if we can get the little toe-rag who beat this kid half to death I dare say we'll get a few brownie points when the new DCI arrives."

At the end of a long and deeply frustrating day, Kevin Mower pushed his files carelessly into a heap on the edge of his desk and glanced around the empty CID office. The tense knot of anger that had gripped him for weeks had tightened all day. The attack on a thirteen-year-old, still too incoherent to talk about what had happened; interviews with her family and friends, all of whom denied any responsibility for her whereabouts as she had been allowed to make her way home apparently alone to the Heights, known locally as Wuthering, at two in the morning; the long list of "lads" her friends had named – or in many cases only half named – as contacts over a drink- and drug-fuelled evening, all now to be traced and interviewed; all this had twisted his guts like a vice.

He glanced at the phone. He had agreed in what he now regarded as a moment of weakness to meet Laura Ackroyd for a drink this evening. The date, if you could call a rendezvous with your boss's girlfriend a date, he thought grimly, had been a mistake from the start. After a day spent probing the meagre life and near-death of Kelly James, he thought it was more than either he or Laura would be able to put up with.

He had already turned down one invitation to the pub from DC Val Ridley, who had become suddenly solicitous for his welfare since the shooting in which DC Rita Desai had died. He had dismissed her curtly, and she had turned away quickly to hide the sudden rush of colour to her pale cheeks though she could not hide the flush as it spread to her neck beneath the short, straw coloured hair, and he cursed her for pushing him, and himself for his clumsiness. If only, he thought uncharitably as he watched her put on her jacket and leave the office without a backward glance, Val would accept that she had nothing to offer that remotely interested him.

The whole station had been devastated by what had happened to Rita and he knew he should not allow his own particular pain to spill its corrosive acid over other people. But the deep burning anger inside flared unexpectedly. He knew he could not control it and at times it frightened him with its sudden violence. He did not know how much longer he could go on.

He started as a burly figure appeared at the doorway and turned on the lights. Detective Superintendent Jack Longley nodded in his direction. He looked as if he had arrived straight from the golf course in light coloured slacks and a red sweater, which clung to his curves too closely. He seemed slightly out of breath and a thin film of sweat burnished his brow and balding crown.

"All right, Kevin?" Longley asked. "She's not dead then, this lass?"

"Not dead, sir," Mower acknowledged. "Not talking yet, though, so if she knows who did it, we're no wiser."

"Vicious bugger, though, by the sound of it?"

"Oh, yes," Mower said. "A real sweetheart. She's a slight kid. How the hell anyone took her for eighteen and let her into the clubs, I can't imagine."

"Time uniformed had another crackdown on underage drinking," Longley said. "They'll be serving Hooch to five-year-olds if we don't watch it."

Longley crossed the room and stood at one of the tall windows, watching the evening traffic drifting around the town hall square. He cleared his throat a couple of times and Mower winced, guessing that the superintendent was about to embark on one of his clumsy attempts at bringing succour to the troops.

"All right, then, are you, Kevin? Coping?" Longley said gruffly.

"Sir," Mower said, getting to his feet and slipping into his designer jacket.

"If you change your mind about taking some time off . . ."

"Thank you, sir, but no thanks," Mower said. "I'd rather keep occupied."

"Aye, well, my door's open if you want to talk . . ." Longley said with something like relief in his voice as he followed Mower to the door and switched the lights out on the empty office. "Good-night then, Kevin. Take care."

He's swallowed the bloody subordinate care manual whole, Mower thought cynically as he stormed down the stairs to the front office, only recalling as he pushed his way out of the main doors that he had not called Laura Ackroyd to cancel their meeting.

Laura was, as usual, the centre of attention as soon as she walked through the door of the Parrot and Banana, Bradfield's slightly tarty shot at a glass and chrome metropolitan

20

pub. In black jeans and a soft sweater somewhere between aubergine and plum, her slim, long-legged figure drew admiring glances even before she turned from the door to let the company take in the creamy oval face, the green eyes and the luxuriant copper hair which she had tied back loosely with a black ribbon.

"You doing anything tonight, love?" demanded one wit as she zig-zagged through the crowd of drinkers to the corner table where she could see that Kevin Mower was a good many drinks ahead of her.

"Nothing you could afford," she countered, to delighted cheers from the young man's mates. Kevin raised an ironic eyebrow.

"You don't look as if you're suffering from your suddenly single state," he said. "What can I get you?"

"Vodka and tonic," Laura said as she dropped into a seat and pushed several long filaments of curly hair away from her eyes. "I'm just pleased to get away from the Mendelsons' enviable but claustrophobic family life for a bit," she said. "I love their kids dearly, but they can get a bit much at the end of a long dull Sunday."

She watched him as he went to the bar to get her drink and was grieved by the uncharacteristic slump of the shoulders and, as he turned back, his strained expression before he caught her eye and made an evident effort to rearrange his features into a smile.

"So you've not found a new flat yet?" Mower asked.

"Nope. I've looked at the nineties post-modern shoe-box, the sixties utilitarian tack coming apart at the seams, and lots of Victorian conversions with black mould oozing from the chimney breasts. Nothing I'd put my worst enemy in so far."

"Can you really not go back to the old place?"

"I don't think so," Laura said soberly. "It wasn't just the place which got trashed, it was me too, in a way. It would never be the same again."

"So, are you setting up home with the boss properly this time?" Mower asked. Laura looked at him consideringly, and concluded that sharing her hopes in that direction was not the tonic which the sergeant so evidently needed. It would be pouring vinegar into an open wound, more likely, although she did not think that he had ever got so far as to discuss living arrangements with Rita Desai.

"I don't really know," she said non-commitally. "Did you go to Rita's funeral? I heard they'd released the body at last."

Mower shook his head.

"I don't think the family would have welcomed me. I was most definitely not the nice Indian boy they were looking for."

"Surely, you could have gone as a colleague?"

"I wasn't sure how much they knew about us. Not that there was much to know when it came down to it. A couple of dates, that's all." He stopped suddenly and Laura sipped her drink to give him time.

"Michael went," she said.

"He had no choice. The super had him in an arm lock."

"You blame Michael for what happened?" It was more statement than question.

"No," Mower said fiercely. "I blame the bastards who shot her."

"Well, you can be sure that Michael will blame himself enough for both of you," Laura said, with a bleak little smile. "You look exhausted, Kevin. Are you OK? Really?"

"I've been at work all day," he said, draining his Scotch convulsively. "A thirteen-year-old got herself attacked and probably raped last night." Laura's eyes widened.

"That'll be our front page tomorrow, will it? I'm sorry. I had no idea. Vicky and David's kids have kept me more than occupied all day. I've not heard the local radio."

"She's going to be OK. She'll probably be able to tell us which little yobbo did it when she wakes up."

Laura sighed and gazed into her glass.

"You can't let the bastards wear you down," Mower said, with an attempt at lightness.

"This time you have, though, Kevin, haven't you?" Laura said.

Chapter Three

Four hours of seminars on creative management and team building in the Old Library, a stodgy lunch in hall and the sight of Dr Magnus Partridge stalking the quadrangle like a elongated crow in his black gown, pushed Thackeray out of the narrow door in the wooden gates of St Frideswide's at five o'clock with a sense of relief. It was not, he thought, that the course did not promise to be interesting, or even useful: simply that his own preoccupations constantly caused his mind to drift away from the best efforts of the lecturers to capture his enthusiasm.

Like a reluctant schoolboy, he seized his freedom as soon as it was offered and even after taking a deep breath of petrol-perfumed air belching from the traffic stream in St Giles, he decided to walk across town anyway in the golden late afternoon sunshine. This city had always had a beguiling charm, he thought ruefully and he felt his heart lift as he made his way briskly through Radcliffe Square where James Gibbs' great dome and the paler spire of St Mary's thrust their masculine and feminine attributes towards a milky blue sky above golden trees. Even when he had felt most alien here, he had still been able to find comfort in the broad green meadows by the rivers and the unexpected mediaeval corners where traffic could not penetrate. Perhaps Jack Longley had been right to get him out of Bradfield after all, he thought.

From St Giles, where Friddies nestled in the lee of more prestigious though not necessarily as ancient colleges, to the side-street off the Cowley Road, which was his goal, was no more than a mile and a half's brisk walk. But it took him from the Oxford of bells and bikes, mellow stone and intellectual grandiloquence to the darker side of the city. Beyond the graceful arches of Magdalen Bridge and up the choked and fume-filled artery that led to the factories and sprawling industrial and housing estates of Cowley, he soon recognised the signs of a world he had barely been aware of as a student but with which he had become very familiar since: a swirling multicultural thoroughfare of large and small shops, pubs hovering on the edge of seediness, of swaggering young men, bustling bargain-hunters, chattering school students, derelicts who had made a small patch of green their own, weary mothers with push-chairs and toddlers, and always the traffic grinding out of town, filling the air with exhausted and exhausting gases and noise. This, he thought wryly, felt far more like home these days than the musty book-lined Old Library and the barbed courtesies of the senior commonroom.

Conway Street was not difficult to find. Just beyond a blank-windowed sex shop, which nudged up against a brightly painted emporium devoted to organic beans and pulses, a narrow one-way street lined with parked cars curved away in the direction of the more sedate and tree-lined Iffley Road. The Victorian terraced houses were narrow too, just a single window and a door opening directly onto the pavement on the street side. One or two of them were in the process of renovation, but most of them, lacking the charm of more picturesque Victorian villas with bay windows and cottage gardens close by, looked neglected, the window-frames peeling and the stucco patchy where the rain and wind had worked their way under the surface.

The door of number 25 had been treated to a recent coat of deep chestnut paint, but as Thackeray pressed the bell he could see that this was little more than a quick dab of lipstick on an otherwise raddled face. It did not disguise the decay beneath. He waited, and then rang again, at which the door was opened quickly.

"Yes?" The voice was sharp and unfriendly, the figure indistinctly female against a gloomy interior.

"Mrs Harrison?" Thackeray asked. "My name is Thackeray. The master of St Frideswide's asked me to come and see you." Slowly the door inched wider.

"I suppose you'd better come in," the voice said. Thackeray had to squeeze past as the woman pressed herself against the wall of the narrow hall. She closed the door behind him and he heard her lock and chain it again.

"In here," she said, leading him into the tiny front room and switching on the light rather than draw open the heavy curtains, which kept out all but a glimmer of the fading sunshine outside. The room was sparsely furnished with a single sagging sofa covered with a bleached quilt, a coffee table and a small portable television perched on a pile of books in the corner next to the boarded up fireplace.

"I'm Penny Harrison," the woman said as she turned to face her visitor and even in the inadequate light from the single naked bulb, which hung from the ceiling, he was shocked by her appearance. She was painfully thin and her hair was streaked with grey, although he guessed that she could not be much older than he was himself. But it was her face which held his appalled gaze until he tore his eyes away in embarrassment. Her eyes were dark and burned feverishly in a face as gaunt and pale as a skull. It was as if she had been reduced by pain or illness to a mere skeleton of herself. Astonishingly, she waved him to the sofa and smiled at him with some warmth.

"I remember you," she said in a low voice in which he recognised a trace of the north. "I remember you playing rugby with Mark. You won't recall, I don't suppose. Why should you? But I met him at Friddies, when he was a research student and I was a fresher. You were there too, weren't you? Though I can't remember your first name. But you came from Yorkshire, like me."

"Good Lord," Thackeray said, astonished. "You were one of the women, the first women . . . Hugh Greenaway never said . . ."

26

"No, well, he wouldn't, would he? We were a bit of an embarrassment, weren't we, the six of us? Me, Jan, Frances, Cath, Indira and poor Liz."

"Liz Selby," Thackeray said. He held out his hand. He could feel the bones of her fingers like a bundle of sticks in his own firm grip. "Michael Thackeray," he said. "I do remember you, all of you, vaguely. And I remember only too clearly what happened to Liz. I'm sorry, Mrs Harrison . . ."

"Penny, please," she said, sitting down beside him.

"It's all a long time ago," he said apologetically, knowing that he was not the only one on whom the past twenty years had taken their toll.

"So what are you doing at St Frideswide's after all this time?" she asked, with a directness which Thackeray found faintly alarming. "You haven't joined the staff, have you?"

"Hardly," Thackeray said. "I'm here on a course. But the new master was my tutor when I was an undergraduate and I bumped into him again last night. He asked me to come to see how you were . . ."

"Oh yes?" she said, with the faintest glimmer of amusement in her eyes and disbelief in her tone. "I'm sure there was a little more to it than that, Mr Thackeray, wasn't there? I always had Greenaway down as a charming but devious bastard."

"Surely not," Thackeray said mildly. "As fellows of St Frideswide's go, I found him one of the more straightforward."

"He's feeling guilty now, though, is he?" Penny Harrison did not sound as if she was much impressed by Thackeray's defence of his tutor.

"I'm not sure about that. What exactly do you think he might be feeling guilty about?" he prevaricated.

Just for a second, Penny Harrison looked as though she might be about to laugh, but in the end she contented herself with a slight smile, which lit up her pale face and reminded Thackeray that at eighteen she must have been the slightly plump and pretty girl with a shock of long dark hair loose to her shoulders he could dimly recall. He had never entirely sorted out the female freshers in his own mind, conscious of them in their bright tops and flares as a flutter of butterflies amongst the dull, male and evidently threatening moths who had made the college their exclusive preserve for so many centuries.

"Well, I suppose the guilt may be the college's perhaps rather than Greenaway personally," she said. "He was away at the time of Liz's death and had the sense to get out completely in the end, so I suppose he could claim a degree of innocence after all this time. But where would you like me to begin on the sins of commission and omission of the rest of them? Their neglect of the girls they admitted in '75 without any thought or preparation? The suicide of Liz Selby? The lack of a single female member of staff we could turn to when all that was going on? Their refusal to discipline those yobs in the rugby team who tormented Liz to death? And of course it all went on long after I graduated, long after Greenaway took himself off to the States."

"You still think it was suicide, not an accident?" Thackeray asked quietly.

"I remember now. You thought she'd been pushed didn't you? I wouldn't have put it past one of those thugs but on balance I always thought she'd jumped. The girl was distraught. I'm not sure why, but it was something to do with a man and she was in a terrible state those few days before she died. But you know Oxford. It wouldn't look good for the college, would it, if one of the first women they let in after nearly six hundred years of unmitigated misogyny decided to jump off the chapel tower? So she fell, didn't she? With profuse apologies from the master to the coroner about the poor state of the ancient balustrade and warnings to students not to take risks after imbibing . . . It was all another of Oxford's little fairytales, all that. Pure Lewis Carroll. All done with mirrors. Just like Alice in Wonderland. And the same hard core of perversity underneath."

"And I thought *I* hated the place," Thackeray said wryly.

"You?" Penny Harrison asked, the slight flush, which had briefly put colour into her face as she had warmed to her theme, fading again. "The place was built for people like you. You're a man."

"I even played rugby," Thackeray confessed. "But I still disliked it. I didn't have the accent or the confidence to cope."

"My father was a coal-miner," Penny said simply as if that explained everything. "Somehow they found out and they really hated that. After the three-day week and the election Ted Heath lost. My God, how they hated miners."

"But you met your husband there," Thackeray objected, wondering how his interview with this rake-like, passionate woman had been hijacked in this way. "It can't have been all bad? Then, at least."

This time Penny Harrison did laugh but the sound carried a harsh echo of something much more painful.

"Well, I didn't think it was all that stuff Greenaway had sent you round to talk about. It's Mark, isn't it? I saw in the *Oxford Mail* that they're launching some big appeal for their six hundredth anniversary. I suppose the new master wants to make sure that I don't do anything embarrassing to muck up the celebrations. Is that it?"

"That isn't exactly how he put it?" Thackeray objected quietly, wondering for a moment whether he had been taken for a ride. "He was more concerned about whether you'd heard anything from Mark. He wasn't there himself when he disappeared . . ."

"No, that bastard Partridge was in charge," Penny said, and there was not a glimmer of humour in her eyes now. "Do you know what happened?"

"Only what Hugh Greenaway told me last night."

"Well, that would be a sanitised version, I expect."

"Tell me yours, then," Thackeray said, his curiosity aroused now. He glanced around the tiny sitting room.

"You live alone?"

"Oh yes," Penny Harrison said. "I've just come out of the Warneford after a little psychiatric episode. This is care in the community and I'm lucky to find it, I'm told. A nurse pops in now and again."

"I'm sorry," Thackeray said, feeling helpless in the face of this relentless assault. "Tell me about Mark. From the beginning."

For a moment her face crumpled, but then she squared thin shoulders inside a shirt which was several sizes too large for her, and folded her hands beneath her chin.

"Mark," she said thoughtfully. "Mark was everything I wasn't: brilliant, self-confident, good-looking, from a nice, comfortable middle-class home. I fell for him, hook, line and sinker. And I'd thought I was such a liberated woman. I spent most of my final year at his flat in Summertown mopping his brow while he finished his thesis. I only got a third, of course, something he never let me forget, although it was his bloody fault.

"We got married as soon as I graduated. He stayed at Friddies, naturally, he was one of their own, and I did teacher training. Got his fellowship here very young. But I'd only been working a couple of years when Caro arrived, and then my son Tom soon after. There's – was – only eighteen months between them.

"We got a little Victorian house in North Oxford and became the normal academic family, kids at Phil and Jim's, agonising over private schools we couldn't afford anyway, bikes in the hall, books in the loo, camping holidays in the Dordogne, never enough money to do the things people think academic families can afford. As soon as the kids were old enough, I did some part-time teaching to help ends meet. State system, of course, and that doesn't gain brownie points with some of the old bastards at Friddies."

"Nothing changes, then?"

"It changes, but so slowly it's almost imperceptible," she said. "And there's always the old guard, sniping from high table about falling standards and Mickey Mouse degrees. The education professor ran a course on comprehensive schools not long ago – you know, those dreadful places, which educate about ninety per cent of kids? – and there were voices asking whether this was really something the university wished to be associated with. Of course, Friddies was always one of the worst, still trying to come to terms with the twentieth century when everyone else had begun to look forward to the twenty-first."

"But Mark changed more quickly?" he asked, knowing that there was much worse to come. She nodded, all the colour drained from her cheeks now, leaving her skin like crumpled parchment.

"Of course I always knew that Mark had girlfriends," she said, not meeting Thackeray's eyes. "You could almost smell it when he came home. But he would never admit anything. Called me a jealous bitch, became more and more difficult to live with as time went by, refused to take me to things at college, as if he was ashamed of me, humiliated me in front of people at those nasty sniping North Oxford dinner parties when I could hardly get a word in edgeways with his brilliant friends. He was the one who always knew everything about everything. All par for the course, really. I should have left him years ago, but I've always been a coward. And I thought it was better for the kids if we retained a semblance of normality. He knew that. Relied on it, in fact."

"Not much of a life," Thackeray said quietly. "But he was a success in Oxford's terms, I assume? So why did he disappear?"

"I don't know," Penny Harrison said with a note of wonder in her voice. "I've gone over it a hundred times and I still don't know. I was already ill. I had my first spell in hospital last winter, just after Christmas. He came to visit once or twice in a perfunctory sort of way, and then I went home and he wasn't there. Two days later, I was summoned to see our bank manager and I discovered that he had remortgaged the house and failed to keep up the payments – forging my signature along the way. Our bank acount was empty. The car had been repossessed. He'd even made off with some money that had been left to the children by their grandmother. He'd vanished and I was destitute."

"You don't know where the money went?"

"I've no idea. His lover, I assume. We certainly never saw any of it at home, and she disappeared at the same time as he did. She was a secretary at the college."

"Have you seen him or heard from him since?" Thackeray asked. He knew that any comment he offered on Mark Harrison's behaviour would be no more than a faint echo of his wife's judgement.

"Not a word," she said. "And I never want to hear from him again. I hope he rots in hell. Why is the college interested anyway? They did absolutely nothing to help at the time."

Thackeray sighed. He thought the plight of Hugh Greenaway's research students a poor excuse to interrogate Penny Harrison much further.

"How have your children taken this? Have they seen their father?" he asked.

"My daughter works in London and wouldn't speak to him if she found him in the gutter," Penny said, her voice like a knife.

"And your son?"

"The college obviously didn't bother to tell you about Tom, did they, though they must know? It was all over the local papers when it happened. Tom walked out of the sixth form when his father left. He couldn't cope. He ended up in a squat not far from here. They found him dead. An overdose of heroin. They called it an accident."

For a moment Thackeray sat very still as an icy hand gripped his heart and squeezed it in a vice. There were, he knew only too well, absolutely no words that could bring any comfort to Penny Harrison. With difficulty, he forced back into the darkest recesses of his mind memories of his own son and made himself concentrate on the woman at his side who had begun to tremble uncontrollably. He took a deep breath to steady himself.

"I'm so sorry," he said. Clumsily he put an arm around her thin shoulders and held her until she regained control.

"I'm sorry," she whispered. "It's very hard to talk about."

"Yes, " he said. "I do know. I'm sorry. I had no right to come here asking questions. I'll tell Hugh Greenaway that you don't know where your husband is and that you don't want to be bothered with their problems." What he would actually say to Hugh Greenaway, he thought, would be a hell of a lot blunter than that.

Gently, he pulled away from her and began to get to his feet but she clung to his arm urgently and then got up and crossed the room to open a battered briefcase, which had been all but hidden amongst piles of books. She pulled out a crumpled newspaper cutting and passed it to him. It was a report of the inquest of Tom Harrison, which had concluded that he had taken an accidental overdose of heroin.

"Don't go," she said. "Please don't go. You don't understand how good it is to have someone to talk to. Why did the master ask you to come here anyway? Why you, if you're just a visitor?"

"I suppose because I ask questions for a living," Thackeray said reluctantly. "I'm a detective."

She looked at him in astonishment but without the suspicion which he met in many people's eyes when he revealed his profession and he felt obscurely pleased at that.

"A detective?" she said, wonderingly, as if she had found some treasure which she did not know exactly what to do with.

33

She was silent for a moment, as though turning an idea round in her mind slowly.

"Can you ask questions for me then? The police here were barely interested when I reported Mark missing. And they never did find out what really happened to Tom."

"What do you mean?"

"The verdict was accidental death," she said. "As you can see." She nodded at the newspaper cutting Thackeray still held in his hand. "There had been a lot of extra pure heroin about and they reckoned that he had overdosed by accident. I never believed that. He was in a distressed state – we all were – but he wasn't an addict. But they didn't seem to accept that. They did so little investigation. None of it made sense."

Thackeray wanted to tell her that it never did make sense to lose a child, never would, that the agonising questions went on for ever, but he hesitated, swallowing the natural sympathy he felt. He had not come to Oxford to get involved in St Frideswide's problems and he felt no inclination to question cases which the local police evidently regarded as closed.

"I'm only in Oxford for a short time," he said. "And Thames Valley Police would be furious if I started some sort of freelance investigation. And rightly so."

"They watch your back and you watch theirs, is that it? I suppose you're all freemasons as well." The question was delivered with a bitter resentment which stung.

"What do you think happened to Tom?" he asked reluctantly.

"I think he was murdered," she said flatly. Thackeray drew a sharp breath. It was not what he had expected.

"Do you have any evidence for that?" he asked. Tom's mother turned those dark eyes full of pain in his direction and this time he met the look directly.

"None at all," she said. "But I know I'm right. And I'd like you to prove it."

Chapter Four

Thackeray stood on the edge of a convivial group of colleagues holding a tiny coffee cup and saucer in one hand and a cigarette in the other, ignoring the veiled disapproval of those closest to him as he inhaled gratefully. Dinner had been a formal affair this evening and the meal, served in the fellows' dining room, an indifferent one. Afterwards, the course members, all male apart from two superintendents from opposite ends of the country, both in severe black suits and pale coloured shirts, had been invited to take dessert and coffee in the senior common room. After toying with stuffed dates and strawberries and prompting raised eyebrows as he studiously ignored the port and Madeira as they were passed several times around the huge mahogany table, Thackeray reluctantly let the crowd take him into a spacious sitting room.

This was a part of the college he had never penetrated as an undergraduate and the soft carpet, deep armchairs and what looked to his untutored eye to be seriously expensive paintings on the walls made a sharp contrast to the rather spartan student room which was his temporary home.

He sipped his coffee thoughtfully and cast a professional eye over the assembled company. Professor Hugh Greenaway had appeared as dessert was served and formally welcomed the course to St Frideswide's with a charm which Thackeray felt was rather more contrived than it used to be. The new master was now on the other side of the room deep in conversation with two men of about his own age who even out of uniform carried the unmistakeable stamp of seniority. Thackeray knew that there were two commanders from the Met on the course and guessed, without much rancour, that Greenaway had unerringly sniffed them out. It was, he thought, what the master of an Oxford college was paid to do.

His own interest lay not in making friends and influencing people but in teasing out a little information from the Thames Valley force without their realising that the deed had been done. He had already identified a chief inspector based at the Cowley police station, a tall, sandy-haired man with a heavy jaw and chilly blue eyes, and he had confirmed from his list of participants that his name was Cliff Gould.

Thackeray spotted Gould standing alone on the far side of the room nursing a brandy glass. He stubbed out his cigarette in an unsullied ashtray of what looked suspiciously like porcelain, and insinuated himself crab-like between the shifting and increasingly animated conversations in the Thames Valley man's general direction. As the talk ebbed and flowed around him he finally got close enough to hold out a hand and introduce himself.

"Bradfield?" Gould said, rocking back and forth on the balls of his feet, although there was no sign of a slur in his voice. "West Yorkshire, then?" Thackeray nodded. "Everything from mosques to sheep farmers going bust," he said, the Yorkshire vowels just a fraction broader than normal. "Must be a bit different here. All this can't take much policing."

Gould gave Thackeray the sort of incredulous stare which he knew he deserved and had intended to provoke.

"You've never heard of effing Blackbird Leys?" Gould asked.

"Ah, right," Thackeray said apologetically. "That was Oxford too, of course. We had some nasty joy-riding an 'all. Kids killed. And I hear even St Frideswide's can give you summat to think about. Someone was telling me in the bar about a don who went missing earlier this year. What was his name? Harrison was it?"

"Something and nothing," Gould said dismissively. "Buggered off with his secretary and his wife went off her trolley. As they do."

"Oh, is that all?" Thackeray said with what he hoped was the right degree of understanding. "A case of the Chinese whispers exaggerating what happened then, I guess. This lad I was talking to was very annoyed with Harrison for mucking up his research project. Talked as though the whole college had been ripped off. Wanted me to mount a posse."

"Their idea of a crime's a bit different from the real world," Gould said. "You've got to be a bit careful driving down the High Street here, though. You never know whether that scruffy beggar stepping off the kerb is the world's greatest expert in Sanskrit tomb doodles or the top man in nuclear fusion or just another old alkie derelict."

Gould allowed himself a thin smile. He was tall enough to gaze over Thackeray's broad shoulder and was obviously losing interest in the conversation.

"But the son? This researcher said Harrison's lad ended up dead. Suicide, was it?"

"Overdose," Gould said flatly. But something he had said, Thackeray was not sure what, had got to him and he suddenly turned his attention to the Harrison family with more venom than his cautious interrogator expected.

"Playing silly buggers in a squat up the Cowley Road, wasn't he? Woolly-minded liberal mother and father too busy to take any notice. The usual North Oxford story. They're almost as much trouble as the London Road hooligans at Oxford United, some of those middle class pot-heads – think it's all a bit of a laugh, shouldn't really be illegal at all, should it? – just like beating up Swindon fans on a Saturday afternoon's a harmless bit of fun for some. Never did anyone any real harm. Till they move onto heroin. Silly cow, Mrs Harrison. I hear she's still harrassing the college to find her husband. Last time she came to the nick to have a moan at us about the boy I told her to hire a private detective."

"A junkie, was he, the lad? Sad, that," Thackeray said.

"Should have had more sense, a boy with his advantages," Gould said unsympathetically.

"Right," Thackeray said. "Accidental death, then, was it? The verdict?" Almost before the words were out he realised he had gone too far. Gould's expression hardened.

"Misadventure," he snapped. "Sounds to me as if you've been talking to Mrs Harrison yourself. She's a pain in the arse, that woman, completely paranoid. A mental case. Messed up with a husband and a son and looking for someone to blame. I don't know how you bumped into her but you want to take anything she says with a bucketload of salt."

"Right," Thackeray said again. Gould drained his brandy.

"I'm off," he said. "My super insisted I come on this course. Waste of bloody time if you ask me, but at least I don't have to sleep here. I'll see you around."

Thackeray did have to sleep there, if he was to sleep at all. The hard student bed at the top of the narrow stone staircase was the only one on offer. But it did not seem alluring as he made his way out of the warm fug of the senior common room into the damp chill of an evening with the smell of autumn about it, leaving most of his colleagues still deep in noisy, increasingly inebriated conversation. But it was not the lack of alcohol so much as the lack of Laura that made him feel hollow inside, and he knew there was no cure for that.

He made his way slowly through the low cloisters, built by mediaeval monks and lined with memorial stones ancient and modern, pausing to light another cigarette and leaning for a moment over the low balustrade, watching his own smoke drift in the dim light cast by a single lamp left on to guide late guests to the archway, which led to the quadrangle and the main college buildings.

He remembered this as a quiet place, not much of a lure to young men alone but a favourite of undergraduates entertaining their girls during the permitted hours. Even now, only the faintest murmur of the city traffic outside the college walls could be heard here, but he was not in the mood to be soothed by the ancient stones and the deeply shadowed arches. There was too much unresolved, and he was annoyed with himself for adding another anxiety here in Oxford to the load he had brought with him from Bradfield.

He shivered slightly as the chill penetrated the jacket of his light suit and he stubbed out his cigarette with a sense of faint sacrilege on the stone flagged floor and realised, as the hairs on the back of his neck stirred, that he was no longer alone.

"Welcome back, Mr Thackeray," a voice said, thin and slightly nasal. "It's been a very long time."

"Dr Partridge," Thackeray said, without turning. "I was surprised to find you still here." Partridge did not reply, although Thackeray thought he detected an indrawn breath. He had no doubt that the older man still expected the sort of deference he had demanded from undergraduates in his day. He had not deserved it then, and would certainly not get it now, Thackeray thought as Partridge moved silently to put his hands lightly on the balustrade at his side.

"I flatter myself that the college still needs me," Partridge said, a touch of complacency in his tone. "A new master, a great anniversary to celebrate, so much to do."

"I'm sure Hugh Greenaway will be delighted by your concern," Thackeray said. That faintly indrawn breath again and Thackeray allowed himself a faint smile, sure that Partridge would not see it in the dim yellow light from behind them. Partridge grasped the balustrade and Thackeray heard his fingernails rasp against the crumbling stone and lichen. He glanced at his face, just in time to catch the fury flickering around the crevice of a mouth and the deep-set eyes. The man had aged badly and was eaten up with resentment, Thackeray thought. He must warn Greenaway that there was not just professional jealousy here but something that went much deeper than that.

Partridge regained control quickly and there was no tremor in his voice when he spoke again. There was no doubt in Thackeray's mind that he had sought him out deliberately, probably waiting here in the shadowy cloister confident that he would pass this way on his way back to his room.

"You once did this college a great disservice, Mr Thackeray," he said.

"That's your opinion, Dr Partridge," he said. "But it's a long time ago, and you got what you wanted in the end."

"Precisely," Partridge said. "My concern now is merely to make sure that you do not repeat the mistake. I understand you have been talking to the Harrison woman." It was a statement, not a question, and Thackeray wondered who had informed Partridge so quickly of his walk towards Cowley that afternoon and whether he knew exactly who had encouraged him to take that walk.

"I think that's my business," he said, keeping his resentment firmly under control.

"It's my business if it impinges on the well-being of this college," Partridge said. "You must understand that the woman is mad. I use the word advisedly, of course: she is being treated for a serious psychiatric illness. One of her obsessions is the wrong she imagines this college has done her. Whatever her husband's sins, and I imagine they were many, I want you to know that St Frideswide's treated Mrs Harrison well – generously even. We did what we could to help when her husband disappeared. She has no legitimate grievance here. I suggest that you treat her complaints very cautiously indeed. The college would not be any more ready now than it was when you were an undergraduate to allow its name to be blackened unjustifiably."

"I hear what you say, Dr Partridge," Thackeray said evenly, swallowing the anger, like the bile, which he felt welling up inside him.

"You are a police inspector now, I understand," Partridge said.

"Detective chief inspector."

"Ah," Partridge said, scarcely veiling his contempt. "Well, I do hope you are not tempted to play Morse around St Frideswide's. I think you would find that an even more fruitless exercise now than it was when you tried to find a scapegoat to blame for a tragic accident in 1975. It was the good name of your fellow undergraduates you threatened then as well as that of the college."

"I'll bear what you say in mind," Thackeray said. "Goodnight, Dr Partridge. Pleasant dreams." He knew the irony in his tone was wasted but could not resist it as he turned on his heel and strode through the archway into the main quadrangle, leaving the senior tutor leaning like a wraith on the balustrade.

Half an hour later, he stood at his bedroom window listening to the city's bells strike eleven with their infuriatingly unsynchronised chimes. The clock in the chapel tower on the other side of the quadrangle chimed slightly later than all the rest, but with a faint tinny apologetic note which could not compete with its more sonorous neighbours. The familiarity of the sounds touched memories, which he had thought long dead and buried. He glanced over his shoulder at his unexpected guest.

"I saw Liz Selby fall, you know," he said. "I was standing at my window, just like this, although it gave a better view of the tower than this one."

"I remember the inquest," Penny Harrison murmured.

He had found Penny sitting, huddled inside her over-sized coat, on the steps at the foot of his staircase. Glancing across the quad he had seen Dr Magnus Partridge, wrapped in his gown, glide through the archway from the cloisters and he had impulsively pulled Penny to her feet and bundled her up the stairs to his room. He did not ask how she had got into the quadrangle. Her connections with the college went back far enough for her to be able to talk her way past the lodge if she had to, or perhaps she knew some more devious route. She had not protested, and when he switched the lights on she had tossed her coat on the floor and flung herself onto the narrow single bed, which stood in an alcove next to the bathroom door.

"I had to see you again," she said, shielding her eyes from the lights with one thin arm. He had shrugged.

"Magnus doesn't like it," he said and was surprised to see her lips twitch in amusement.

"Magnus wouldn't," she said. "Poor Magnus has never recovered from the arrival of what he always insists on calling "gels" all those years ago. Mark and I used to play hide and seek around the cloisters to make sure we ended up in the same room for the night. Magnus specialised in ambushing lovers. He was a poor twisted bastard, even then."

"Magnus thought that Liz Selby's death was no more than the modernisers deserved," Thackeray said, turning away to the window and glancing at the chapel tower from which he had seen a figure flutter to earth like a wounded bird against a golden late evening sky.

"Why were you so convinced it wasn't an accident?" she asked. "I was at the inquest too, you know, though I wasn't called to give evidence. You seemed so sure."

"I heard them fooling about out there," he said. "There'd been a rugby club party that evening and they were very drunk. I'd have been there myself but finals started that week and I was off the booze. When I looked out of the window I saw them with a girl, making a lot of noise. Something made her run and several of them followed her. I was sure that they went into the chapel after her, but afterwards they swore no-one did. She ran off alone, they said. They saw her on the roof, shouted at her to be careful, and then she fell."

"And you didn't believe them?"

"No," Thackeray said flatly. "It wasn't true."

"She didn't jump?"

"No, she didn't jump. She seemed to go over not quite backwards, but looking behind her, almost as if she was saying something to someone I couldn't see. She didn't jump. But I've always thought she could have been pushed."

"You mean murdered?" Penny Harrison looked horrified.

"If she was chased up there, to that rotten stone balustrade, even if she wasn't actually touched, it was not an accident," Thackeray said. "I never thought it was simply an accident. But I couldn't persuade the police or the coroner I was right. I took my exams and went home to Yorkshire. I never came back."

"She was in a terrible state that week. I always assumed she must have killed herself," Penny said. She paused. "Were you? Did you and Liz . . . I mean?"

Thackeray smiled this time and shook his head.

"I was a good Catholic boy in those days. I took some stick from the rugby team because I used to go to confession on a Saturday night instead of getting plastered in the bar. But it was on the field they tried to get me, some of them. I was never quite sure who was friend and who was foe in the ruck."

"Oh, I'm sure you could count Mark in on that sort of unpleasantness," Penny said. "I got the same sort of treatment until I modelled myself in his image."

"Yes, well, I never did that," Thackeray said. "I was too bloody-minded to conform. In any case, I had a girl at home, the girl I married eventually. I went to bed with my arms outside the bedclothes. To be perfectly honest, with rugby and finals coming up, I was hardly aware that the college had taken women that year."

"Huh," Penny said. "And we thought we were changing the world. Liz was very fierce, you know, one of the bra burners, started a women's group – for all six of us."

"Which is why the rugger buggers hated her, I imagine. She put the fear of God into them."

"But not you? You were one of them."

"I told you. I was hardly aware of your existence."

Thackeray turned away from the window and for a moment their eyes met and he was startled by the longing he glimpsed there.

"Why did you come?" he asked.

She shrugged and threw herself back on the bed with her arms above her head. The invitation was overt. But her heart did not seem to be in it and when he sat on the bed beside her and took her hand she turned her face away to hide the tears. It would be easy to take her in his arms, he thought, and maybe that would give both of them something they wanted, but he knew that would be a temporary fix, little more than a guarantee of a good night's sleep. What would Laura call it? A one-night stand? And the teens and twenties would have an even cruder name for it, but be just as forgiving, more forgiving than he could ever be.

"I'm not sure there's anything I can do to help," he said, his face closed and remote.

"I forgot to give you Tom's address," she said, pulling her hand from his and sitting up briskly, offering a glimpse of the competent woman she must once have been. "His friends are still there. A girlfriend called Jancie. Jancie McLeod. And I thought you'd like to know that my daughter is coming to see me this weekend. You might like to talk to her? No-one can say she's a bloody neurotic. I meant what I said, you know. You couldn't get at the truth when Liz died. You owe it to me to find out what happened to Tom."

"I'll take you home," Thackeray said, with chilly finality.

Chapter Five

Back at Kelly James's bedside, Sergeant Kevin Mower was beginning to piece together what the girl could remember of her Saturday night out. But as he looked at his notes he felt as if he were trying to assemble a jigsaw created by a particularly malign jester, the sort who might deliberately distort the outlines here or fudge the colours there and occasionally cut a vital piece in jelly instead of wood. The effort set his nerves on edge and more than once he had needed to get up and walk off some of the tension which threatened to overwhelm him.

Some things he accepted that Kelly might not remember, fuddled as she had evidently been by alcohol and – though she denied it – drugs. Others might have been obliterated by the blow to the head, which had rendered her semi-conscious when she had arrived at Accident and Emergency. But there were other questions at which the baby blue eyes under the bandaged head flickered away before she framed her reply, where there was a hesitancy, which was different from the hesitancy with which she seemed to wrack her brain when she genuinely had difficulty in recalling what had happened. Kevin Mower was convinced that Kelly James was lying about something and he guessed that it was sex.

When he and Val Ridley had arrived at the hospital he had brought the initial police report of the incident with him. He sent Val ahead of him to the ward and sought out the young Asian doctor who had admitted Kelly in his cluttered office beyond the cubicles overflowing with human misery. The doctor glanced at his watch with eyes like black slits in crumpled brown paper bags. A vein throbbed at his temple.

"Two minutes?" he said. "The waiting time is four hours out there." Mower nodded.

45

"How bad is Kelly James?" he asked.

"Extensive bruising around the face and body, bruises and lacerations to the head, concussion, two cracked ribs, a broken arm. How much more do you want?"

"A weapon?"

"Hands and feet, I'd guess," the doctor said, the weariness dulling his voice. "And cuts to the back of the head when she fell. Nothing that indicates your proverbial blunt instrument. The usual Saturday night drunken injuries. The only difference is that she's a girl."

"Was she raped?" Mower asked. The doctor shrugged.

"Impossible to tell medically," he said. "She'd had sex but there was no obvious bruising or sign of force. And she was not a virgin. In fact, I think she's had an abortion not long ago. You'll have to ask her whether she thinks she was raped or not." The doctor's expression was impassive but between the two men lay a cultural chasm as deep as the Persian Gulf.

"Some parents," Mower said mechanically.

"Yes." The doctor nodded, long fingers fiddling with the stethoscope in the top pocket of his white coat.

"But we have samples?"

"Oh, yes, they've been passed to the forensic people. You'll have DNA if you need it. But I guess you'll have to test half the men in Bradfield to pin him down. I don't think Kelly was in a fit state to know who she was with let alone what he was doing to her. Her blood sample will make interesting reading." He stood up dismissively, a tall thin exhausted man with melancholy eyes.

"I've got the rest of Bradfield waiting out there," he said.

Going up the stairs to the ward, Mower had hesitated for a moment, almost losing his balance and clutching the bannister rail for support. He felt as deeply weary as the casualty doctor had looked. Since Rita Desai's death he had slept only fitfully, his nights shattered by vivid flashbacks to the day she was shot. The dreams were filled with an overwhelming sense of panic as he tried again and again to reach the body he had in reality first seen already sprawling lifeless in the dust. His illusory self clearly believed that some intervention on his part could snatch her back from the threshold of death. He woke each time, aching with the knowledge that he would never reach her in time.

He took a deep breath before resuming his ascent to the ward where Val Ridley was sitting at Kelly's bedside waiting for her to wake. The girl's mother hovered at the end of the bed where Kelly lay with her eyes so tightly shut that Mower wondered if she was shamming. The drip had gone now and according to the hospital, the girl was fit to talk.

"All right if I go outside for a fag?" Lorraine James asked, with a defiant glance at the nurse busy at the next bed. Her hands were shaking and Mower could see that the nails were bitten to the quick.

"Fine," Mower had said, happy to question Kelly without any prompting from a parent. He glanced at the apparently sleeping girl and then at Val Ridley, who was sitting on the edge of the visitor's chair also looking pale and tense. They watched Lorraine hurry out of the swing doors.

"You're not going to like it," he said.

"Try me." Her face was as expressionless as it usually was when she had to work with Mower. Quietly, so that Kelly could not overhear, he told Val what the doctor had said. She shrugged.

"They're sleeping around before they're out of primary school, some of these kids," she had whispered in response. They had turned back to the girl's bed and found her suspiciously wide awake, watching them with huge, wary eyes, the whites blotched with blood.

"Are you feeling better?" Val asked. "Do you think you can answer some questions about what happened?" The girl nodded, a small painful movement as if she was not yet fully aware of how much her bandaged head and bruised neck hurt.

47

Excruciatingly slowly, they prised out of her what little she could recall of her Saturday night out, a succession of raucously crowded pubs and bars followed by a steamy session at the Underground, a new club close to the university but favoured by youngsters from the town rather than students, and well-known to the police for its readily available drugs.

Who she had been with proved to be more difficult to establish. She reeled off the names of a dozen girlfriends easily enough, including the two fourteen-year-olds with whom she had set off from the Heights at about seven that evening. Most of them were names her mother had already supplied, friends and acquaintances Ridley and Mower had either spoken to already or put on their list of interviews to be conducted. But with boys names she was more hazy, or more reticent. As the girl's eyes flickered this way and that, it was difficult to tell whether Kelly really could not or would not remember.

"There was Degsy," she said.

"Degsy who?" Val came back for perhaps the fifth time, an edge of impatience creeping into her voice in spite of the girl's evident misery as she added the name to the pathetically short list in her notebook.

"I dunno".

"Does he go to your school?"

"Nah. I think he's left school."

"Older than you, then?"

"Yeah."

"But you'd know him again?" Val insisted.

"I dunno," Kelly said again. "He were with some other lads, lads from Leeds or somewhere – Craig and Kenny and one called summat like Basher."

"White lads?" Kevin Mower asked sharply.

"Yeah, 'course," Kelly said. "Pakis don't go to t'Underground, do they?"

"So three? four? – lads from Leeds. Maybe? Did you leave with them, or with your girlfriends?"

"Chance'd be a fine thing," Kelly said morosely. "I couldn't find nobody when I wanted to ger'off home. I don't know where Tracey 'n' Cath went. I looked all over."

"How much had you had to drink, Kelly?" Val asked. The girl glanced away.

"I don't know, do I? You lose count after a few bottles, don't you? What's it matter, any road? It weren't the drink that put me in here, were it?"

"That's a matter of opinion," Val muttered. "So, anyway, you wanted to get home and you couldn't find your mates. So what did you do next? Can you remember that?"

"I went outside to look for them, didn't I? It were right hot in t'club."

"But you didn't find them?"

"No, I bloody didn't. There were lots of folk milling about, like, down Manchester Road, but I couldn't see anyone I knew. So I walked home, didn't I?

"Why didn't you get a taxi, Kelly?" Mower asked and realised it was a stupid question even before he had asked it. The girl looked at him with contempt.

"I didn't have owt to pay for a taxi wi', did I? I were spent up. Any road, them Paki drivers charge five quid to go up to t'Heights. That's if you can get them to go there at all. It's a rip off, innit? An' I don't like the way some of them look at you. As if you're a slag or summat."

Val Ridley glanced at Mower at that and met a flicker of cynical amusement, which irritated her.

"Did anyone speak to you on the way up the hill?" she persisted, with a sharp edge in her voice. "Can you remember seeing anyone, anyone at all, on your way home."

Kelly shook her head painfully again, and her eyes suddenly focussed on the door to the ward. Mower and Ridley turned as Lorraine James came back in, fidgeting with her bag and nervously running a hand across her pale, lank hair.

"She looks tired out," she said sullenly to the two police

officers. "She should be resting, not trying to answer questions. Nurse said so."

"Just another minute, Mrs James," Mower had said. "Then we'll leave it till tomorrow."

"Come on, Kelly, try to think back," Val Ridley said. "Did anyone follow you? Did you see anyone at all? Can you remember?"

"I don't know," the girl said. "It were right dark up t'hill past the Red Lion. I can't remember what happened after that, can I? I can't remember owt about it till I woke up in here."

Mower gave up at that and the girl turned away and closed her eyes as they got up to go. Lorraine James followed them out of the ward.

"We'll need to talk to you again, Mrs James," Mower said, his tone unfriendly, as the doors to the ward swung closed behind them and they waited for the lift.

"What for?" Lorraine asked querulously, pulling her cigarettes from her pocket and putting one in her mouth in spite of the prominent no smoking notices on the walls. But she held her lighter tightly in one hand in response to Val Ridley's frosty stare.

"Well, for one thing I'd like to know who got Kelly pregnant recently."

Lorraine looked at him, her pale eyes full of dislike, though she made no attempt to deny Mower's allegation.

"What's that got to do wi' owt?"

"She's thirteen, Mrs James," Val Ridley said, exasperated. "If she's been sleeping around it might have a lot to do with what happened on Saturday night."

"I don't see how," Lorraine said.

"Even so, I think we need a chat with you and Kelly's dad. Was he not able to get in to see her today?" Mower persisted.

"Her dad?" Lorraine asked. "I ain't seen Kelly's dad for ten years or more."

50

"I thought . . ."

"You mean Carl?" Lorraine laughed, a harsh sound which started her coughing and she pulled the cigarette from her mouth in annoyance as the three of them stepped into the lift.

"Carl's my boyfriend. He's not Kelly's dad."

"Right," Mower said, pressing the button for the ground floor. "So shall we say tomorrow morning? Ten o'clock suit you both? You're not at work are you?"

"Not till later on, me," Lorraine said.

Back in the main CID office, Mower hung his jacket with his usual care on the back of his chair, sat down, leaned back and groaned. Val Ridley glanced at him sharply.

"Are you OK?"

"Terrific," Mower said.

"You're a liar," his colleague said, thin-lipped, scanning Mower's haggard face. "For God's sake, Kevin, if you need some time off, take it. The brass won't mind. You're not doing yourself any favours struggling on."

"Leave it, will you?" he said. He would have said more, so suddenly did the embers of rage flare into life, but they were interrupted by an obviously excited DC Tom Wilson, fresh-faced, bright-eyed and so eager that Mower choked back his anger and turned away to hide his despair. His stomach, which had been nagging him all day, gave an insistent gripe of pain that made him flinch.

"Have you heard?" Wilson said. "You'll be made up, Val. Just what you always wanted."

"What on earth are you on about?" Ridley asked CID's newest recruit.

"The new boss? You haven't heard? DCI Jackie Bairstow?"

"Jackie as in Jacqueline?" Mower asked, curious in spite of himself.

"Got it in one," Wilson said. "Drafted in from York or some-where to stand in while Mr Thackeray's away."

51

"Jesus bloody wept," Mower said. "That's all we need so soon after we manage to lose our last female recruit. She'll go through this place like Queen bloody Boadicea."

"She well might," a sharp female voice said unexpectedly from behind them. The tone was far from friendly. All three detectives spun round to face a small slim woman, grey-haired and sharp-eyed in a black trouser suit and red silk shirt who had evidently entered the room unnoticed.

"Sergeant Mower, I presume? DCI Bairstow. My office," she said. Mower got to his feet quickly, rigid with embarrassment.

"Ma'am", he said, as Val Ridley tried to hide a triumphant smile.

"She's trouble, Laura," Mower said, putting down his bottle of Mexican beer and spitting out a lime pip with a grimace. "She's taking no hostages. If you get a chance you need to tell Michael Thackeray to watch his back."

Laura Ackroyd sipped her own vodka and tonic and glanced around the glittering new café-bar at the Theatre Royal with interest. She had been watching television with Vicky and David Mendelson, feeling contentedly stuffed after one of Vicky's flamboyant Italian meals, when Mower had called her. She had been tempted to turn his invitation for a drink down flat. One night with Kevin was enough, she thought. But the edge of panic in his voice persuaded her to agree. She was surprised to find that the cause of his anxiety was not Rita Desai but Jackie Bairstow.

"Aren't you just a exhibiting a classic case of female boss shock?" she asked. "I can just imagine the effect on some of my lot at the *Gazette* if they appointed a woman editor. They'd be weeping into their pints at the Lamb for months. Not that there's much chance of it, of course, provincial newspapers being stuck even more firmly in a time warp than the police."

"Come on, Laura," Mower said. "Give me a break. It's not like that any more."

"I tell you what," Laura said. "I'll do an interview with her for my women's page. Headline: Top Cop In No Balls Horror. Will that do?"

Mower allowed himself a faint smile.

"You think I'm paranoid," he said. "But you're out of date, you know. I've worked with women all my career. Even worked for them once or twice. I don't give a damn what she is, male, female, gay, black, white. That's not what this is about."

"So what is it about?" Laura asked, her tone marginally more sympathetic. Mower, she thought, was looking even more ragged than the last time she had seen him, his eyes red-rimmed from lack of sleep and his usually immaculate hair unkempt.

"She wants Michael Thackeray's job, that's what it's about. And she'll use Rita's death to make sure she gets it. She's an acting DCI and she wants to be made up fast. This mess in Bradfield is her opportunity and she's not going to miss it." Mower took a gulp of his beer and put the bottle down with a thump, as if to emphasise the urgency of what he was trying to convey.

"You're serious, aren't you?" Laura asked, wondering whether Mower's judgement was sound enough to make her as worried on Michael Thackeray's behalf as Mower evidently was.

"Deadly serious," Mower said. "She had me in, spent five minutes reviewing the current cases, and fifteen asking me about the illegal immigration scam, how we got ourselves into a situation where Rita could be shot down like that . . ." Mower stopped and picked up his bottle and gripped it so hard that his knuckles turned white.

"Take it easy," Laura said. "Surely she'd need to fill herself in – "

"She virtually asked me straight out if it was Michael Thackeray's fault." Mower's voice was hoarse.

"Did she?" Laura said softly. "And what did you tell her?"

"You know what I told her, for God's sake. It was no-one's fault. No-one could have predicted what happened. That's what I've already said in my statement for the inquest, and to Jack Longley for the internal inquiry."

"But she didn't believe you, your new DCI?"

"She didn't want to believe me, more like." Mower slammed his bottle down on the table again. "Given what else gets airbrushed out of the picture why should this be any different? One dead. Terribly sorry, folks. No-one to blame. Another?" he asked, and without waiting for an answer got up and pushed his way to the bar. As Laura watched him order fresh drinks, she allowed her own shoulders to slump for a moment as dejection threatened to overwhelm her, but by the time Mower returned with her vodka and what looked like a double Scotch for himself, she determinedly rearranged her features to conceal her own feelings.

"If you tell the truth, Michael will be OK," she said with more confidence than she felt. "I don't see what your new boss can do to rearrange the facts."

"Maybe," Mower said with uncharacteristic uncertainty. His hand shook as he drained his glass and put it down on the table. "I dare say you haven't seen as many facts rearranged as I have."

"Come on, Kevin. You're bound to feel dreadful about what happened. Can't you take a break too? I'm sure it would do you good."

Mower's anger flared to the surface then, and for a moment Laura was afraid that he would hit her, so fierce was the rage which flashed across his features. Instead, he siezed the edges of the table and pushed himself abruptly to his feet, his dark eyes on fire.

"Nothing will do me any fucking good, because nothing, absolutely fucking nothing, can undo what's happened," he said in a whisper fierce enough to have the occupants of neighbouring tables turn quickly in his direction. "And I'm sick and bloody tired of everyone telling me what can make it better. Because nothing fucking can."

He turned on his heel and pushed his way roughly through the crowded bar to the door, which slammed noisily behind him. Laura drew a sharp breath and remained where she was, her cheeks blazing, until general interest in her and her abruptly departed companion subsided. Then she finished her drink, gathered up her jacket and bag and made her own way out to where she had parked her car. Of Kevin Mower, there was no sign.

The VW Golf, which she had bought on the spur of the moment to replace the beloved green Beetle she had recently lost, still felt alien. She sat for a moment to collect her thoughts and then pulled out her mobile phone and dialled another mobile number. It was seven thirty and, unused to the ways of Oxford colleges, she was not sure that he would not be already at dinner. But Thackeray answered quickly and she heard his voice soften when he realised who it was.

"How's it going?" she asked.

"The course is OK," he said. "But it's strange being back in college. There's all sorts of ghosts, and a master who wants me to act as an unpaid Sherlock Holmes and find a missing don for him."

"You're joking," Laura said.

"I wish I were."

"Miss you," she said.

"Why don't you come down for the weekend? I'll take you punting on the Cherwell, do the things I never got around to doing when I was a student."

"Great," she said lightly. She could not imagine even a young Thackeray indulging in the university's more frivolous pleasures. "What do I need? A floaty dress and a big floppy hat?"

"I think Zuleika Dobson's just a folk memory these days."

"Pity. Anyway, I'll see if I can get Friday off and you can play hooky from your classes. I bet you never did that when you were a student, either. But Michael . . ." She hesitated, knowing how much he disliked her interfering in his work, but anxiety overcame discretion and she rushed on.

"I'm worried about Kevin Mower," she said. "I saw him for a drink and he seemed almost distraught. And – you probably know this – but there's someone doing your job, a woman, and he seems to be having difficulties with her. Shouldn't he be taking some time away from all this? Get some counselling, whatever it is the police do these days for post-traumatic stress?"

There was a silence at the other end which Laura could not interpret.

"He was offered time off," Thackeray said at last. "I made sure of that. And counselling. But he wouldn't have it. I don't think he can admit how close he'd got to the girl, Rita, even to himself. When it happened he was pole-axed, but then – within hours – it was the old Kevin, cracking jokes, layer on layer of defence . . . I can't get near him, Laura, and I'd be surprised if you can."

Chapter Six

Coming out of his seminar at lunchtime the next day, Thackeray found himself waylaid by a young man of Chinese appearance and a rather taller fair-haired young woman, both in jeans and sweatshirts and carrying bulging briefcases of books and papers.

"Mr Thackeray?" the young woman said, tossing long blonde hair away from a thin, intelligent face, with bright, angry eyes. "I'm Annie Costello and this is Danny Chang. We're two of Dr Harrison's research students and the master said we should talk to you about him."

Greenaway was determined to have his pound of flesh, Thackeray thought wryly.

"Let's get out of here. I'm not keen on the lunches down in the buttery," he said. He led the way out through the college gates and down St Giles to the Eagle and Child where they found a table at the far end of the apparently endless series of narrow brown rooms, which at this time of the year were packed with tourists. He bought the two students the pints of beer they asked for, and himself a tonic with ice and lemon, and squeezed himself onto a wooden bench against the wall.

"So tell me about yourselves and Mark Harrison," he said, feeling their anxiety washing over him in waves. Annie, the more confident of the two, or perhaps merely with a better command of English than her companion, explained exactly how their supervisor's disappearance had disrupted their research projects.

"He was supposed to check some of my results," she said. I gave him my only copy – stupid thing to do. Now I back everything up on disk about fifteen times. He kept promising to get back to me right through the Hilary term. He was away a lot and I got on with other aspects of my work. There was plenty to do and I had no reason to be particularly worried about the disk. But he never gave me the disk back with the results – and then he just went, no word, nothing, and didn't come back. And no-one could find the disk. I kept nagging them to search his office, but at first they wouldn't, said he'd be back, and when they did finally look they couldn't find anything. All that work. Months and months of work. Jesus, I could kill him."

"Was it unusual for him to keep you waiting for your work?" Thackeray asked.

Annie hesitated, the pale blue eyes flicking towards Danny Chang and back to Thackeray.

"He wasn't the easiest supervisor to cope with," she said cautiously. "He went abroad so much, so there were times when he simply wasn't around. But when I started, he was helpful enough when he was there . . ."

"But?" Thackeray prompted.

"Three of us complained to the senior tutor a year or so ago that it was getting more and more difficult to get time with Dr Harrison, he was away so much."

"Where was he going? Do you know?"

"The Far East. Indonesia. All over."

"Surely Friddies doesn't need to go recruiting foreign students like some cash-strapped former polytechnic?" Thackeray said, surprised.

"No, I don't think that was what he was doing. Dr Partridge just said "college business" – but that doesn't mean much," Annie said.

"And did your complaints have any effect?" Thackeray asked. The girl shrugged.

"Not really," she said. "I don't think Dr Partridge was very interested in our problems. As it happened we were all women. You never get the impression that he likes women much."

Thackeray allowed himself a small grim smile but decided that this was not the time or the place to fill the students in on the college's history of misogyny.

Danny Chang had been listening to all this, sipping his drink as if he did not much enjoy it and nodding his head from time to time, but saying nothing. But when Annie had finished he offered a small fierce grunt of agreement.

"I am sorry to say that the college has not been helpful," he said. "Not until now, that is. Now I understand you will kindly make some effort to find Dr Harrison. It is most irregular, what has been happening. My father in Taiwan is most concerned."

"Did you give him disks, too?" Thackeray asked.

"No, I gave him the final chapters of my thesis, already typed up, ready for a final revision. He was to annotate them. In fact, I believe he did annotate them. He told me to that effect. But again he was very slow, and when he went there was no sign of the work. I have had to find another supervisor and begin to discuss the work all over again with her. It has held me up, and that is expensive for me, so far from home. I hoped to submit my thesis last term. Now it will be Christmas before I finish – or maybe longer than that. My new tutor says there are points which Dr Harrison should have brought out much earlier." The young man stopped and gazed down at his still almost full glass, avoiding Thackeray's eye.

"It is very hard for my family, if I am here even longer," he said, quietly at last. "They are not wealthy. They have spent a great deal of money on my education. Money they cannot afford." Danny's soft round face was impassive but, when he finally looked up, his dark eyes were stunned with misery.

Thackeray looked at the two students in silent fury as the full implications of Harrison's disappearance for his students sank in.

"How many research students did Dr Harrison have?" he asked.

"I think six," Annie Costello said. "One had finished his thesis, so was not really affected, but the rest of us are in diffi-culties. Some results are lost, experiments were not recorded,

59

parts of theses have disappeared – and so much time has been wasted. And then there are his undergraduate tutorials. I don't know what's going to happen to them when term begins."

"But do you have any idea why he should take your work away with him?"

"I shouldn't think it was deliberate," Annie said reluctantly. "It was probably just that he had stuff with him when he disappeared . . ."

"But he'd not been doing his supervision properly for months?"

"Not really, no," the girl said. "But it's difficult to complain. This is Oxford. These are supposed to be eminent people, the best in their field. Complaining isn't encouraged, you know?"

"I can imagine." Thackeray said, with feeling.

He let the two of them go when they refused his offer of another drink and sat on alone in his corner, back to the wall, letting the chatter of a group of tall, bronzed young tourists in a tongue he guessed was Swedish wash over him, insulating him from further contact with the human race.

Annie and Danny had depressed him, not because they had problems: those, he thought, were by no means insuperable, especially if Hugh Greenaway was alerted to the simmering revolt which threatened the college's reputation. The master would be only too aware of how damaging it could be to the college if one or other of the disgruntled postgraduates took their complaints to the press.

What had thrown him, he thought, was simply the fact that Annie and Danny were alive, while Rita Desai, who was much the same age, with the same vitality and all the possibilities of life ahead of her, was not. He drained his glass and put it down on the table, fighting the urge to have it refilled with something much stronger than fizzy water. Glancing at his watch he realised he had missed the start of his next seminar and felt relieved. He found little satisfaction in trying to boost a career which now seemed so fragile. It was just as well, he thought, that Laura was coming down to see him. He needed her.

In a small back street in Jericho, a stone's throw from the back gate to St Frideswide's, Thackeray hired a bike and, rusty after twenty years out of the saddle, wobbled his way through the town centre and along the historic High Street. He had come to Oxford without his car and now he knew the decision was a wise one. The sun was shining, the traffic was light since the recent restrictions on cars in the city centre, and he was occasionally overtaken by frantically pedalling young people late for work or pleasure even though term had not yet begun. Nothing much changes, he thought wryly as he braked noisily as a young woman waving an umbrella aloft marched determinedly across the road in front of him followed closely by a straggle of Japanese tourists clutching plastic macs and festooned with photographic equipment as their tour took them from the Queen's College to the Examination Schools.

At Magdalen Bridge the traffic thickened again and he kept close to the kerb as buses and cars swept past him unnervingly close. Feeling his life at some risk, he dismounted and pushed the bike round the roundabout at the far side of the bridge and into the narrow funnel of the Cowley Road. He had rented the bike on a whim, thinking that he might take advantage of the fine afternoon to ride one of the river towpaths and find enough peace and quiet to contemplate his future. But once in motion the challenge which Penny Harrison had flung at him proved impossible to resist and he determined to visit her son's house-mates to see whether they could shed any light on his death.

The squat was part of a Victorian terrace in a narrow street where the gardens were distinguished by the variety of the rubbish piled up in them rather than any horticultural endeavour. Number 45 boasted a particularly eclectic collection of mangled bikes and prams, plus a heap of black rubbish bags evidently waiting collection.

He knocked on the streaked blue front door, which offered neither handle nor letter box to the outside world. To his left the tall windows of the front room were masked by what looked like blankets nailed up across the glass, though from the other side of the door he could hear an insistent musical beat, which did not alter as he banged again, much harder this time. The response to this renewed assault was animal rather than human. A dog began barking and appeared to hurl itself heavily at the door, frantically scrabbling its claws against the woodwork.

Tired of bruising his knuckles, he stepped back towards the gap in the low wall where the gate should have been and looked up at the windows on the first and second floors but failed to distinguish any signs of life.

Looking around, he saw a narrow alleyway to the right, which he guessed must lead to the back of the terrace but as he headed towards it he was stopped in his tracks by a shrill voice.

"You from the council?" it said. "'bout bloody time. I've complained often enough." It took a couple of seconds to locate the source of this querulous complaint, which came from an indistinct figure sheltering behind a half-open window at the house next door.

"Can you open the door and tell me what the problem is?" Thackeray asked, wondering if impersonating a council official carried the same sort of penalties as impersonating a police officer. The window slammed shut and he made his way to the front door of Number 43, which eventually opened no more than a crack, held fast by a heavy chain. A bright eye peered at him for a moment before the chain was released and the door swung open to reveal a small elderly woman with a bird's-nest of grey hair obscuring sharp blue eyes and a face so seamed that it looked more like crumpled tissue paper than a human visage.

"Mrs . . . er . . . ?" Thackeray said cautiously.

"Lettie," the voice said sharply, the delivery fast and staccato. "Lettie O'Grady. Miss. Not married. Could never see the point. I've phoned often enough. Don't you keep any records? Don't you know what they're getting up to round here at all? It's not right, you know, all that noise, all that mess, all hours. I've lived here for more than fifty years and it's getting worse and worse."

Thackeray looked at Miss O'Grady's house, which, in terms of general dilapidation, did not look much different from its neighbour. But the front path, he noticed, was swept clean, and in the tiny patch of earth alongside a few plants struggled to bloom, and he knew that such things counted.

"Can I come in?" he asked. Lettie O'Grady nodded sharply and, leaning her weight heavily on a walking stick, she led him into the living room which was mainly taken up with a huge double bed from which quilts and blankets tumbled in a tangled and slightly malodorous heap.

"Can't get upstairs no more," Lettie said, waving him towards a communicating door that led into an untidy but, he was relieved to see, relatively clean kitchen. "Have to live down here – with all that noise." She gestured at the wall, through which the steady thumping beat he had heard outside reverberated even more loudly.

"You can get that stopped," he said, raising his voice to overcome the sound. Lettie banged on the wall vigorously with her stick and the sound subsided fractionally in response. She waved Thackeray into a rickety chair at the cluttered table but continued to hobble around the room herself, picking things up and putting them down again with nervous intensity.

"There's someone in then," he said.

"Always someone in," Lettie said venomously. "Squatters, aren't they? No right to be there. Got in there when old Jim

63

Forrester died and they couldn't find his next o'kin. They stay in and guard the place, don't they? Got a huge great dog. No-one dares go near. Squatters on that side, students on the other. I've lived here fifty years, and it's getting worse and worse."

"It was one of the squatters I wanted to see," Thackeray said. "A young woman called Jancie McLeod."

"I don't know what any of 'em is called. Come and go all hours, they do."

"Were you here when one of them died?"

"Ambulance," Lettie said and cackled with laughter. "I thought they'd come for me."

"You didn't know the lad? Tom, he was called."

"I don't sleep, you know. In case they come for me in the night," Lettie said unexpectedly, her eyes suddenly glittering.

"In case who comes?" Thackeray said sharply. "Has someone threatened you?"

"Them that's watching," Lettie said. "They think I don't know. But I do. I see them. Black eyes on the telly. Through the letterbox. Watching. I see them all."

Lettie glanced out of the kitchen window into the small back garden where huge clumps of michaelmas daisies were just coming into bloom amongst the overgrown grass and weeds.

"Out back," she said fiercely. "When that dog's not there, they're watching." For a moment Thackeray almost believed her, but when he asked her to describe the watchers she simply giggled and cut herself a slice from a stale looking loaf and crammed it into her mouth.

"Are you going to get rid of them?" she asked when she had finished.

"The watchers? I'm not sure . . ."

"No, them noisy kids," Lettie said, the manic gleam in her eyes gone now, and her voice sharply aggressive again.

"Can I get to the house from the back?" Thackeray asked, glancing out to where a wooden fence separated the two back gardens.

"Oooh, yes," Lettie said enthusiastically. "Climb over the fence. You can get in that way." She banged her back door fiercely with her stick until it swung open on a sagging hinge and peered out.

"They're not watching," she said confidently and gave Thackeray an ineffectual shove towards the fence. Thackeray looked cautiously into the next-door plot, which was almost as cluttered as the front garden and heavily soiled with dog mess.

"Christ," he muttered as, confident there was no aggressive canine presence lurking amongst the overgrown shrubs, he hauled himself over the fence. But whether or not Lettie's watchers were present, he had hardly taken a step towards the back door before it was flung open and a menacing growl stopped him in his tracks. A heavy black alsatian quivered on the threshold, his collar held with what Thackeray thought was insufficient commitment by a tall thin young woman in jeans and a loose and far from clean white top.

"If that bastard touches me I'll have you in court and the dog put down before you know what's hit you," he said quietly. The girl tightened her grip marginally on the dog's collar.

"Who the hell are you?" she asked.

"I'm a friend of Tom Harrison's mother," Thackeray said. "I knocked on the front door but no-one answered. I'm looking for Jancie McLeod."

"How do I know you're not from the effing council?" the girl asked, her eyes almost as unfriendly as those of the dog, which was straining against her grip.

"You'll just have to believe me," Thackeray said, walking slowly towards the door and ignoring the dog's low growls. "Penny Harrison asked me to come. And I'm not going to go away until I've seen Tom's girlfriend." He stopped a good yard from the threshold, meeting the dog's eye until it glanced away and sat on its haunches, quivering with tension.

"Are you Jancie?" he asked the girl, taking in the emaciated figure and the huge dark eyes in the pale face. She nodded imperceptibly.

"Are you here by yourself?" She nodded again.

"You can talk to me out here if you'd rather," Thackeray said. "I don't need to come inside."

Jancie shivered convulsively and turned away, fondling the dog's huge head as she did so. It followed her obediently into the house. "You can come in," she said over her shoulder. "Bisto'd kill you if you tried to hurt me."

"Bisto?"

"He was gravy coloured when he was a puppy," she said inconsequentially.

She led Thackeray through a kitchen that resembled somewhere that had been shelled during the worst days of Sarajevo, into the main room with its blanketted windows and a stereo system that made the air throb with sound and Thackeray's ribs vibrate. Without being asked she switched the music off and Thackeray swallowed hard to clear his ringing ears. The girl flung herself down on a sofa piled with blankets and multi-coloured cushions and Bisto took up a position beside her from which he could watch every move Thackeray might make.

He tipped a pile of magazines and papers off a wooden chair close to the door and sat down. He glanced around the room, taking in the slightly scented air, and the used syringe just visible beneath the sofa.

"So what's she on about now, Tom's mum?" Jancie said, her voice brittle. "She can't accept it, can she? The rest of us have to, but she can't."

"What are you on, Jancie? Heroin?" Thackeray asked. The girl looked at him blankly for a moment but did not reply. He wanted to grab her by those thin shoulders and get a good look at the arms which he was sure were riddled with injection scars, but he knew that the dog would not allow him to get anywhere near her.

66

"What Penny Harrison can't come to terms with is that her son was a junkie," Thackeray said, more harshly now. "So which of you started first, you or him?"

"You don't know anything about anything that went on here," the girl said. "None of you do."

"Penny blames herself for Tom's death," Thackeray said. "I told her it wasn't her fault. But was it yours, Jancie? Did you get him hooked?"

The girl stared at him with pitiless contempt.

"He wasn't a junkie," she said. "We told the police that."

Thackeray pulled the local newspaper cutting that Penny Harrison had given him out of his pocket and looked at it again. He knew that the girl must have seen it.

"That's not what the coroner concluded," he said.

"The inquest was rubbish," Jancie said. "They said if he wasn't injecting – and the pathologist said he wasn't – *and* he wasn't! – then he must have been smoking the stuff. And he wasn't doing that either. I told them that, but they wouldn't listen, would they?"

"So how did he come to die of a massive overdose of heroin?" Thackeray asked. "Injected heroin?" The girl looked at him, her eyes filled with misery, and shrugged those thin shoulders.

"Was it deliberate? Did he kill himself?" Thackeray persisted, thinking that if his girlfriend believed that of Tom Harrison it was not information he much wanted to pass on to the boy's mother.

"No," the girl said, evidently outraged at the suggestion. "Of course he didn't kill himself. I was pregnant, wasn't I? I was going to come off the stuff and we were going to have the baby. Tom was really excited about it. He'd never have killed himself. Someone killed him, didn't they?"

"You mean you think he was murdered?"

"Sure," Jancie said, with a shrug. "And we know who did it, don't we? But no-one believes us, so what's the point?"

"You know?" Thackeray tried to keep the incredulity out of his voice, but the girl just shrugged and he noticed that her hands were beginning to shake as she fondled the dog's ears.

"It's a long story, all to do with a dealer, and me coming off drugs, and Tom thumping him in the mouth. So surprise, surprise, one day I find Tom dead, and a nice little stash all ready for me . . ."

She stopped and ran a hand through her hair.

"Sod off, now," she said wearily. "I don't want to talk about Tom any more. I need a fix."

"When's the baby due?" Thackeray asked, catching a glimpse of the scarred arm he was expecting to see as Jancie fiddled nervously with her sleeve.

"I got rid of the baby," she said, avoiding his eyes.

Of course you did, he thought to himself helplessly as he watched her scrabble behind the cushions and pull out a syringe and a small packet. By rights, he should confiscate her drugs and arrest her, he thought bitterly, knowing that he would do no such thing.

"Are you at least going to tell me who you think killed Tom?" he said. "His mother needs to know what really happened."

"No she doesn't," Jancie said, rolling up her sleeve to expose inflamed veins and infected scars. She twisted what looked like the cord of a dressing gown between her hands with increasing agitation. "It wouldn't do her any good. It wouldn't do any of us any good. It's over now. Tell her to just accept that it was an accident, why don't you? That's the best thing."

"You're wrong," Thackeray said. "It's always better to know the truth."

"That's what Tom said about his father," Jancie said. "And look where it got him. Bloody nowhere, is where. Now sod off, can't you! Go!" Her voice rose and the dog, picking up her mood, gave a low, menacing growl and Thackeray knew that he would get no more out of the girl now.

"I'll come back when the others are here," he said, getting cautiously to his feet, one eye on Bisto.

"Please yourself," the girl said, wrapping her cord around her upper arm even before he had reached the door. "That's what men do, isn't it?"

Back in the narrow street, made narrower by a clutter of parked cars, Thackeray cursed when he discovered that the bike, which he had carefully locked to the gatepost, had gone. A remnant of plastic covered cable was all that remained of his transport and he saw his deposit disappearing into the hire shop's till with the same inevitability.

He glanced at his watch. If he hurried and caught a bus through the rush hour traffic, he might just get back to the college in time for a shower and a chat with the master before the evening meal was served. He kicked the remnants of his bike lock angrily into some bushes and set off down the narrow street. But before he had gone more than a few yards he felt the hairs on the back of his neck prickle. He turned quickly, certain that he was being watched, and wondered for a moment whether Lettie O'Grady's complaints of being spied on were as hallucinatory as he had imagined. But the road was deserted and he could not see even the slightest twitch of a curtain at any of the houses nearby. With a shrug, he began to walk briskly again, back towards the Cowley Road.

There was no warning as he was struck a tremendous blow on the back of the head, which brought him to his knees. With a rugby player's instinct, he twisted as he fell, but caught no more than a glimpse of a figure, dressed in black, and with some sort of a scarf covering most of his face, before another blow from the weapon his assailant was already raising above his head caught his shoulders and sent him sprawling across the pavement, leaving him face down and gasping for air in the gutter against the wheel of parked car. Dazed and helpless, he braced himself for further blows but the assault stopped as suddenly and inexplicably as it had begun. But by the time Thackeray had propped himself upright against the car, and wiped what he realised was blood out of his eyes, the street was as deserted and silent as it had been moments before.

He sat for a moment with his head between his knees, taking in gulps of air and trying to reorientate his fragmented senses, before he hauled himself to his feet and reached for a hankerchief and his mobile phone. But as he dabbed ineffectually at the blood, which seemed to be seeping rather than pouring from the bruise on his head, he began to wonder whether dialling 999, which had been his first instinct, was such a good idea. He was not, he realised, badly hurt. And he did not feel in the mood to explain to the Thames Valley police just why he had been visiting Tom Harrison's girlfriend, or on whose behalf.

"You're old enough to have more bloody sense," he muttered to himself as he put the phone away again. He did not think he would share his humiliation today.

Chapter Seven

The three remaining squat blocks of flats known as the Heights lowered above Bradfield, a monstrous if well-meant monument to 1960s attempts to relieve the town from its legacy of ill-lit, ill-ventilated and damp back-to-back mill-workers terraces. Named after local writers, the fourth block, Brontë House, had been pulled down a few years before, sagging terminally under the weight of dereliction, with water pouring through its prefabricated structure and crime endemic on its concrete corridors. So far, the other three blocks had survived as the prospects of replacing them with more acceptable homes had slithered out of the cash-strapped town council's grasp.

Kelly James's family lived on the fourth floor of Priestley, a stiff climb up a bleak concrete staircase smelling alternately of urine and disinfectant depending on whether or not this was the day its turn came for a brisk hosing down. Kevin Mower led the way to the front door along the walkway open to the sharp Pennine breeze from the west. The door was opened by a pasty-faced Lorraine James, still in a grubby dressing gown.

"Oh, it's you," she muttered, reluctantly pulling the door back so that Mower and Val Ridley could enter. "I'd forgotten you were coming. Carl's still in bed."

"Can you get him up, Mrs James?" Mower said, not bothering to hide his irritation. He had slept badly again and felt only marginally in control of his faculties. "I told you we needed to talk to you both this morning."

"He'll not be right chuffed," Lorraine said sulkily, but she left them in a sparsely furnished living room from where they could hear her in the adjacent bedroom attempting to persuade Hegerty to wake up.

"It's obviously not the day either of them have to sign on," Val Ridley muttered, surveying the scruffy living room with distaste.

"I thought she said she had a job," Mower said.

"Yeah, well," Val said, casting a bleak eye over the room. A couple of school photographs on the mantelpiece showed two children in school uniform, a boy of mixed race and an older girl with gold blonde hair, half smiling at the camera. "It looks like Kelly's got a little brother," she said. "Half-brother anyway."

After a deal of muffled thumping and mumbling in the bedroom next door, Lorraine came back into the room, dressed now in jeans and a sleeveless top, closely followed by Carl Hegerty, in baggy shorts and a T shirt, still rubbing sleep out of his eyes.

"Have you not found the beggar who beat up our Kelly yet?" he asked aggressively.

"We need to ask you a few more questions about Kelly's friends," Mower said, more calmly than he felt.

"Well, we wouldn't know, would we?" Hegerty said. "We don't go out clubbing with her, do we?"

Val Ridley glanced at the photograph of the two children and raised an eyebrow.

"Your son's at school, is he, Mrs James? He gets himself out in the morning, does he?" Lorraine glanced at Carl before replying.

"Darren doesn't live here no more," she said. "He's in care."

"Why's that, then?" Val Ridley asked.

"He and Carl don't get on," Lorraine muttered, glancing at her boyfriend with an anxious expression. Mower wondered why Lorraine was so afraid of him.

"Little bastard, he were," Hegerty broke in, flinging himself onto the sagging sofa, which took up much of the small room. "Never did what he were told. Started staying out all bloody night. Nowt to do wi' me. He's not my lad. She couldn't control him. I'd ha' skelped him if he'd bin mine." He looked meaningfully at Lorraine, who shrugged helplessly and lit a cigarette.

"So you never hit Darren or Kelly, Mr Hegerty?" Kevin Mower asked. Hegerty shook his head.

"Nah," he said.

"And you Mrs James?" Mower persisted.

"Not now," she said quickly. "I'd belt 'em when they were little. What d'you think? But Kelly's taller than me now. They'd belt me back if I tried owt like that. In fact, Darren did once or twice. Gave me a right black eye. That's why he had to go."

"And he's how old now? Eleven? Twelve?" Val Ridley asked, glancing again at the photograph of the two children with the identical faint smiles for the camera but with eyes that seemed to be wiped clean of all emotion.

"Coming up to twelve," Darren's mother said, without enthusiasm. "Next week, his birthday, innit?"

"What's all this about, any road?" Hegerty asked, his initial aggression returning. "You don't think we beat Kelly up, do you? We told you. We come home and went to bed. We knew nowt about it till the next morning."

"Wouldn't you usually have expected the three girls to come home together, Mrs James?" Mower asked, ignoring Hegerty. "If they went out together, you'd expect them to see each other safely home?"

"I suppose so," Lorraine said, dragging heavily on her cigarette.

"But the other girls say that's not what usually happened," Mower came back quickly. "They say if they "scored", they'd usually come back on their own. They didn't seem to accept that they had to look after Kelly. Didn't you know that?"

Lorraine shrugged.

"She did as she liked," she said. "Don't they all?"

"She wasn't expected in by a certain time?" Mower asked.

"What's the point of that? They teck no bloody notice, do they?"

"So you can't have been very surprised when she came home pregnant?" Mower persisted.

"I were bloody furious," Lorraine said. "Silly little cow. I'd told her time and time again to teck care."

"Little slag," Hegerty muttered under his breath.

"So who paid for her abortion?" Val Ridley broke in sharply.

"Paid for it?" Lorraine looked blank. "She got it on t'National Health, didn't she? She were only twelve, for God's sake. Social worker said she could go back to school straight away if I looked after the babby for her, didn't she? Daft cow. What would I want to do that for? I told her to get rid."

"And did Kelly tell you who the father was?" Val persisted.

Lorraine shrugged and glanced at Hegerty.

"She never said nowt to me," she said.

"And even after that you still let her stay out all hours?" Val asked sharply.

"She were on t'pill then, weren't she? Doctor put her on t'pill after."

"So that was all right then," Mower muttered, only half under his breath. Val Ridley glanced at him. His face was pale and there were beads of sweat on the dark hairline.

"And you're sure she never told you who the father of the baby was?" she asked. Kelly's parents shrugged in unison.

"She's say nowt about it to me," Lorraine said. "Said it were none o' my business. Wouldn't tell anyone, so far as I know."

"So you don't know if she was still knocking around with the same lad? Or any lad, for that matter?" DC Ridley persisted.

"She said nowt to us about a boyfriend. Never." Lorraine lit another cigarette from the butt of the previous one and

74

inhaled deeply. "She were going out wi' her mates as far as I were concerned. All lasses together. She said nowt about boys."

Mower got to his feet abruptly.

"Right, we'll leave it there, for now," he said. Val Ridley followed him to the door slightly reluctantly and after the door had slammed shut behind them she stood for a moment looking over the walkway railings. Their car was parked a hundred feet below and she could see that the side window had been smashed in. There was no-one in sight.

"Bloody little toerags," she said angrily. "Look what they've done." Mower gripped the balustrade as if he needed help in staying upright.

"I had to get out of there," he said. "Those two were getting to me."

"Call themselves parents," Val Ridley said angrily. "One kid in care and the other running wild and getting herself pregnant, raped, beaten senseless? Just what did happen to Kelly anyway? We don't even know that, do we? She can't bloody remember. Or won't. These people don't need a police force. They should be in a bloody menagerie."

Mower looked at her wearily. In other circumstances, as a child of a block very similar to Priestley House and a London neighbourhood as reviled, he would have challenged her assumptions as simplistic. But today, as on so many days recently, he could barely find the energy to go through the motions required of him. He was drowning, he thought, and if he went down one more time, he knew he might not come up again.

"Sod you," he said under his breath as he turned away and headed down the bleak concrete stairs to assess the damage to their vandalised car.

"So you think she was asking for it, do you?" DCI Bairstow asked sharply. "That's not very politically correct of you."

Val Ridley flushed slightly and brushed a non-existent lock of hair from her eyes.

75

"Normally, I'd agree, ma'am," she said. "And I didn't mean it quite like that. But she was drunk. Out of her skull, one of her friends said. And I guess she'd been on more than the booze. She says she doesn't remember what happened. We can't charge anyone with rape if she doesn't know whether or not she was raped. Quite honestly, I wouldn't waste much time on this one."

Jackie Bairstow leaned back in her chair and turned a chilly gaze on Kevin Mower, who was standing uneasily by the door of the DCI's office.

"What do you think, Kevin?" she asked. Mower ran a hand across his dark hair and straightened up imperceptibly.

"I think Kelly James was raped. Possibly raped repeatedly, if the medical evidence we've got now is right. And now she's frightened out of her wits," he said slowly. "I don't know why, but I think we should find out. Ma'am."

DCI Bairstow got to her feet, smoothed down her tight black skirt against slim thighs and tossed her silver hair, cut in a sleek bob, away from her face as she slipped into her jacket. Val Ridley suspected that this little performance was strictly for Mower's benefit. She also knew that given Mower's present state of mind, the DCI was wasting her time, and she smiled faintly at her superior intelligence.

"I didn't put you down as the crusading type, sergeant," DCI Bairstow said. "But I'll talk to the super. Keep it a high profile case for a day or two longer. See where we get. OK? You never know, this might just be a first effort by a serial rapist. We wouldn't want to risk down-playing that, now would we, because we all know where that leads? Straight to a Ripper scenario." Jackie Bairstow gave the distinct impression that was a scenario she might relish as she ushered the two detectives out of the door ahead of her.

"By the way, Val," she said, putting a hand on the detective constable's arm. "As the only women in CID, you and I should get together some time to talk about a few issues. OK?"

"Fine," Val said faintly.

"Jesus wept," Mower said as he watched the DCI's retreating back and she passed out of earshot. "What the hell have we got here?"

Laura Ackroyd and Vicky Mendelson stood in the late afternoon sunlight, which was streaming through the tall windows of a Victorian front room. The bare boards had thrown up clouds of dust as they had stepped inside and they danced now in the golden light while they surveyed the peeling Laura Ashley wallpaper and mahogany fireplace and fretted cornices of the room with a critical gaze. The ground-floor flat was part of a tall detached villa off Aysgarth Lane and little seemed to have been done to it since the house had been split up into flats thirty years earlier.

"It's a bit more spacious than your attic was," Vicky said, spinning round slowly with her baby daughter in her arms. "More central too. Can you afford it?"

"They're not asking much more than I'll get for my place, according to the agents," Laura said. "But it needs a lot of modernising."

"New kitchen, new bathroom. But it looks sound enough. And you get the garden, as it's the ground floor. That's good."

Laura shrugged slightly and ran her fingers lightly over the dusty mantelshelf, tracing out an L and an M and then obliterating the marks irritably with a puff of breath.

"Is your man any good at DIY?" Vicky asked, avoiding Laura's eye. Her friend gazed out of the window at the late summer garden.

"Don't ask," she said at last. "I don't know, Vicky. How would I know? I don't even know whether I'm looking for a flat for myself or for the two of us."

"Well, if you want my opinion, which I don't suppose you do, I think it's time you decided, one way or another. I thought it was twentysomething men who couldn't get their minds round commitment. Michael's too old to be messing you about like this. Perhaps you should have gone for that job you turned down in London, after all."

"Maybe," Laura said dully. Then she squared her shoulders and turned back to Vicky with a rueful smile. "Come here, Naomi Laura," she said, taking the child from Vicky and giving her a hug. In a fit of affection, and some astonishment at the red hair the baby had been born with, the Mendelsons had named their daughter after their friend. "Let's go and have a look at the flowers, shall we, sweetheart?"

The three of them made their way out of the back door, down three stone steps and onto a patch of long grass, which must once have been a lawn, surrounded by overgrown rose bushes, their autumn flush of flowers just breaking bud in a riot of pink and gold.

"I could have a dog here," Laura said, breathing deeply. "You'd like that, Naomi, wouldn't you? Would you come and see Laura's doggie?"

"Doggie," the child said happily.

"And some kids," Vicky said fiercely, watching the sun set fire to her daughter's and her friend's copper curls. "It's big enough, this place."

"Oh, let's not try to cross too many bridges at once," Laura said, dispirited again, as she felt the relentless biological clock ticking discordantly against her conviction that Michael Thackeray wanted no more children. "I'll tell Michael about it when I see him at the weekend. See what he thinks."

"He's not still depressed about the girl who died, is he?" Vicky asked. "No-one's blaming him for that, are they?"

"Probably no-one but Michael himself," Laura said. "And he has an infinite capacity for that."

Laura dropped Vicky off at home just as another friend delivered her two young sons to the door after school.

"I'll see you for supper about seven," Vicky said as the small boys enveloped her in excited chatter about their day. "Give Joyce my love."

Laura crashed through her unfamiliar gears in a three-point turn and accelerated away to join the early rush hour traffic in the town centre and then ground up the long hill towards the Heights. There, outside a tiny bungalow in the shadow of the blocks of flats, she locked the new car carefully, although she knew that not much she could do in the way of security would prevent her wheels disappearing if one of the local gangs of youths decided they had urgent need of cash that afternoon. It was a good job that not many of the pensioners on what those same youths derided as "death row" could afford cars, she thought.

She knocked at the front door of the bungalow and was irritated to find, when she tried the handle, that it swung open.

"Nan, you're incorrigible," she said as she went into the tiny sitting room, softening the complaint with a smile and a kiss for Joyce Ackroyd, whose face lit up at Laura's arrival. "You must lock your doors."

"Oh, if they want to get in, love, they'll get in," Joyce said blithely from her chair by the gas fire, as she drank in the sight of her only granddaughter and one who resembled her not only in looks – though Joyce's red hair was pure white now – but also in temperament.

Laura turned away and was surprised to see that Joyce was not alone. Another woman, comfortably plump, unashamedly middle-aged in her unfashionable pleated plaid skirt and lavender sweater, but with a very determined line to her jaw and sparkle to her eyes, was sitting in a chair half concealed by the door. She seemed slightly startled by the interruption.

"This is Cathy Draper," Joyce said. "She's one of the volunteers at the advice centre they've set up in Holtby House. We were just talking about battered women."

"I came to see how you were settled again after the Portuguese trip," Laura said ruefully. "I needn't have worried, need I? I can see you're raring to get back into the fast lane."

"Aye, well, you know me," Joyce said, shifting slightly uncomfortably in her chair. "My leg's fine now. The doctors say the bone's healed better than I've any right to expect at my age."

"Good," Laura said, knowing that any further disability would seriously threaten Joyce's cherished independence, something Laura feared almost as much as she knew her grandmother did.

"Your mother was very kind when I was over there," Joyce said. "Even your dad put himself out. Now and again. But quite honestly, I'd be dead of boredom if I had to live out there much longer than it took me to get back on my feet. The highlights of the day seem to be the arrival of the *Daily Telegraph* at lunch-time and deciding whether to have a G and T or a Scotch and soda on the terrace before dinner."

"Yes, well, tell me about it next time my boss has bawled me out because my copy's missed its deadline by thirty seconds," Laura said. "There are times when extremely early retirement has its attractions."

"What you need is your union recognition back so you can deal with bullies like Ted Grant," Joyce said.

"Yes, right," Laura said, realising that Cathy Draper was listening to these inter-generational exchanges with some bemusement and not wanting to encourage one of Joyce's lengthier political tirades, honed by years of town hall politics. "I only really came up to tell you that I'm going to be away this weekend, so don't expect me on Sunday. I'm going down to Oxford to see Michael."

"Huh." Joyce's extended convalescence in Portugal with a broken leg had obviously done little to reconcile her to what she had long regarded as her grand-daughter's unsatisfactory relationship with Michael Thackeray.

"What's he doing down south then?" she asked. "I'd have thought with young girls being raped and beaten up willy-nilly he'd have been leading the investigations up here. It's not as if the Heights suffers from over-policing, is it?"

Cathy Draper leaned forward in her seat at that and cleared her throat, as if unsure whether the sparring Ackroyd women would welcome an intervention on her part.

"Michael'll be back in a week or so," Laura said. "In the meantime, his stand-in is a woman, which should please you, as the oldest feminist on the block."

"That'll be Chief Inspector Bairstow, will it?" Cathy Draper ventured at last. "I had the police over earlier this afternoon asking about the safety of the young girls on the estate. They seem to be worried that it might happen again."

"Really?" Laura said, her reporter's instincts stirred by that. "What's the basis for that assumption then? I thought they were looking for one of Kelly James's pick-ups who'd gone over the top."

Cathy looked flustered by Laura's sudden interest.

"It was just a remark the young woman detective who dropped in made," she said. "Something about her Inspector Bairstow fancying it was a serial rapist. Personally, I'd have thought it was more likely Kelly got beaten up by that thug her mother's living with. I had her in not long ago complaining he was abusing her. Hitting her, I mean. But she wouldn't go to the police. Not that hitting her means he'd go as far as rape . . ."

"Kelly, you mean, or her mother?" Laura asked sharply.

"Oh, the mother," Cathy said quickly. "She never said anything about Kelly. And she wouldn't make a complaint to the police. They're their own worst enemy, some of these women. They put up with far too much."

"Did you tell the police all this?" Joyce asked as Cathy, her face flushed, ran her hands around the neck of her sweater as if it has suddenly become too tight.

"No, they didn't ask . . . I didn't think . . . Do you think I should have done?"

Chapter Eight

Michael Thackeray combed his damp hair carefully over the bruise at the back of his head, wishing that he had something stronger than paracetomol in his luggage to control the thumping headache and aching muscles, which were the main legacy of the assault he had suffered just hours earlier. Stripped off for his shower, he had twisted his neck painfully to see the full extent of the damage across his back and shoulders before washing the congealed blood out of his hair. It was a good job they had missed his face, he thought as he surveyed the swellings, which were rapidly turning from an angry red to purple. At least, if he moved carefully enough to avoid wincing, he could conceal the fact that he had been attacked, for the time being at least.

Standing naked in a chilly college bathroom examining the damage reminded him of how many times he had done the same thing after a rugby match. Safe from the scrutiny of his team-mates and their fiercely competitive stoicism, he had more than once gone to bed with his self-esteem as bruised as his body. He had been frustatingly aware that there was nothing he could do to enhance his standing with those who despised him. That was the nature of blind prejudice, he thought. At that age, he could no more contemplate changing his accent, his ancestry or his religion than a Jamaican or an Indian could change the colour of his skin. He had thought those things immutable, although in the end some of them had been eroded by time and bitter experience. And it had taken a long time at St Frideswide's for his pride to reassert itself and for him to learn to give as good as he got physically on the field and stay clear of his tormentors off it.

Dressed now in a white shirt and dark suit, even though he had more difficulty than usual in persuading his hair to lie flat, he concluded that no-one would guess he had been sprawling in a Cowley gutter so recently as he took a parting glance in the mirror over the empty fireplace in his room. As for the headache, he would try to kill two birds with one stone on his way to the master's lodgings.

St Frideswide's general office was situated near the main gate close to the porter's lodge, and Thackeray had already noticed that, presumably for the duration of the course, it was staffed until the course members went to dinner. At six-thirty he strolled across the quadrangle, through the deep shade cast by the chapel tower and out into the rosy sunshine of the September evening, which lit up the golden stone of the arched gateway through which it was possible to glimpse the broad and busy expanse of St Giles and the town beyond.

He tapped gently on the glass of the office door and went in. A woman was working at a word processer on the far side of the room and looked up with a smile of interrogation as Thackeray stopped by the inquiry counter.

"Can I help you?" she said. "Are you on the police course?" Thackeray nodded.

"A silly request, but the chemists will be shut now and I need painkillers of some sort. I haven't brought anything with me and I've got a thumping headache."

"Been over-indulging in the buttery?" the woman asked. She was small and blonde and friendly and there was no offence in the question. "You're all a bit senior for such under-graduate games, aren't you?" She opened a drawer in her desk and rooted about for a moment before pulling out a packet of Panadol.

"These any good?" she said, crossing the room and handing them to him. "I should take two if it's really bad."

"I'm sure," Thackeray said. "You're obviously used to handing out the tender loving care. Comes with the job, does it?"

"The kids who come from boarding school are the worst," she said. "They've always been able to run to matron. Suddenly there's no matron and they seem to think that any female over twenty-five is a substitute." The woman smiled, obviously not minding her motherly role in college life too much.

"You still get a lot of public school people, do you? I was here in the seventies and the place was overrun with them then." Thackeray wondered if he had overdone the implied disapproval as the women hesitated for a moment. But then she smiled again.

"So I believe," she said. "I wasn't around then. But I'm told letting in girls has civilised the place a lot."

"The first women arrived in my final year," Thackeray said. "The rugby men gave them a hard time."

"They still do, if they can get away with it," the woman said. "I mean it's nothing to do with me . . ." She shrugged.

"But you hear things?"

"Of course," she said. "Mr . . . ?"

"Thackeray. Michael Thackeray." He held out a hand and she took it, obviously slightly taken aback at the old-fashioned courtesy.

"Sue Bentley," she said.

"I was surprised to hear about Mark Harrison disappearing like that," Thackeray said, leaning confidentially on the counter and speaking more softly. "He was here when I was. I played rugby with him. I couldn't believe he'd go off like that, leave his family, his students . . . I suppose you knew his girl-friend?"

Sue's face tightened perceptibly and she looked down at the counter, drawing a pattern with one finger on the surface.

"This is a small college," she said. "But of course you know that. We all knew Dr Harrison. And Emma Capstick." She said no more and Thackeray knew that he would have to use more persuasive tactics.

"The master asked me if there was anything I could do to help find them," he said. "I don't suppose he has so many tame coppers around very often, and certainly not many who actually knew Mark. He's very worried about the effect of his disappearance on his students."

"So he damn well should be," Sue Bentley said explosively. "No-one seemed to be giving them a moment's thought when those two disappeared. Or Emma's family, for that matter."

"She has a family?"

"Oh, she wasn't married. It wasn't that. She was only twenty-four or so. She'd only had one other job, I think. Something out Burford way. She was only a girl, really. She seemed content just to have a good time until she took up with Dr Harrison. That was my impression anyway. Not that she talked about it much. But it was obvious that she was really in love . . . And then one Monday morning at the beginning of the vacation, they'd just gone. No word to his wife, apparently. No word to her mother. She lives somewhere in the Cotswolds. I saw her just the once when she came in to see Dr Partridge, no doubt trying to find out what the hell was going on. Obviously, things weren't going very well for her, though whether that was because of Emma or not I don't know."

"So you had no warning at all? One day they were there . . . ?"

"The Friday. Emma was at work. Said she was going to the Playhouse with Dr Harrison on Saturday night. Didn't like it much when I gave her a look. I didn't think it was right, what they were doing. He was far too old for her. She was far too impressionable. I suppose I'm not very trendy, but it seemed all wrong to me." Thackeray hid his surprise at that and wondered whether, by Sue Bentley's old-fashioned yard-stick, he was also too old for Laura.

"And on Monday they'd gone?" he persisted.

"On Monday they'd gone. Vanished without a word."

"Do you know where Emma's mother lives? Do you have an address in your files?"

86

Sue looked unsure for a moment and then shook her head.

"Dr Partridge took her file away soon after they went," she said. "If you want to see it you'll have to ask him."

"Thanks for your help," Thackeray said, giving her one of his rare smiles, quite oblivious of the effect it had on her.

"If you need more pain-killers later there's a late-opening chemist up the Woodstock Road, you know. Just opposite St Anne's . . ."

"Thanks."

Thackeray looked thoughtful as he made his way to the master's lodge. Hugh Greenaway opened the door himself and nodded him through into the drawing room where the French windows stood open to the mild evening air and the scent of flowers from the walled garden outside.

"Are you enjoying your resurrection as a student?" he asked, waving Thackeray into a chair and pouring him a tonic with ice and lemon without being asked. Thackeray nodded, trying to disguise gritted teeth as he tried to find a position that did not set the muscles across his shoulders protesting.

"It's a useful course," he said. "If I'm going to be allowed to resume my career."

"There's no serious risk of your not being allowed to, is there?" Greenaway asked, handing him his drink.

"In the present climate, who knows? It depends if they want another scapegoat or whether the bastards who actually fired the shots will suffice. Neglect of duty means pretty much what they want it to mean if they want you out." He sipped his drink and gazed into the tranquil garden where a blackbird was hopping across the lawn with its head on one side, listening for subterranean activity.

"It would be a pity if they wanted you out," Greenaway said. "Even now there aren't that many intelligent policemen around."

"Well, let's hope they're not wasting public money sending me down here then," Thackeray said, uncomfortable with the turn the conversation had taken. "Now, can I tell you where my freelance investigations have taken me – though it's not very far, it has to be said?" He sketched in for Greenaway the conversations he had had with Penny Harrison and Tom Harrison's girlfriend, leaving out both the girl's evident addiction and his own less than dignified encounter with an unknown assailant in the street.

"The wild card in all this seems to be Emma Capstick, the young woman he apparently ran away with. While there may be good reasons why Harrison wouldn't want to contact his family, or the college, there's no reason why the young woman should want to go to ground, is there?"

"Not that I know of," Greenaway said. "I didn't know her, of course. She came to work here long after I went to the States and had disappeared before I came back. But everyone speaks highly of her work. And most people seem to have liked her, for what that's worth. Apart from Magnus Partridge, of course, who's never knowingly liked a woman in his life, I suspect."

"Can you dig out her home address for me from your files? Or her mother's address, if you've got it? Apparently, Magnus Partridge took her file away from the office after she vanished and no-one there seems to know where her family lives."

"Magnus seems to have done a remarkably thorough job of covering up what happened rather than illuminating it," Greenaway said. "His only concern seems to have been to protect the college from embarrassment. Which is fine to an extent. It seems that none of us can survive without an element of spin these days. But he seems to have spun a web of such dense obfuscation that innocent people have been strangled by it. First Penny Harrison. Now it seems this girl's family as well."

"It seems entirely possible that Harrison's son was actually killed by it," Thackeray said grimly.

Greenaway raised an eyebrow at that.

88

"I only wanted a little clarification for the college's purposes," he said mildly. "I'd like my postgraduates to get their work back and some amends made. I wasn't looking for a crusade. There's no point in going out of our way to court bad publicity."

"If I find evidence of a crime . . ."

"Of course," Greenaway said smoothly. "But let's keep focused on Mark Harrison's whereabouts, shall we? Beyond that, I think we should leave it to the estimable Thames Valley force."

"Then it's to be hoped they've woken up a bit since the last time I had anything to do with them," Thackeray said sharply.

"That was a very long time ago," Greenaway said. "Let's see if we can locate Emma Capstick rather than the ghost of Liz Selby, shall we? I'd like to think she's still alive even if equally deluded. Do you feel like sharpening your forensic claws on Magnus right now?" Greenaway smiled maliciously. "If I tell him to answer your questions, he'll have to do it, won't he?"

"It would be a pleasure," Thackeray said.

Greenaway punched in some numbers on the phone which stood on a mahogany side-table.

"Could you ask Dr Partridge to spare the master ten minutes before dinner?" The answer was evidently satisfactory as Greenaway resumed his seat and sipped his sherry with a look of anticipation on his face.

"He's sixty-six years old," he said. "He's been here more or less without interruption since he was an undergraduate and it's another year before I can insist that he retires. He comes from an unbroken line of deeply conservative fellows from a very narrow spectrum of private schools, which have been sending scholars here for three hundred years or more. His attitudes are antediluvian, his prejudices entrenched, his attachment to the university's more arcane traditions absolute. He's a misogynist, a racist and a snob. And he has allies in almost all the older colleges. In any normal university he'd have been put out to grass in the 1980s when so many academics were culled. Here, he can go on to the bitter end, driving generation after generation of more enlightened people slowly round the bend – or into getting out themselves like I did."

"There aren't many safe havens these days for people like him," Thackeray said.

"Damn right," Greenaway said, a trace of his American years showing through. "And if I get my way – and I guess that's why I was elected – this won't be that sort of safe haven for very much longer."

The doorbell rang and Greenaway moved swiftly to answer it and usher his senior tutor, dark-suited and gowned, into the room. Partridge nodded coldly at Thackeray and accepted the glass of sherry, which Greenaway handed him without comment.

"Do sit down, Magnus," Greenaway said irritably. "Thackeray and I are discussing Mark Harrison's unfortunate absence, and I hope you can help us clarify a few points."

"Of course, master," Partridge said, wrapping his gown around himself like protective armour before sitting down. "What can I do to assist?" The effort of making the offer left Partridge looking as if he had just detected a very bad smell wafting from Thackeray's direction. His thin, seamed face, like cracked parchment, remained impassive and his eyes were cold and grey like still water on a winter's day.

"You can tell me for a start whether there was anything in Harrison's professional as opposed to his personal life which could have made it necessary for him to disappear so abruptly," Thackeray said, his own voice harsh with dislike. "Had he had his hand in the till, or the wine cellar or up too many students' skirts?" He was being deliberately crude in the hope that it might goad Partridge into giving somthing away, but he under-estimated the elderly academic's composure.

"He had committed none of those crimes as far as I am aware," Partridge said. "They are not misdemeanours with which the college has been unfamiliar on isolated occasions over the years, and they can all normally be resolved without recourse to a dramatic disappearance. Is that not the case, master?"

"Oh, I have it on good authority that even rape has been brushed under the carpet during the college's illustrious history," Greenaway said with distaste. "In the interests of not damaging the academic career of some brilliant young mind, you understand."

"Some slut of a kitchen girl in 1876, I believe," Partridge said. "There was quite a fierce debate at the time about the seemliness of allowing females onto the premises, even in a subservient role. They excluded them for some little time thereafter, I believe."

"But not for long enough to keep Emma Capstick off the premises," Thackeray said. He was afraid that his old dislike of Partridge would overwhelm him if he did not keep the conversation moving forward briskly.

"That is where you need to look, I think, if you really seek to elucidate Dr Harrison's motives for leaving so suddenly," Partridge said. "There is really no mystery here, you know. Very often the correct solution is the most obvious – in this case some sort of romantic entanglement through which he was persuaded to leave with the young woman and not return. My own considered view is that he is unlikely to come back and the whole unfortunate episode is best forgotten."

"Unfortunately there are half a dozen postgraduate students with a highly developed sense of grievance who would not agree with you, Magnus," Hugh Greenaway said. "I'm not sure a college has ever been sued by an aggrieved student but if there's going to be a first time these young people certainly have solid grounds."

"Sue the college?" Partridge said, evidently outraged. "What a preposterous notion. I think, master, you may have spent too much time in the United States of America."

"Years of their work has gone missing," Greenaway said angrily. "We have some obligation in those circumstances. They could claim negligence on our part with some justification."

"Could Harrison actually use the work to further his own career?" Thackeray asked. "Is there actually any reason why he might have deliberately decamped with unfinished postgraduate work?"

"There are probably institutions, which call themselves universities in America or the other former colonies, where he could pass it off as his own," Partridge said with distaste, but Greenaway demurred.

"It's unlikely the students had come up with anything mould-breaking in a PhD thesis," he said. "And he only seems to have taken some of the work. Nothing in a completed state. I think that is a dead-end as far as motivation is concerned."

"Can you let me have the file on Emma Capstick, Dr Partridge?" Thackeray put in quickly.

The senior tutor flashed him a look of intense dislike.

"I will endeavour to locate it," he said.

"Were you aware of this liaison, before they disappeared?"

Partridge gave another grimace of distaste before nodding almost imperceptibly.

"I had occasion to suggest to Dr Harrison that it was not appropriate to pursue matters on college premises," he said. "What they did elsewhere was their own affair, of course . . ."

"But they had been using Harrison's rooms?" Thackeray knew that most colleges disapproved of the use of the convenient provision of sleeping accommodation by fellows for extra-marital adventures.

"That was certainly my impression, yes," Partridge said.

"But there were no other "misdemeanours" in college which you knew of?" Thackeray persisted.

"He appeared to be a popular tutor," Partridge admitted grudgingly, and Thackeray guessed that was not an adjective which had ever sprung to the lips of the senior tutor's own students.

"And Emma Capstick had not given cause for dissatisfaction in the office?"

"Like most young women these days, she exhibited a taste in clothes which one could only describe as exhibitionist," Partridge said. "But her work was apparently entirely satisfactory."

"So tell me about the trips he was making abroad. Was that on college business?"

Partridge hesitated for a moment, unwilling to answer, but a glance from Greenaway seemed to assure him that there was no help available in that direction.

"You seem astonishingly well informed already," he said sourly. "As the master knows, Dr Harrison was helping me with the sexcentennial appeal. This is not a rich college, as you may remember. Some ill-advised support for the Parliamentarians during the Civil War lost us land, apparently irretrievably, when the Royalists controlled the city, and poor investment decisions by one of the masters in the eighteenth century worsened the financial position. Hence, this rather undignified appeal. I'm sure Professor Greenaway will not wish me to go into detail, but it is a well-known fact that we have alumni, to use the American expression, in many parts of the world. Dr Harrison's particular assignment was to make contact with some of those potential benefactors to inform them of our proposals . . ."

He turned away from Thackeray in evident irritation. "Which reminds me, master, there are matters which we need to discuss about the Feast next week. If we could have a private word."

Greenaway glanced ruefully at Thackeray who took the hint and stood up to go.

"You remember the Feast of the Munificent Carp?" Greenaway kept a straight face but Thackeray could see the glint of laughter in his eyes. "Perhaps you'd like to attend as my guest? It's quite an evening. The Monday after your course finishes? It falls the same night as St Giles's Fair this year, which is unfortunate, but the fellows refused point blank to change the date. The celebration is only held every five years and apparently tradition would not permit a change of date. I fear it will be a slightly noisy evening."

"Thanks, I'll have to check that out," Thackeray said noncommitally. He turned back to Partridge.

"If you could let me have that file on Emma Capstick tomorrow morning," he said in a tone which left no doubt that if authority were needed it could be brought to bear. The senior tutor gave him a look of pure venom, but he nodded his agreement.

"Of course, inspector," he said.

Thackeray ploughed his way through dinner, taking only a desultory interest in the conversation about crime management and clear-up rates, which ebbed and flowed around him. In spite of Sue Bentley's painkillers, the aches and pains in his head and shoulder were becoming fiercer and he could feel the muscles stiffening up. By the morning, he thought, he would find movement difficult and he wondered how Laura, when she arrived, would react to the sight and distinctly limited capacity of a seriously battered lover.

At the end of the meal, he decided to skip coffee in the senior common room and was making his way down the stone stairs to the quadrangle when someone clapped him heartily on the shoulder, making him yelp with pain.

"Christ," Thackeray said, half turning to see who had overtaken him and finding himself looking up into the unfriendly features of Thames Valley's Detective Chief Inspector, Cliff Gould.

"You're a jumpy beggar," Gould said.

"I went jogging round University Parks this morning to work off some of this stodgy food," Thackeray said quickly. "Slipped and wrenched my shoulder. It's bloody painful."

"Sorry," Gould said perfunctorily. "But I wanted to catch you before I bugger off home. You seemed very interested in Mark Harrison the other night, I recall."

"Well, only because I knew him slightly when I was an undergraduate here."

"You were here, were you?" Gould said, evidently surprised. "Well, well, it's astonishing where Oxford graduates finish up these days, isn't it? You did graduate, I take it? Not like that fictional copper who gets Thames Valley such a bad name?"

"I graduated," Thackeray said. "So what's new about Harrison, then? You haven't found him, have you?"

"No, no, not the father," Gould said. "But you said that the mother was still determined to create a fuss about the son. Not happy with the inquest verdict. That right?"

Thackeray nodded, wishing his headache was not making rational thought so difficult.

"Well, I checked out what went on when I went into the nick this morning and I thought if you saw her again you could disabuse her. Tactfully, I suppose, given her mental state. Not the details, of course, but just the fact that I'd put it at ninety-nine per cent certain that the inquest jury got it right about young Tom Harrison."

"You mean he accidentally OD'd on heroin?"

"Exactly. Not much doubt, according to one of my drug squad colleagues. Strictly off the record, they've still got the house under surveillance. They think his girlfriend's dealing, and it's quite likely he was too. It's a pot his mother won't get any joy from stirring up again."

"If I see her again I'll tell her that," Thackeray said, thinking that Lettie O'Grady's conviction she was being watched was not perhaps as outlandish as it had first seemed.

"Why don't you do that?" Gould said, gripping Thackeray's shoulder again and this time he knew the pressure was not accidental. "Mind how you go with your jogging," the Thames Valley man said as he strode away towards the main gate, leaving Thackeray to walk slowly to his room, wondering just why the local police were taking the trouble to warn him off so emphatically and what, if anything, he could do about it.

Chapter Nine

"Two men?" Val Ridley said incredulously, distracted from her paperwork by Kevin Mower's whistle of surprise.

"That's what the tests say." Mower was hunched over the medical report on Kelly James with an expression of faint distaste on his face. "She had sex with two men that night."

"So where does that leave us?" Val said helplessly. Mower, she thought, looked even more cadaverous than he had the night before. There were dark circles under his eyes and his hand shook slightly when he picked up the papers and handed them to her. "So is it gang rape or just a party girl?" she asked, when she had skimmed through the results of the forensic tests the police had asked for.

"Or is she on the game?" Mower offered sourly.

"I told you we shouldn't waste time on this one. I never thought she'd been raped."

"Come on, Val. Someone beat her half to death, whatever she'd been doing," Mower snapped. "You can't just wash her out of your hair. That's not on. Do you want to go and talk to her again? See if you can get any more out of her?"

"No, I want to talk to her boyfriend," Val said. "I finally got an admission out of one of her mates this morning that there is a boy she's been seeing on and off, a black lad called Gary Miller, lives on the Heights as well."

"Do we have any evidence that "on and off" included Saturday night?"

"This girl said she didn't see him, but that's no guarantee he wasn't there," Val said reluctantly.

Mower was filled with an overwhelming sense of futility as he contemplated the prospect of driving back up to the Heights to interview Gary Miller. It did not take anyone with eyes as sharp as DCI Bairstow's to work out that Mower was at the end of his tether. The growing piles of paperwork on his desk, the two days' dark stubble on his chin, and a shirt, which had not only not been ironed but had not noticeably been washed for several days, said it all. But when Jackie Bairstow had taken that particular inventory that morning she had not commented beyond an imperceptible tightening of the lips and a raised eyebrow in Val Ridley's general direction. Mower had appeared oblivious, but Val herself doubted whether by now the DCI's manifest ambitions included Mower in a Bradfield CID reconstructed to her own exacting specifications. Kevin Mower, she thought, ran a severe risk of being downsized in some way if Michael Thackeray did not return to Bradfield soon, and that aroused emotions in her own breast which she hesitated to examine too closely.

"Come on, Kevin," Val said, quietly enough not to be overheard. "Come with me. You need to be out of here." Mower gave her an ironic glance and rubbed a hand wearily over his unshaven chin.

"In more ways than one," he said.

DC Ridley drove with Mower slumped in the passenger seat beside her. As she changed down a gear to follow a lorry belching black deisel fumes up the hill to Wuthering, she glanced in his direction more than once but he just as resolutely gazed out of the window to his left and avoided any possibility of conversation.

With her mind only half on the road, Val allowed her thoughts to roam. She had been surprised the previous evening when DCI Bairstow had followed up her half-promise and invited her for a drink after work. Settled in a modern bar some distance from CID's usual watering-hole, she had felt Jackie Bairstow's evaluating gaze rake her from the top of her short-cut blonde hair to the slightly scuffed heels of her sensible shoes as she had carried the drinks carefully over to their corner table.

"How do you find CID, then? As a woman?" Bairstow had demanded without preamble. Val had shrugged lightly. If six years working with male detectives had taught her anything, it was to give as little as possible away.

"I'd have thought you'd have gone for sergeant by now," the DCI had persisted. "A bright woman like you."

"There's plenty of time," Val had said, sipping her gin and tonic thoughtfully. "I don't have any outside commitments."

"Not married?"

"Not now," Val said. "Once. But it didn't last long. He didn't like the hours or the company I kept."

"I know what you mean," Bairstow had said. "So you should go for promotion now. That's what I did, and look where it got me." She had got them a second drink and talked apparently inconsequentially about her own career, and some of the men she reckoned had stood in her way, but all the time Val was aware that she was being subtly pumped for information about her colleagues in Bradfield generally, and about Kevin Mower and Michael Thackeray in particular. Aware that the drink was loosening her tongue, she had tried to shift the conversation back to less dangerous ground.

"You really think I should go for sergeant, do you?" she asked.

"Of course you should," Bairstow said. "They need women in senior positions, just like they need blacks, to prove they're not discriminating. Not that it's easy," she added with a bitterness Val had not heard before. "They have you down as a dyke as soon as you put your head over the parapet and show the slightest sign of ambition. You need to be ready for that, especially if you don't have a resident bloke. I don't suppose it's any different in Bradfield."

"Mr Thackeray's been very supportive," Val said, knowing her loyalty would sound false even before the words crossed her lips. Jackie Bairstow drained her glass.

"And what did he want in return?" she asked. "Or was it Kevin Mower who was on your case?"

Val flushed slightly, knowing that she was giving away more than she intended and that the DCI's sharp eyes would miss nothing.

"There was nothing like that," she said. It was the truth but she knew that somehow it did not sound like it. As far as Mower was concerned, the truth was a matter of infinite regret she shared with no-one.

"Yes, well, I should start thinking about that promotion if I were you, Val," Bairstow had said as she got to her feet. "You never know when a vacancy might come up." Recalling Bairstow's words, Val glanced again at her passenger as she pulled into a parking space at the foot of Holby House.

"Come on, Kevin, for God's sake," she said. "At least go through the motions, or La Bairstow'll feed you to the wolves at county before you know you're on the menu."

Gary Miller opened the door of his parents' second floor flat when they knocked and glanced without much interest at the warrant cards they flashed in his direction. Dressed in track-suit and trainers, he stood a good four inches taller than Mower, with shoulders considerably broader, and dark eyes veiled by a crop of Ruud Gullit dreadlocks.

"I wondered how long it would take you to get round here," the boy said without any sign of alarm. "Someone's told you about me and Kelly, have they?"

He let them into the flat's cramped sitting room with a bouncy, balls-of-the-feet stride, turned down the TV and flung himself into an ample sofa, which he still succeeded in making look too small for his body. After glancing at Mower, who had dropped into another chair and appeared to be taking little interest in the proceedings, Val Ridley concentrated on the boy.

"So if you expected we'd want to talk to you, that's bound to make us wonder why you didn't come forward and tell us about you and Kelly yourself, Gary," she said. The boy shrugged massively.

"You joking?" he asked. "You think I don't know what you'll try to pin on me now?"

"Were you with Kelly on Saturday night?"

"Sure I was. She's crazy about me, isn't she? Her and half her mates, as it goes. I saw her at the Underground soon after we went in, ten, eleven o'clock maybe."

"And?" Val prompted, risking a glance at Mower who was watching the boy with eyes like smouldering coals.

"And what? We talked, we danced some, we went to chill out in my car for a bit."

"Chill out?"

"You know," the boy shrugged carelessly. "She was gagging for it."

"She's thirteen years old!" Mower said suddenly, his voice thick with emotion, although it was probably not that which made Miller sit up suddenly, the first sign of worry in his eyes.

"You're joking?" he said.

"No jokes, Gary," Val said sharply. "Are you telling us you've been having sex with a thirteen-year-old? That's a serious offence in itself. How old are you, Gary?"

"I'm nineteen," Miller said sulkily. "She told me she was sixteen. Jesus God, she looks sixteen, seventeen even, with tits like that. I wasn't the first, you know. Little slag . . ." He trailed off and tried to resume his nonchalent pose, but the conviction had suddenly drained out of him, leaving him tense and jumpy.

"So you had sex? In your car?" Val asked.

Miller nodded.

"And then what?"

"Then we went back to the Underground. I was on the guest list so there was no trouble getting back in."

"And then? Did you take Kelly home at the end of the evening?"

101

"No, I didn't," Miller said, suddenly vehement. "I didn't stay, did I? I went on to a party out Milford way, me and some lads I met . . ."

"With Kelly?"

"No. That's the point. It were just lads who went on. We didn't want to spoil our chances, did we?"

"You mean the next chance?"

"Yeah, well, why not?" Miller said, glancing away uneasily.

"So these lads you met, and the people at the party – they can vouch for your movements later that evening, can they?" Val snapped back.

"Yeah, sure they can," Miller said. "I don't know where they live, like. I just met them, black lads I'd never seen before, and they persuaded me to drive out to this party, I'm not right sure where we went, as it goes . . ."

Sergeant Mower stood up suddenly and stood over Miller.

"So let's get this straight Gary, shall we?" he said. "You saw Kelly at the club. Took her out for sex. And then buggered off with some brand new friends to a party, you're not even sure where, and never saw Kelly again that evening? Is that it?"

"Yeah, that's about it."

"Bollocks," Mower said. "I don't believe a bloody word of it. If you went off anywhere with anyone, I guess you didn't have any luck and came back looking for Kelly later. You knew she was willing so you thought you'd have another go, and organise something for your mates as well, maybe. It turned into a gangbang, didn't it, Gary? That's how Kelly James ended up half dead?"

For a moment Val Ridley thought Mower would smash a fist into the cowering boy's face, but when she put a restraining hand on his arm he drew back, and she felt him shiver as the anger drained out of him. He swallowed hard.

"Have you heard of DNA evidence, Gary?" he asked.

"Yeah, yeah," Miller said faintly.

"So that's what we'll be looking for, isn't it?" Mower said. "Gary Miller, I'm arresting you on suspicion of unlawful sexual intercourse with an under-age girl, rape and a serious assault." He repeated the caution in a monotone.

"Come on, Gary," Val Ridley said when he had finished. "Let's be having you."

The boy stood up to his full height, his face impassive but his eyes full of rage.

"Yeah, yeah," he said again. "Fit me up, why don't you? But I'll tell you something. When I prove what you're saying ain't nothing but shit, which it is, I'll have you two racist bastards. You can bank on that. I never hurt Kelly, and you can't prove I did."

DCI Jackie Bairstow, trim in a black trouser suit over a beige polo-necked sweater, with never a sleek grey hair out of place, regarded the two detectives facing her in Michael Thackeray's office later that afternoon with undisguised disfavour.

"It would have made more sense to talk to the girl as soon as you got Miller's name, sergeant," she said. "Not after you arrested him."

"We had no choice, guv," Mower said defensively. "He admitted having sex with the girl anyway."

"But that's not exactly the same as rape and grievous bodily harm, is it? Tell me exactly what the girl said when you tackled her about Miller?"

"She didn't say much, ma'am," Val Ridley said. "As soon as we mentioned his name she collapsed in floods of tears. When she'd calmed down a bit she backed up his story to the extent that she admitted that she'd been out in the car with him and they'd had sex but then she said they went back to the club and she lost track of him after a while. When I suggested that he and his friends might have caught up with her on the walk home, she went bananas again, said she never saw him, or anyone else, and anyway he would never hurt her."

"So we've got precisely nothing on the more serious charges?"

"We got a DNA sample authorised and taken," Val Ridley said, knowing that this would prove nothing they did not know already if the girl stuck to her story.

"Has he got a brief?" the DCI asked, irritably.

"Da Silva from Aysgarth Lane," Val said. "He sat in on the interview. Now he's clamouring for his client to be bailed."

"We'll have to let him go," Bairstow said. "Bail him until we get the DNA results and get a chance to put a bit more pressure on the girl. Without her evidence we'll get no-where on the serious offences. Get her parents to talk to her, for God's sake."

She glanced at Mower with ill-concealed dislike.

"I'll come down with you," she said.

In the custody area, the three CID officers were confronted by a well-dressed young Asian man who announced himself as Gary Miller's solicitor. When DCI Bairstow told him that his client would be bailed for three weeks he nodded grimly.

"We'll be lodging a complaint, chief inspector," he said, as the custody sergeant made his way to release Miller from his cell.

"What sort of a complaint?" Jackie Bairstow asked sharply.

"I understand Sergeant Mower here came to Bradfield from the Metropolitan Police," Da Silva said. "My client says that he has brought some of the Met's bad habits with him."

"What the hell do you mean by that?" Mower broke in.

"We'll be making a complaint of racial harrassment," Da Silva said as Miller followed the custody sergeant into the room.

"Bloody right," Miller said, catching the end of the conversation. "The only reason you've got me down here at all is because I'm black. You're all t'bloody same. As bad as Kelly's dad, aren't you, when it comes down to it?" He flung his dreadlocks out of his eyes and glared at the officers.

Mower took a step towards him and then, apparently realising just in time what he was doing, spun away and flung his way out through the swing doors, back towards the CID offices. DCI Bairstow followed hard behind him.

"Sergeant," she said, eyes flashing. "I'll not tolerate that sort of complaint about my officers. Is that clear? You should know the endless bloody trouble it's caused elsewhere."

Mower turned to meet her, the colour draining from his face.

"And you should know that even a male officer is innocent until he's proved guilty," he said. "I'm not a bloody racist. Ma'am." He turned on his heel and left the office without looking back just as Val Ridley came back in. The two women's eyes met.

"Kevin was never going to be best pleased about that sort of complaint," Val said.

"So I gathered," the DCI said dismissively. "But if you can't play by the book, perhaps you shouldn't be in the job at all."

"Kevin was having it away with Rita Desai, the DC who was shot," Val said quietly. "You don't get much less racist than that.'

"Oh, thanks a lot, Val," DCI Bairstow flung back angrily. "And how the hell was I supposed to know that? In any case, it makes no difference, does it? He wouldn't be the first to like a bit of Tandoori chick one day and give her brother a good thumping the next, would he? These things aren't logical, are they?"

A floor above CID, Superintendent Jack Longley put his phone down with a thoughtful look on his face. His usually benign features were strained and he drummed his fingers irritably on the desk before picking up the receiver again and punching in the number of a mobile. He appeared slightly surprised when it was answered almost at once.

"That you, Michael?" he asked sharply, glancing at the clock which indicated five to five. "Longley here. I thought you'd be stuck into your seminars or whatever."

"Just finished for the afternoon, sir," Thackeray said. He had taken the call as he walked across the quad back to his staircase.

"Bloody holiday camp by the sound of it," Longley said. "And from what I hear, you've not been paying too much attention to your studies."

"Sir?" The surprise in Thackeray's voice was sharp in spite of the less than perfect line.

"Had a call from some beggar at Thames Valley," Longley said. "Says you've been poking your nose in where it's not wanted. What the hell's going on down there?"

There was a long silence before Thackeray replied.

"The college asked me to make enquiries about a missing person the local police lost interest in months ago," he came back, his words evidently measured with some care. "More than likely they were right in thinking it was just a domestic, a husband who took off with his girlfriend leaving all sorts of loose ends behind. But all of a sudden Thames Valley are getting twitchy about it."

"Aye, well, I should concentrate on your own problems if I were you," Longley said. "Which is the other reason I called. I want you back here on Tuesday, two o'clock. The super from complaints and discipline wants to start preliminary interviews. Wants to see you and me."

"Right," Thackeray said. "They're not wasting any time, then?"

"No reason why they should," Longley said. "It's in everyone's interests to have it all out in the open, yours and mine. Clears the air. Puts a stop to the speculation. Makes the parents feel better an'all."

"I doubt that," Thackeray said.

"Aye, well, it's the least we can do," Longley conceded. "So

I want you here for a spot of lunch before we get grilled ourselves. Meet me in my office at twelve."

"Sir," Thackeray said.

"And Michael, do yourself a favour, will you?" Longley said, with just the suspicion of hesitation.

"What's that?" The voice came back strangely disembodied as the line began to break up and fade.

"Stop blaming yourself."

If Thackeray replied, his response was lost in a crackle of static as the connection broke. Longley slammed the receiver impatiently back on its rest.

"Which doesn't bloody mean you can blame me, either, you priest-ridden bastard," the superintendent muttered. "We need our lines straight on this one if we're to get off the hook. And for me to avoid getting lumbered with that bloody Bairstow woman permanently."

Chapter Ten

Laura Ackroyd had arrived in Oxford not knowing quite what to expect of a city she had heard so much about but had never visited before. She remembered her father's furious reaction when she had adamantly refused to listen to her sixth form teachers' advice to apply for a place at the university. Her resolve to go back to the north of England after seven unhappy years at a boarding school in the south had been based, she could admit now more than a dozen years down the line, partly on prejudice and partly on a bloody-minded determination not to allow Jack Ackroyd to make decisions for her any longer.

Driving through the leafy Victorian suburbs of language schools and other educational auxiliaries and into the broad expanse of St Giles, she had slowed down to take in her first view of the city itself. Ahead of her a collection of ancient buildings, from eighteenth-century town houses to late mediaeval colleges, any one of which would have had the architectural historians drooling, gave her a glimpse of what she had turned down. It was a world away from Bradfield University's uninspiring Victorian buildings and add-on sixties' slabs. And yet she knew that while she had revelled in her student life, Michael Thackeray had been unhappy here amongst the golden stone and clusters of towers and spires. Beauty and truth might not be all you need to know, whatever the poet said, she thought.

Standing now alongside cluttered pigeonholes in the badly lit porter's lodge of St Frideswide's, she could see Thackeray striding across the quadrangle towards her, tall and broad, with unruly dark hair. Her heart leapt, as it always did when she saw him unexpectedly. She nodded her thanks to the man behind the counter and stepped out under the dim stone archway to meet him.

He took her in his arms and for a moment they stood locked together in silence, neither of them wishing to break the spell with all the complications of speech. Eventually, he let her go, kissing her hair and holding onto her hand as he allowed her to draw away.

"I haven't booked anywhere to stay," she said. "I wasn't sure . . ."

"You can stay here and share my monastic single bed, or we could book into a hotel," Thackeray said lightly. "Come up to my room. See what spartan horrors you missed by not coming to Oxford yourself."

He led the way, conscious that their progress across the quad was being watched by the familiar gowned figure of Magnus Partridge, who had stepped out of the library doorway just as they left the lodge. Laura looked about her curiously, taking in the rectangle of grass browned by the summer heat, the aged oak beside the chapel doors, and the ranks of small, blank gothic windows, which broke up the stone walls of soft golden stone.

She followed Thackeray up the steep stone stairs to his set of rooms, slightly overwhelmed by the damp aura of antiquity that seemed to seep from the walls. He opened the doors and she dropped her bag on the bed and stood at the narrow double window looking down at the way they had come.

"Who's that?" she asked, conscious of Thackeray standing behind her, but still too full of undefinable emotions to do anything more than make inconsequential conversation. She nodded at Partridge, who was still standing in the library doorway like an emaciated vulture.

"An old dinosaur who was here when I was," Thackeray said. "Should have been put out to grass by now. He thinks the college belongs to him and all change should be resisted to the last man – and I do mean man. People like him have never come to terms with the arrival of women students."

"Are there many like that?" Laura asked.

"Fortunately not," Thackeray said. "The rest of the university seems to be tip-toeing into the twenty-first century – tentatively, at least."

"Not always a good thing," Laura said. "Don't they have a Rupert Murdoch chair of English or something? Ironic or what?"

Thackeray laughed and put his arms round her.

"Thank God you've come," he said. "You cheer me up."

"Who was Frideswide, anyway. I've never heard of him."

"Her," Thackeray said. "A mediaeval virgin who sought refuge in the city. Became an abbess or prioress or something of that sort. The cathedral's dedicated to her."

"I don't suppose there's many of them around these days. Virgins, I mean." She wriggled around to perch on the window-sill facing him, and the sunlight caught her hair as she turned, setting it alight.

"What have you been doing? Flagellating yourself in the chapel every night? I'm not sure this sort of monkish cell is exactly what you require," she said, her eyes bright with mockery.

"Well, I'm sure you can put that right," he said, kissing her lightly on the lips. He had years of experience of blotting things he did not wish to think about from his mind, and this weekend he was determined to bury his anxieties and enjoy Laura's company.

She put both hands on his shoulders, too intent on his face to notice him flinch as she touched his bruises.

"Try me," she said, returning his kiss with interest.

"This is exactly why people like Magnus Partridge fought tooth and nail to keep women out," Thackeray said as he carried her to the bed in a small alcove to one side of the study area and began to undo the buttons on her shirt.

"More fool him," Laura said, letting him kiss her breasts as she struggled to wriggle out of her jeans. "Oh God, do that again," she said. "And again and again. I've missed you." But before he could oblige her even once they were interrupted by a sharp knock on the door.

"Christ, who's that?" Thackeray groaned through gritted teeth as he got to his feet and adjusted his dress, leaving Laura in a fit of giggles to wrap herself in the bedclothes and turn her back to the door.

Outside on the landing he was astonished to find Penny Harrison, looking even more haggard than the last time he had seen her and hugging a unseasonably heavy coat around her emaciated frame. She was accompanied by a much younger woman, attractively round faced and dark haired in a way that reminded Thackeray instantly of the Penny Harrison of twenty years before. He glanced back into his room in helpless embarrassment but to his relief saw that Laura had made herself decent enough to be sitting on the edge of the bed looking dishevelled and not entirely innocent as she did up the zip on her jeans.

"Mrs Harrison," he said, keeping a firm grip on the door to allow Laura a little more time to compose herself. "I wasn't expecting you."

Penny Harrison's burning intensity did not leave him much room for manoevre. She almost pushed her way into the room with her daughter following close behind.

"This is Caro," she said. "She's just arrived from London. I was sure you'd want to see her straight away."

Thackeray shrugged helplessly, aware that neither Harrison was going to be deterred by any excuse he might invent to put them off.

"Come in for a minute," he said. "This is a friend of mine, Laura Ackroyd, who's also here for the weekend. Laura, this is Penny Harrison, and her daughter Caroline." The three women nodded warily at each other and Laura looked hesitantly at Thackeray.

"Is this something private?" she asked.

"No," Thackeray said firmly. "I was going to tell you about it. I'd like your opinion."

111

"Is she in the police too?" Penny Harrison asked.

"No, she's a journalist," Thackeray said. "But if what you want to tell me is private, she will respect that."

There was a moment of awkward silence before Caro Harrison, business-like in a short-skirted dark suit over a silk chemise, took charge.

"I'm sorry if we've burst in on you unexpectedly, but my mother was in a dreadful state when I got to her place and I thought it was best to come and tell you whatever I can if you really think you can help find my father."

"You've no idea where he is, then?" Thackeray asked. "Sometimes people contact their children even when they don't want to have anything to do with their . . ." He hesitated, searching for the least offensive description of the status Mrs Harrison had inadvertently gained.

"Their shafted wives?" Penny Harrison offered. "It's usually wives, isn't it? Is that what you mean?"

"Mum," her daughter protested uneasily.

"Oh, you've no idea the expressive vocabulary I acquired while I was in hospital," Penny Harrison said, letting her coat fall open to reveal a thin cotton dress underneath.

"Sit down here, Mrs Harrison," Laura said, leading the older woman to the room's only comfortable chair, which sagged in a corner by the empty fireplace. She could feel the stick-like arm trembling under her touch in spite of the thick wool of her coat. "Let your daughter talk to Michael. There's no need to distress yourself."

"So has your father ever contacted you since he went – or your brother?" Thackeray asked Caroline.

"No, not a word to either of us," she said, her face closed and eyes cold. "The only person we heard from was the brother of the woman dad is supposed to have run off with, a man called Capstick, David Capstick. He seemed to be absolutely furious that his sister had vanished, although I could never work out quite why he was so angry. Angry rather

112

than anxious, if you know what I mean. It's not as if she was married or anything, and had abandoned a brood of kids. As I understand it, she was a free agent, as far as it goes. She apparently lived with her mother."

"Did you or Tom ever meet Emma Capstick?" Thackeray asked, ignoring the faint moan of protest from Penny Harrison. But Caroline shook her head, flinging her dark hair away from a determined jaw, an unconscious action, which reminded Thackeray even more forcibly of the girl her mother had once been.

"Never," she said. "I never even knew she existed, and I don't think Tom did either. Although with what happened to Tom it was difficult to know what he knew or thought. I only saw him twice after he left home, and I think he was stoned out of his head on the first occasion. He didn't seem to be making much sense." Thackeray didn't think that he was imagining the note of contempt in her voice, the contempt of the survivor for a weaker personality. He guessed that even though she looked like her mother, she had inherited her father's determination. She had not buckled under stress, and clearly had no intention of doing so in future.

"So where did you meet David Capstick?"

"He called me in London. Said Tom had given him the number. And then he came round one evening. I didn't invite him, he just turned up on the doorstep and I felt I had to invite him in for a drink."

"How long was this after the two of them vanished?"

"Oh, about two weeks, I suppose. He said he'd tracked Tom down but hadn't been able to get much sense out of him, which didn't surprise me. Mum was in hospital at the time, so he'd not found her, of course. So he landed up on my doorstep demanding information. Quite persistent, he was. He said I must have had a postcard, something, and why was my father preventing Emma from contacting them."

"He and his mother had heard nothing?"

"Apparently not," Caroline said. "He gave me his address and phone number to get in touch if I heard anything but of course I haven't. He rang again a couple of times, but I'd no more to tell him than I had the first time. I've not heard from him for a while now, a couple of months, at least. But of course he's not the only one who wants to find them, is he, Mum?"

Her mother gave Caroline a startled glance but did not answer.

"The college, the bank, the building society, and quite a few people who used to be friends," she went on. "He'd borrowed money all over the place for some scam he had going, something which was supposed to make us all rich. He even persuaded the barman at the local pub to invest. Of course, they never got a penny back. And he's left my mother penniless. There's not even an insurance policy untouched."

Caroline Harrison's fury distorted her face into an ugly mask and Thackeray's wondered if the anger was entirely on her mother's behalf or perhaps because of the disappointment of some financial expectations of her own.

"So you seem to be assuming that he decided to disappear when his creditors began to close in?" Thackeray asked.

"It must have been that, judging by the mess he left Mum in when he went. She was bloody lucky the bank was sympathetic and didn't sue her for what he owed. Technicall,y she was liable for some of the debts. What he did was criminal. I mean seriously, fraudulently criminal. And from what the bank manager let slip when I spoke to him, he'd ripped the college off as well. But no-one seemed interested in tracking him down and charging him with fraud or whatever. That's Oxford for you, I suppose. Cover it up. Avoid the embarrassment. Don't tarnish the precious university's reputation. In my job, if I'd done what he did, I'd be in gaol by now."

Thackeray turned away, avoiding Penny Harrison's look of distraught appeal, and gazed out of the window at his colleagues who were streaming across the quad to lunch. The abstract concerns of the course, the obsession with statistics, trends and objectives, seemed as remote as Mars in this tiny room awash with anger and despair. He knew that his own very personal motives for joining the police still stood in spite of the speed at which the force seemed to be moving on and the risk that he would be crushed by one management juggernaut or another. In his view, if the job was not about helping the people threatened and damaged and dispossessed by crime, and tracking down those who did the damage, then it was not worth the candle. All the community liaison, political correctness and public relations priorities in the world should not alter that, he thought, though he increasingly suspected they might be used as an excuse to try.

He knew that Laura and Caroline were watching him, the one with troubled eyes, the other furious, and he was not sure how he could meet their expectations. There seemed so little he could do to prevent Penny Harrison's disintegration from running its course. Indeed, he was far from convinced that finding her husband or disinterring more, probably bad, news about her son, would do her any good at all.

"It's very difficult," he began cautiously. "If they really don't want to be found, if they've gone abroad for instance, which is not impossible for an academic, is it? Unfortunately people can simply disappear if they are really determined about it."

"Her brother did say he couldn't find her passpport," Caroline Harrison said quietly. "My father certainly took his."

Thackeray turned away from Caroline to her mother and took Penny's thin hands in his.

"You know there's very little chance of finding them," he said. "But I'll go and talk to Emma's mother and see if there's any clue there that the local police have missed. But you mustn't get your hopes up. It's a very long shot, probably a final shot. You do understand that?"

Penny Harrison nodded lethargically.

"And Tom?" she said.

Thackeray sighed.

"I'll see what I can find out, though the local police are not very happy about me digging around that case. I guess they have their own inquiries going on into the drug scene down there."

"He was not an addict," Mrs Harrison said flatly, clinging onto Thackeray's hand.

"If you tell me he wasn't, I'll believe you. That's all I need to know."

Caroline glanced sharply at Thackeray, a hint of alarm in her eyes, and he guessed that she feared Tom had in fact been more than an addict.

"Come on, Mum," she said. "These people have other things to think about." She nodded her thanks to Thackeray and helped her mother to her feet. Before they went, she took a business card from her bag and wrote something on the back.

"That's my address in London and the address David Capstick gave me," she said. "It's probably better if you contact me if you're able to find out anything new." Thackeray nodded, understanding exactly what she did not want passed on directly to her mother.

"I'll do that," he said quietly.

When the two women had gone, Thackeray shut the door gently behind them and leaned against the dark oak. Laura was sitting on the bed again with a faintly quizzical smile on her face.

"Well, well," she said. "What have you got yourself into? I thought freelance investigations were more my scene than yours, chief inspector."

"I wish I knew what I was into," Thackeray said. "This is all the blasted master of St Frideswide's fault. He asked me to track down an errant don and one half of Oxford seems to be cheering me on and the other half trying to stop me." He told her briefly exactly how Mark Harrison had disappeared and whom he seemed to have damaged in the process.

"Charming fellow," Laura said when he had finished.

"Oh yes," Thackeray said. "He was always a charming fellow, even when I knew him as a student, one of those surface smoothies with generations of greed and viciousness underneath."

"So there's a personal angle to this, is there?"

"Oh, not really, after all this time. I learned to look after myself after coming up against Harrison and his rugby cronies. He probably did me quite a lot of good in the end."

He held out his hand to Laura and pulled her to her feet. His tone had been cheerful but Laura did not entirely believe that his run-in with Harrison had been as benign as all that.

"In my day, they went to some trouble to stop us entertaining girls in our rooms," Thackeray said, changing the subject smoothly. "They may be somewhat more laid-back now – apart from that old spoil-sport Magnus Partridge, of course. But I think, on balance, I'll treat you to a couple of nights at the Randolph. It's just round the corner and there won't be so many ghosts there. Or so many interruptions."

"Isn't that where Zuleika Dobson . . . ?"

"Oh, I'm sure she did," Thackeray said with a faint smile. "They've got pictures of her all over the walls – or they used to have in my day. Anyway, I think I'll keep you out of sight, my sweet, just in case you have the same sort of effect on the town as she did."

"Flatterer," Laura said lightly, knowing that the unalloyed pleasure of their reunion had been tarnished. She glanced around the bare little room and shivered. "Let's go," she said. "This place gives me the creeps. And that bed's like a board."

"You amaze me, you know," Laura said angrily later, running her fingers over the bruises across Thackeray's back and shoulders. "You'd play hell with me if I did what you've just done. How many times have you told me I'm too impulsive, I'm irresponsible, I rush into things, and here you are doing exactly

117

the same and for what? A woman on the edge of a nervous breakdown and her hard-faced daughter who seems more worried about losing her inheritance than she is in her mother's condition."

Thackeray groaned slightly as Laura's fingers stirred more than a faintly pleasurable pain across his shoulders.

"It's nothing. No worse than I used to pick up every weekend when I played rugby. Still, you'll understand now how I feel when you take risks," he said, his voice half muffled by the ample pillows on one of the Randolph Hotel's extensive and seductively comfortable beds.

"Why are you doing it? I thought you hated your time at St Frideswide's."

"I did, I did," Thackeray groaned. "I'm doing it for Greenaway, I suppose. He was someone who made being here worthwhile."

"But is it worth the risk? Look at the state you're in."

"I don't know," Thackeray said, turning over and pulling Laura towards him until she was lying beside him. They were both half dressed but their anticipation of a passionate afternoon locked safely away from the world had been interrupted by Laura's dismay when Thackeray had slipped off his shirt and exposed the damage his attacker had inflicted the day before.

"Calm down," he said. "I'd no idea I was taking a risk when I went to see a rather pathetic junkie up the Cowley Road. I take more chances than that every time I set foot in Wuthering, as you very well know. We know that people up there have got guns. The risk comes with the territory."

"As Rita Desai discovered," Laura said soberly. "It could have been you that day too."

"It could be me any day. But it doesn't happen very often. Most coppers die peacefully in their beds." He neglected to add that for many it was a premature death, hastened by stress, erratic meals and booze, and that could have been him too.

118

"So you're going to carry on with this little Oxford crusade, are you?" she demanded, still angry.

"I'd like to talk to Harrison's girlfriend's mother tomorrow. She lives out in one of the Cotswold villages, so if you'd like a trip . . ."

"Bastard," Laura said, although her hands, which continued their exploration of Thackeray's body, were saying something else entirely.

"And that'll be the end of it?" she asked. Thackeray pulled her closer and kissed her and she felt herself melt inside.

"Maybe. I'll talk to Hugh Greenaway again. I owe him that, at least. You can't argue with that." His tone was matter-of-fact even as he slid an exploratory hand between her thighs.

"I don't think," Laura said thickly. "I don't think, at this precise moment, I can argue with anything."

Chapter Eleven

They had lain in bed late that morning and breakfasted in style in the hotel's ornate dining room from which they could watch the citizens of Oxford hurrying about their Saturday morning pleasures and the tourists making their way into the museum on the opposite corner.

"Did you really hate it so much here?" Laura had asked, captivated by the shadowed facade of Balliol College across the busy street, and the sunlight that glanced off the gothic pinnacles of the Martyr's Memorial and created a dappled shade beneath the trees lining the far side of St Giles. It seemed an exuberant commemoration of a grisly page of history.

"I was too young too appreciate it," Thackeray said. "I think a lot of people are when they come here. Kids of eighteen are interested in the opposite sex not the finer points of late mediaeval architecture. Anyway it was some of the people I hated, not the place. Oxford's very beautiful, but could still be very cruel, in my day anyway."

"A bit Jude the Obscure?"

Thackeray gazed at Laura across the scattered remnants of their breakfast, revelling in the chance to enjoy her company unencumbered by the chains of past lives, which so often weighed them down in Bradfield. He had put the next week's anxieties firmly out of his mind, determined to savour the weekend.

"I wouldn't go that far," he said. "That was deeply Thomas Hardy. But Friddie's was conservative in many ways, suspicious of anything that didn't fit a very male, public school version of the world. Even in the seventies they found an unsophisticated northern lad like me quite hard to take but the arrival of Penny Harrison and her bra-burning friends frightened some of them witless."

"She was one of those?" Laura was surprised.

"Until she fell for Mark and he knocked that sort of nonsense out of her," Thackeray said dryly.

"And look where that got her." Laura had been more moved than she was prepared to admit by Penny Harrison's evident disintegration.

They had driven in a companionable silence out of town to the west, turned down Burford's steeply sloping high street and across the narrow river bridge into the high open country beyond where the fields spread out in golden splendour in the later summer sunshine. After a few miles, a narrow turning took them down a winding, leafy lane, which dropped steeply into Church Campden village. It lay in a narrow green valley beneath a high dry plateau dotted with sheep and criss-crossed with crumbling stone walls. It was no more than a huddle of cottages surrounding a squat church tower and a single pub, all built in a mellow cream stone, which glowed in the bright morning sunshine, and they had no difficulty in identifying Shepherds Cottage in a pretty terrace close to the church gate.They parked beside the green, where a rushy stream opened out into a pond dominated by a couple of proprietorial swans and a gaggle of squabbling mallard.

"Picture postcard stuff," Laura said as they stretched their legs and took stock. The air was warm and damp and vegetation ran rampant through the churchyard and the cottage gardens.

"A long drive into Oxford to work, if this is where she lived," Thackeray said more practically.

"Perhaps a good reason to leave?"

They took a well-tended gravel path, which skirted the deep green waters of the pond. The cottage doors opened directly onto the lane leading to the church and the morning sun caught the narrow windows making it impossible to see whether or not there was any life inside.

Thackeray lifted the tarnished brass knocker of Shepherd's Cottage and let it fall with a sharp tap against the wood of the old-fashioned pine door. There was no immediate response, and he tried again. This time they heard some muffled noises on the other side and eventually the door was unlatched by a heavy grey haired middle-aged woman dressed in a felted blue dressing gown, and, as far as they could judge, little else.

"Yes?" the woman said. Her face was plump and puffy and her eyes red-rimmed and there was absolutely no welcome, or even animation in her features.

"Mrs Capstick?" Thackeray asked, and when the woman nodded he explained briefly why he was there. For a moment, Laura thought she would shut the door in their faces, so little interest did she appear to take in what she was being told, but eventually she shrugged slightly and pulled the door open with a hand which shook, apparently uncontrollably.

"You'd better come in," she mumbled, as if the words hurt her.

She led them from the tiny hall into a cramped and cluttered livingroom where she chased a elderly collie off the sofa.

"I don't know why the college is bothering about Emma now," she said, her voice barely audible as she lowered herself into an armchair close to the gas fire. The room was hot and stuffy and smelt strongly of dog and faintly of almonds. Amongst the ornaments and bric-a-brac that cluttered every surface Laura saw several half-consumed candles.

"They took no bloody notice when she went, did they?" Emma's mother said more forcefully. She glanced at Laura,

"D'you want to make a cup of tea?" she asked. "You'll find everything in the kitchen through there. I'm not well, you know, or I'd do it for you."

Laura hesitated for a moment, biting back the sharp rejoinder, and glanced at Thackeray who tried to stifle a smile and nodded imperceptibly.

"I suppose," she said ungraciously, and picked her way through the piles of magazines and dirty cups on the floor into the tiny kitchen at the back of the house. There she had to sort gingerly through stacks of dirty dishes to identify three moderately clean mugs, which she washed at the sink with an ostentatious amount of splashing about in hot water before making a pot of something she tentatively identified as tea from amongst a jumble of mainly herbal mixtures in the cupboard. She took a half full bottle of milk from the fridge and sniffed at it suspiciously. She could not find a jug to put it in.

She carried the mugs back on a tray, with milk in the bottle and sugar in its packet, to find Thackeray listening to what appeared to be a lengthy litany of Mrs Capstick's health and welfare problems, and how inconvenient it was to find herself unexpectedly without her only daughter on the premises.

"There was no indication she wanted to leave home?" Thackeray asked.

"She never said anything to me about going," Mrs Capstick said. "Never saw her pack her bags or anything. Mind, I go to bed early so I suppose she could have put everything in the car that night when I was asleep."

"She took everything with her then?" Thackeray asked.

"Everything of any value that I could see," Mrs Capstick said, her face creased with bitterness. "She could write, couldn't she? Or telephone? But we've not heard a bloody word, have we? Not a word. She knows I can't cope here on my own. I can't get out, can't do any shopping. Selfish little cow. That's what my David says, and he's right, isn't he? Selfish cow."

"David?"

"My son. Lives over Gloucester way. Got a wife and three little ones, he has, so how's he supposed to be able to help? He's been very good. Comes over and brings my groceries for me. But it's not the same as having Emma living here, is it? Not

123

the same at all. I don't know how long I can go on like this, I really don't. My health's never been good and this looks like finishing me off." She held a trembling hand in front of her face and shrugged.

"She went in her car? What sort of car was that, Mrs Capstick?" Thackeray asked.

"Oh, a little blue thing she got when she went to work in Oxford. Said it was worth it because the money was better than she earned when she had that first job in the estate agents in Burford. But by the time she'd bought her petrol I doubt if she was any better off. And it was a much longer day. She didn't get back till ten or eleven some nights, said she had to do overtime, but I reckon now that if there was this man involved she was with him, wasn't she? She always was a two-faced little thing when she was a girl, you know. Told me once she wasn't our daughter, she belonged to the people who live in the big hall down the road. Slapped her face I did and told her if we weren't good enough she should go and knock on the door down there and see how far that got her."

"And your husband, Mrs Capstick. Where's he now?" Thackeray asked.

"Oh, he blew, didn't he, years ago. Emma takes after him, doesn't she? Left me with two teenagers to bring up. Another selfish beggar."

"And Emma's car, Mrs Capstick. Do you know the make, the year, anything about it?" Thackeray persisted.

"Blue," she said. "A French thing. I told her, I didn't see why British wasn't good enough. Her dad used to work at Cowley when he was younger. She just laughed."

"Renault? Peugeot?"

"That's it. Peugeot."

"I don't suppose you know what the registration number was, do you?" Mrs Capstick shook her head.

"You'll want to see her room, I suppose," she said, as if it did not matter much to her either way. "The sergeant who

124

came had a look at her room. But I don't think he found anything interesting there. Go up, why don't you? I won't come with you. The stairs are difficult. I try not to go up there more than I have to. It's the door on the left at the top."

Laura followed Thackeray up the steep narrow staircase and into a tiny bedroom where the single bed had been stripped down to the matress and every shelf appeared to be bare.

"My God, someone's cleared this place out pretty thoroughly," she said, closing the door and glancing round in surprise. "She doesn't expect her to come back, does she?"

"I'm surprised she found the energy to tidy up," Thackeray said.

"Perhaps brother David did it. There doesn't seem to be much love lost there."

Laura opened the wardrobe and fingered a few faded garments, which were still hanging on wire hangers.

"She must have taken most of her stuff," she said. "Most of this is junk. The only shoes left are a couple of pairs of old trainers and a pair of fur-lined boots. She's left a winter coat too. She can't have been going anywhere chilly."

Thackeray was going through the dressing table drawers, which like everything else, were almost empty.

"Didn't expect to be needing her car either," he said quietly. "As her brother said, there doesn't seem to be any sign of a passport but she's left the registration and insurance documents, with another two months to run."

"So why didn't she sell it if she wasn't expecting to need it again? Isn't it odd no-one's found it? Even if she left it at the airport or something, surely someone would have begun to wonder about it by now and contacted her mother?"

"You'd think so," Thackeray said. "I dare say I can find out if it's turned up anywhere. I'll get Kevin Mower to run a check."

Laura looked hard at Thackeray for a moment.

"No, it's not strictly by the book," he said. "But as it may not matter after Tuesday, who's going to quibble?" He told her about his date with Superintendent Longley, keeping his voice as light as he could.

"You seriously think they'll take disciplinary action against you," she asked.

"I don't know," Thackeray said carefully. "Jack Longley warned me off that line of inquiry. I suspected his motives, and in the end, in the heat of the moment, I took no notice anyway. And Rita died." He gazed out of the window, refusing to meet her eyes.

"You couldn't have known there was anyone with a gun inside." Laura knew that there was no easy reassurance. "It's the heat of the moment thing they might get you on, isn't it? After finding my car wrecked?"

"According to this lot on the course, you should make a major risk assessment before you even flag down a speeding motorist these days."

"Come on, Michael. Cynical doesn't suit you," Laura said.

He put an arm round her.

"I suppose when it came down to it I did what I thought was right. I reckoned I had two good reasons to investigate."

"And as it turned out, you were right," Laura said. "They can't hang you for that. I'll take a sickie on Monday and drive you back to Bradfield. How about that? So we can devote ourselves to this little Sherlock investigation till then."

Thackeray smiled faintly.

"I got the feeling down there you didn't relish a role as my side-kick, Dr Watson," he said.

"Not if it means making the bloody tea," Laura said. "As I recall, Watson never had to sink that low. Apart from that, I might just about cope."

"So, what do you reckon to young Emma then?"

126

"It sounds to me as if she's well out of this family, even if her taste in men is somewhat dodgy. Mark Harrison sounds like a right bastard. I'd quite like to help him come to grief, if that's feasible."

"I rather doubt it," Thackeray said, but his mood had lightened, as she had hoped it would.

Chloë Sanderson leaned back in her swivel chair and gave her visitors a long calculating once-over. She was very tall, very dark and quite evidently mistress of all she surveyed, which amounted to a conglomeration of prefabricated buildings tucked away at the back of a small park in Cowley and filled with a milling mass of the younger members of East Oxford's multiracial community. The noise, until she had shut the door on it, was overwhelming.

Chloë tossed her elaborately beaded hair out of her eyes and shrugged.

"I would never have said that Tom was the sort of boy to kill himself," she said. "But then who knows what's going on in people's heads?"

"How long did he work here?" Thackeray asked. He and Laura were sitting side by side on a low couch where Thackeray had to tuck his knees almost under his chin. Laura had taken the easier option and curled her legs beneath her.

"Well, now, work it wasn't. More like therapy," Chloë said slowly. "You know he ran off from home? I guess he had a sort of breakdown when his father left. He may not have called it that but that's what it was. He came down here with that sad girl he lived with and I gave him some odd jobs to do. Paid him peanuts. He wasn't old enough to get benefit, and he wasn't really fit to work. But he came in a lot just for something to do. Got involved with some of the kids doing music and drama, you know? He played guitar. As they do."

"But not suicidal?"

"Angry more like. Angry with his father. Angry that his

127

mother was ill. Angry about the girl he lived with, what was she called? Jancie? He thought she was injecting heroin. Asked me how to get her to stop, as if I had the answer."

"And was she?" Thackeray asked. "Then, I mean? I've absolutely no doubt that she's injecting it now."

"Oh, I guess so," Chloë said. "There were all the signs when I saw her. Which wasn't often. We make very sure they don't bring anything in here. But it's there on the street for anyone who wants it."

"Was Tom on drugs?" Thackeray asked.

"I don't think so," Chloë said. "Stoned occasionally, I'd say, but then who isn't?" She gave Thackeray a sideways smile. "But not the hard stuff. I was shattered when I heard what had happened."

"So you thought it was odd? Out of character?"

"I suppose I did, yes," Chloë said slowly. "But if you want to know what really happened to Tom, I don't have any answers, I'm afraid. If it was drugs, the person who'll know is Jancie. But if she's in deep herself she won't tell you, will she? There are some very nasty people out there on the street, Mr Thackeray. And they know how to keep the lid on anything they want the lid kept on, believe me.'

"You want to go and see the girl again, don't you?" Laura asked when they were back in her car. Thackeray shrugged.

"I've been warned off by the local nick," he said.

"I haven't," Laura said. "There's nothing to stop me knocking on her door."

They drove slowly back down the Cowley Road where the early evening crowds were beginning to pack into pubs and late opening shops.

"Just knock and ask her if she'll come out for a drink or something," Thackeray said as Laura followed his instructions and turned into the narrow side-street and found a parking space. But when she knocked on the door of the squat it was opened not by Jancie but by a young man with short-cropped blond hair and a thin emaciated-looking face.

"What?" he asked with a distinct lack of charm, but when Laura mentioned Jancie's name he turned away and she thought she caught a glimpse of tears in his eyes.

"She's not fucking here, is she?" he said. "They took her to the fucking hospital."

"Why was that?" Laura asked, feeling a chill, which she was sure had nothing to do with the evening air.

"Took an fucking overdose, didn't she? Silly stupid cow. Wouldn't let me go in the fucking ambulance, would they. Bloody pigs."

"When was this?" Laura asked, feeling stupified.

"This morning, wasn't it?" the boy said.

The door slammed in Laura's face with a finality that shook her as hard as it shook the thin wooden panels and as she turned away she saw Thackeray get out of the car, as if he sensed that something was very wrong. She told him quickly what the boy had said.

"One overdose might be an accident, but two?" he said, his face grim. "Jancie thought Tom had been murdered. Perhaps she was right."

"And someone's shut her up, you mean?"

Thackeray didn't answer for a moment. Then he strode back down the street to the squat and hammered on the door until the wood threatened to splinter under his assault. The same boy opened it and Thackeray recognised the fear in his eyes.

"What's happened to Jancie's dog?" he asked. The boy shrugged. "Where's Bisto?" Thackeray persisted.

"God knows," he said. "I found Jancie lying in the hall. If effing cops stopped calling round we wouldn't have all this trouble, would we?"

"What do you mean?" Thackeray asked, making sure that his foot in the door prevented it being slammed in his face as it had been in Laura's.

"Well, that's what you are isn't it?" the boy challenged. "You should know what happens round here if people think you're talking to the cops. Big Al doesn't like it."

"Big Al?" Thackeray pounced. "Who the hell's Big Al?"

"Sod off," the boy said, putting his whole weight against the door but meeting the solid resistance that Thackeray had honed in the scrum.

"Has Big Al got something to do with Jancie's overdose?" Thackeray persisted, holding the door firm as a rock against the boy's weight. "Come on," he said impatiently. "Has another of your friends got to die before you start helping to sort out this mess?"

"It's nothing to do with me," the boy said. "I don't know anything about it."

"That dog would have killed anyone who attacked Jancie," Thackeray said with feeling, recalling Bisto's unwavering and deeply unfriendly yellow eyes. "Only someone she allowed into the house would have got close while he was there."

"The dog's gone," the boy said, his face closed. "I told you. I'd gone to cash my giro, hadn't I? I came back and found Jancie in the hall. There was no sign of the effing dog. Now will you get off my back?"

Thackeray eased his weight off the door slowly. He could feel the limb he was standing on creaking beneath the weight of this unauthorised interrogation and his natural caution asserted itself. He guessed that if the house was still under surveillance he was already in more trouble with the local police than he wanted to be. He let the boy push the door closed and he heard a bolt slide shut on the other side. Whatever the boy was prepared to tell him, he was convinced he knew much more. But the fear in his eyes told him it would be the devil's own job to persuade him to talk.

Chapter Twelve

Laura leaned her head against the cool glass of the intensive care ward where the girl she knew only as Jancie lay hooked up to various items of high tech medical equipment as pale and still as the corpse that it looked as though she might soon become. Behind her, Thackeray was talking quietly a uniformed police officer who had been in the corridor outside the ward when they had arrived.

Oxford's main hospital, a brutal white brick complex on the hill to the east of the historic city, had been easy to find and easy enough to penetrate. But it was clear as soon as they had made their way from casualty, where she had been admitted, to the intensive care unit where she now lay, that Jancie was in no fit state to talk to them or anyone else. She was deeply unconscious and, according to the doctor who had admitted her, unlikely to wake up soon, if at all.

"Shit," Thackeray had said with uncharacteristic vehemence and had turned away almost directly into the arms of a tall uniformed police sergeant who was regarding him with the utmost suspicion. It took the production of his warrant card and some hard talking on Thackeray's part to persuade the Thames Valley officer that he was there with Jancie's best interests at heart.

"The drug squad wanted her watched, otherwise I wouldn't be wasting valuable time up here," the sergeant conceded at last. "Apparently she's got some pretty unpleasant friends."

"The least unpleasant of whom, as I understand it, is already dead," Thackeray said.

"The lad, what was his name? Tom Harrison?" the sergeant said thoughtfully. "I was on duty that night. Went round to the squat. This must be the same girl. She was completely hysterical when the paramedics told her he was dead. She had this

131

bloody great German Shepherd dog with her. I told her if it so much as growled at one of my lads I'd have it put down."

"I've met the dog," Thackeray said with feeling. "But what's odd about this . . ." He nodded at the intensive care cubicle where two nurses were busy around Jancie's prone body. "What's odd is that the dog's disappeared. I'd have expected him to stay with her if she was unconscious. Most likely go for anyone who came near her, in fact. But the lad who's still in the house says he's gone."

"So what are you suggesting, sir?" the sergeant asked carefully. "We'd likely put this down as an attempted suicide, given the psychological state she was in when her boyfriend OD'd. Or just another fatal accident. She's a long-term addict, well-known for it."

"You were happy with the coroner's verdict on Tom Harrison then?" Thackeray asked, conscious of the intense interest his questions were arousing although the sergeant remained outwardly impassive. "His mother isn't, you know, which is how I come to be involved. And nor was Jancie. And now she's found unconscious . . ." He stopped, happy to let his suspicions hang in the air for the sergeant to work out for himself.

The sergeant looked away for a second and when he turned back Thackeray saw the scintilla of doubt in his eyes.

"I wasn't sure when I first saw the body," he said. "I was one of the first on the scene. He obviously wasn't injecting regularly. There was just the one puncture wound – messy, but just the one. At first I thought he might have killed himself. But there was no corroboration, and the girl swore at the inquest he wouldn't have done that. I think the jury just gave the lad the benefit of the doubt and brought in the misadventure verdict as the kindest one for the family."

"Even though it implied he was an addict? Some kindness."

"Well, you never know how juries' minds work, do you," the sergeant said.

"No-one considered he might have been murdered?"

"The injection might have been given by force, you mean?" the sergeant asked warily. Thackeray waited. The sergeant was a thick-set, stolid man and must have been coming close to retirement. If boats were to be rocked he was not someone who would set anything in motion without careful consideration.

"He had a belt around his upper arm," he said. "As they do, you know? Not tight, but it had been. I thought the arm looked quite badly bruised for just the one injection. But you can never tell." The uncertainties were evidently beginning to burgeon.

"Did the pathologist mention that at the inquest?"

"No," the sergeant said. "I don't think he mentioned anything about bruising."

"And Jancie?" Thackeray asked. The sergeant shrugged.

"Jancie's arms are black and blue," he said reluctantly. "Though that's not unusual. These kids neglect themselves."

"She didn't neglect her dog," Thackeray said sharply. "Jancie's not dead yet, but I guess the dog is. If you find him dumped somewhere – poisoned, cracked over the head, whatever – then it's as good an indication as you're likely to get that this wasn't an accident, or a suicide. It's attempted murder. Not that I'd dream of telling Thames Valley CID how to do their job – but you might like to."

The sergeant smiled faintly at that but Thackeray knew the challenge interested him. He left it there for him to consider in his own good time and walked Laura back to the lift with an arm around her shoulder.

"There's nothing else I can do for Jancie," he said. "Either she'll recover, or she won't. If she does, she'll no doubt be able to tell the local force what happened, and they'll give her some protection. If she doesn't, I might just have raised enough doubts to get them digging a bit deeper.

"So we don't go looking for Big Al?"

"I don't think that would be a good idea," Thackeray said. "We'll leave that to the local drug squad."

Sunday dawned grey and wet, and Laura realised that when the sun ceased to shine on the city's ancient stones it was as if a light had been switched off, turning gold to grey and warmth to a chilly dampness, which numbed the bones. The trees in St Giles outside their bedroom window dripped forlornly, and the tourists, wrapped in ungainly layers of garish waterproof clothing, wandered miserably past the hotel windows in search of the common or garden attractions and bright lights of the shopping centre.

They ordered breakfast in their room, made a half-hearted effort at eating and fell back into bed where even their love-making seemed to lack the passion they usually shared so intensely. Later, Laura lay in bed with the bedclothes pulled up to her chin and watched Thackeray through half-closed eyes as he came naked out of the shower. There were times when she felt that however much she cared, there were layers of him that she had not even begun to touch, parts so deeply concealed that she despaired of ever uncovering them.

She went through in her own mind the practical things she needed to discuss with him – his divorce, the flat she was tempted to buy but which she wanted to share with him, and above all their future together, and knew that this was neither the time nor the place. Rita Desai's death had disturbed him in ways she could only dimly understand and until the questions it had left behind were resolved she knew that nothing else could be.

She sighed and sat up in bed, trying to look more cheerful than she felt.

"You look distinctly battered," she said as he turned to reveal the still angry bruises across his back though she knew that the wounds she couldn't see were far worse than those she could. He shrugged himself into one of the hotel's towelling robes and sat on the bed beside her.

"Do you fancy a little shopping now we've finished the other thing?" he asked. "I think I need to see Hugh Greenaway before we go back to Bradfield. He'll wonder where I am if I disappear on Monday. And there are some more things I need to clarify about Harrison."

"The elusive Dr Harrison," Laura said. "The damage he's done is quite incalculable, isn't it? Spreading out like ripples on a pond."

"If a bit simpler to understand than the one about the butterfly flapping its wings in Peru," he said dryly. "You should never underestimate people's capacity for selfishness."

Dr Magnus Partridge gripped the arms of his leather armchair as if to prevent himself slithering helplessly from its glossy seat to the floor. He faced the master of St Fridewide's and Michael Thackeray across the stone fireplace in the master's study, his pale, thin features illuminated by two spots of burning colour high on each cheekbone.

"He betrayed my trust," he said in a voice that had become little more than a sybillant whisper. "What we planned was perfectly legitimate. Absolutely correct. We have former members of the college all over the world. They told us they were extremely honoured, in most cases, to be asked to contribute to the sexcentennial appeal. They were delighted to receive a visit from a fellow of Dr Harrison's eminence. I have letters, many letters, to that effect. What I did not appreciate at that time was that our supposedly esteemed colleague was retaining some of the proceeds of his travels for himself."

"And when you found out, he decamped with the loot?" Greenaway asked, his anger contained behind a rigid jaw, eyes like ice, fingers drumming almost imperceptibly on the arms of his chair.

"No," Partridge said. "I didn't discover what had happened until after he had gone." As he admitted the extent of his failure he seemed to shrink into his chair and metamorphose from the martinet who had intimidated so many generations of students into a frail grey-haired old man stretched to the limit of his powers.

"So there was no confrontation?" Thackeray asked. "You had no idea what he was going to do until he'd gone?"

"Precisely," Partridge said. "Then I went through the books."

"I shall want to go through the books," Greenaway said harshly. "What you are describing is fraud. On what sort of scale? Have you any idea?"

"Not clearly, master," Partridge admitted. "I did not feel able to approach donors and ask them for details of what they thought they had contributed to compare with the records Harrison left behind. It only became clear that there were large sums missing when his wife came to the college and began to complain about financial irregularities in his domestic affairs. It appeared that there was a bank account in their joint names, which her bank informed her was overdrawn by a considerable sum. She said she had no idea where the money had come from to open the account in the first place or where it had subsequently gone. Dr Harrison seems to have forged her signature at will. I made some inquiries and discovered that substantial sums had been paid in at the end of each and every one of Dr Harrison's trips abroad."

"But the money had vanished?" Greenaway said, his tone resigned now.

"Evidently. The funds came from overseas and had apparently been moved overseas again, plus additional funds up to the account's overdraft limit."

"Switzerland?" Thackeray asked.

"So I believe," Partridge said. "Dr Harrison's bank was not forthcoming on the finer points of the transactions."

"So when you said that the college assumed that he had gone abroad, that was a more reasonable assumption than you actually gave me to believe. You had some evidence?" Thackeray snapped.

"Not evidence, I suspect, which would stand up in a court of law," Partridge said, flashing Thackeray a look of intense dislike. "But reasonable grounds for my assumption that he had left the country."

"Did you inform the police about any of this when he disappeared?" Thackeray asked. Partridge glanced at Greenaway and shook his head almost imperceptibly.

"There was the reputation of the college to consider," he said. "And the terrible repercussions to the whole appeal process if any of the donors found out that some of their money had been misappropriated. I did not feel able to tell anyone."

"Not even the newly appointed master, it appears," Greenaway said to Thackeray. He turned to Partridge, his expression grim.

"I will see you and the bursar in my office at nine in the morning," he said getting to his feet and dismissively waving Partridge to the door ahead of him. "I shall want to see all the records of the appeal, of course. I think the most appropriate course of action is to appoint a firm of auditors immediately to go through all the college accounts."

Bobbing his head in frantic acquiescence like a distraught turkey, Partridge left the lodge and Thackeray heard the front door slammed behind him with unusual force. Greenaway came back into the room, poured himself a large Scotch, and flung himself into his chair.

"Stupid, incompetent old fool," he said. "He's let Harrison run rings round not only him, and presumably the bursar, but probably dozens of eminent MAs in the Near and Far East And he's right, of course. If it gets out, our reputation for probity will be ruined. It'll be difficult to raise another penny."

"Nothing much changes in Oxford, does it?" Thackeray asked, not really expecting a reply. "There's Magnus, been here his whole life, sitting at the centre of his spider's web of friends and contacts, from here to Whitehall and Westminster and back, wheedling out any confidential information he needs to know – details of bank accounts, no problem. Then, smoothing things over, covering things up – theft, fraud, what I'm still convinced might have been a murder in my day. You don't need freemasons here, do you? The whole place is a bloody enormous grand lodge."

"I thought when you were a student here I'd persuaded you that evidence came before conclusions," Greenaway said irritably. "A useful strategy in your professional life too, I'd have thought. Or am I to believe what I read in the liberal press about the police arriving at their conclusions first and finding the evidence to fit later?"

Thackeray leaned back in his chair and gave his former tutor a slightly shame-faced smile.

"All right," he said. "I'm overreacting. I've got a long memory as far as this place is concerned, too long perhaps. But am I to take it that finding Mark Harrison is no longer as high on your agenda as it was?"

Greenaway shrugged slightly.

"Believe me, Michael, it grieves me to even think of agreeing with that old fool. And you need have no doubt I'd have handled it very differently if I'd been here at the time. But I wasn't. And now, months later, with the celebrations so close, I have to concede that he has a point. We need a scandal like that on the eve of our six-hundredth anniversary year like we need a hole in the head. I need some time to think about what to do next."

"There is just one problem," Thackeray said. "I told you at the beginning of all this that I'm a policeman first and your private investigator second."

"And?" Greenaway prompted, his expression darkening.

"I'm not sure," Thackeray said. "But I want to satisfy myself that Harrison's girlfriend actually went with him. If I know she's safe and well, then you can bury the rest of it beneath your six-hundred-year-old cloisters for all I care. Save your precious reputation. But if there's anything more sinister been going on than a collegiate and individual rip-off of a few oil sheiks and shipping millionaires thousands of miles away, then forget it. I'll have to go to the local police and tell them what I know."

"Give me a day or two to sort out the books," Greenaway said. "I'll make no decisions before we talk again. OK?"

"I'm going back to Bradfield tomorrow for a couple of days to sort out some problems of my own," Thackeray said. "I'll come and see you when I get back."

He got to his feet. He knew that Greenaway was not pleased as they made their way to the door in silence. They were, he supposed, disappointed in each other. They turned on the doorstep and Greenaway held out a hand. Thackeray took it with a half smile.

"You should know better than to entrust your secrets to a known troublemaker like me," he said.

"I was looking for an honest man," Greenaway said. "I'd forgotten how unbending honesty can be. But don't worry, Michael. Partridge is finished. This is certainly the excuse I've been looking for to get rid of him. And believe me, the college is changing. And if I don't find it's changing fast enough I'll kick some ass, as they say across the pond, until it does."

"Not before time," Thackeray said.

"Oh, and, Michael? Good luck with the troubles in Bradfield," Greenaway added as his guest turned away with a salute of acknowledgement. But he left Thackeray wondering just which channels the master had been using to make himself so familiar with his affairs at home.

Chapter Thirteen

DC Val Ridley ran down the stairs to the front office at police headquarters looking more composed than she felt. She was answering a call from the desk sergeant who had reported the arrival of a woman reluctant to give her name but anxious to talk to someone about the case of Kelly James. Sergeant Mower half slumped across his desk with his head ostensibly in his backlog of paperwork had shrugged dismissively when she had taken the call.

"You deal," he said. Val had been tempted to argue but one look at Mower's dejected figure told her it was a waste of time and the knot of anxiety in her own stomach tightened perceptibly as she turned away.

Val found a gaunt middle-aged women sitting uncomfortably on the edge of an interview room chair, puffing nervously on the butt of a cigarette. The heavy make-up did not conceal the care-worn seams around mouth and eyes, the dark roots of her bleached hair were in urgent need of retouching and her short skirt revealing cruelly veined legs. She was, Val guessed without being told, one of the women who kept what could only ironically be called family life afloat on estates like The Heights.

"You wanted to talk to someone about Kelly James?" Val asked. The woman nodded uncertainly.

"I'm her auntie," she said. She stubbed out her cigarette with chewed fingernails in the tin ashtray on the table and lit another. Her breathing was husky. Val waited. She knew the signs.

"We won't involve you if you'd rather talk anonymously," she said eventually as the silence began to drag.

"Yes," the woman said quickly. "I don't want them knowing I came in here. It's not quite right – her auntie, I mean. I'm

Lorraine's auntie, not Kelly's." She pushed the dry blonde hair away from her eyes. "Lorraine had Kelly when she was no more than a kid herself."

"I understand from the hospital that they're going to let Kelly home tomorrow or the day after," Val said. "No serious harm done, apart from her broken arm." She noticed that the woman's hands were shaking.

"Depends what you mean by serious harm," the woman said, her eyes angry now as she sucked hard on her fresh cigarette.

"Is there something else we should know?"

"I'm surprised you've not checked Lorraine's boyfriend out. That Carl," she said. "I know for a fact he's been thumping our Lorraine."

"How do you know that?" Val asked carefully.

"I were there when she were round at her mum's a week or so ago, weren't I? Her mum told me she thought summat were going on there. Bloody great bruises, she had. Tried to hide them wi' that instant tan stuff, but it were so hot that day that it had all run off wi' sweat. He's a violent beggar, is that Carl. And if he can thump one, he can thump another, can't he?"

Val nodded non-commitally.

"Has he been in trouble with the police?" she asked.

"Not that I know of. But wi'a temper like that on 'im, I reckon it's only a matter of time. You can check that out yourselves, any road, can't you, with all your computers and stuff?"

"Yes, we can check it out," Val said. "Is there any particular reason why you think he might have been abusing Kelly as well as her mother?"

"They don't need reasons, do they? some of these lads. The drink's a good enough reason. He spends more time in the Heights social club than he does at home, from what my sister says. He's no different from t'rest of them up there in them flats, is he? No job. Scrounging a living from a bit o'this and a bit o'that. None of it legal, like as not. It's Lorraine's got the job

141

to keep that family going, isn't it? Carl comes in pissed and gives her a good thumping and a good seeing to an' all, I dare say."

"Has Lorraine complained to the police?"

"If every woman on the Heights who got thumped complained to t'police you'd have your work bloody cut out, wouldn't you?" she asked contemptuously. "Any road, our Lorraine won't complain. She thinks the sun shines out of that lad's backside. But if he's started on our Kelly an'all . . . She's not his daughter, you know?" Thumping children who were not your own was evidently where Lorraine's auntie drew her somewhat ambiguous moral line.

"Kelly says she can't remember what happened that night," Val said.

"And you silly beggars believe her?"

"It's possible after concussion," Val said. "And she'd been drinking, and probably taking pills."

"They'll be teckin' pills before they're out of nappies soon," the woman said. "You should do summat about that, an'all. We had our fun, but we didn't need all these bloody drugs to enjoy ourselves, did we? You can't step out o't'front door up on Wuthering after dark without some little toerag trying to flog you summat he shouldn't be. I don't know what you lot think you're going to do about it."

"We're working on it," Val said wearily. "Give it time. It's down to the people who live up there as well as the police, you know." She knew she was wasting her breath on the official line before Lorraine's aunt's face began to twist in contempt.

"Aye, well, you know what happens if anyone grasses them lads up, don't you? But when it comes to kids like our Kelly, that's different, isn't it? It's not right, what happened to that lass."

"But what it comes down to with Kelly is just guess work, really isn't it? You've got no proof Carl has ever laid a finger on her." Val tried to provoke the woman into providing more than speculation which, she guessed, would take the investigation nowhere.

"Ask her, why don't you?" Lorraine's aunt said angrily. "Ask her while she's still in t'hospital. She won't tell you owt once she gets home again, will she? He'll see to that. And Lorraine'll cover for him. She's right daft about that lad. I can't see what she sees in him myself."

Val let her visitor go and made a criminal record check on Carl Hegerty, but he turned out to have no more than a couple of shoplifting convictions as a juvenile offender. However uncertain his temper might be it had not yet officially come to the attention of the police. She went back up to the CID office and was surprised to find that Kevin Mower was not at his desk.

"He's in with the DCI," one of her colleagues offered. "Our Jackie didn't look right chuffed."

Val glanced at the scattered papers on Mower's desk and did not have to expend much energy working out the reason for Jackie Bairstow's disfavour. She wondered how much longer Mower could survive and whether the attempts she was making to watch his back were really in his interests, or her own.

"Tell him I'm in the canteen", she said, putting her notebook into her jacket pocket and going downstairs to buy herself a large mug of tea and an extremely sticky bun. The stress was getting to her just as much as to Mower, she thought, as she chewed a sugary mouthful and wondered how many inches it would put on her bum. She did not have long to wait for Mower. He swept into the room and dropped into the chair opposite, his dark eyes full of anger.

"Bloody woman," he said, reaching over to take a bite out of Val's bun as he loosening his tie.

"Ha, the great feminist I thought you could hack it with women bosses," Val scoffed.

"I can. I have. But not this one. It's perfectly obvious she hates my guts. So what's going on with Kelly? Anything new. Madam upstairs wants progress, so she says, though she's got nothing constructive to offer on how we might get it."

"Well, maybe I have," Val said, taking her bun out of his hand and indulging in another massive bite herself. With her mouth full, she told Mower what Lorraine James's aunt had told her.

"Is she suggesting Hegerty bloody raped her?" Mower asked incredulously.

"We don't know that anyone raped her," Val reminded him. "She's not complained of rape. Yet."

"Let's go and see the blasted girl again," Mower said, jumping to his feet, full of nervous energy now. "I can't hang about here doing paperwork. It's driving me round the twist."

Val followed him uneasily out to the carpark, pulling her black jacket on as she went, and caught the keys when he threw them to her across the roof.

"I don't think I'm in a fit state," he said. She glanced at him sideways as he dropped heavily into the passenger seat and she guessed that was the closest he had come to admitting the truth to himself for days. She put the key in the ignition but did not turn it.

"You shouldn't be on duty," she said, expecting an angry outburst but it was a blunt statement of fact, which this time he seemed to accept.

"I can't stay at home," he said, and this time the truth came tumbling out. "It was bad when it happened but it's getting worse. Every time I try to sleep I wake up again shouting . . . I'm back in that bloody truckers' yard with Rita. The whole thing plays through again in slo-mo, clear as a bell, and all the time I think I can do something to stop it even though I know I can't. It's as if I'm two people – a spectator and an actor in the same bloody film." His voice trailed away and he leaned his head back, eyes closed, a single tear trickling silently down his cheek.

"You've got to get help, Kevin," Val said, digging in her bag and handing him a crumpled tissue. She put a hand tentatively on his. "You need to see someone. If you don't the Bairstow woman'll have you out, one way or another. Even unfounded complaints of racial harrassment aren't going to do you any good with her. And if she can get you for incompetence . . ." She shrugged, leaving the threat hanging in the air. But Mower just looked at her blankly.

"She's already got me lined up for your job," she said angrily, trying to jolt him into some sort of reaction. "She virtually told me so when we had our little heart-to-heart in the pub. Get some help, why don't you?"

Mower scrubbed his eyes with the tissue and disentangled his other hand from hers.

"Right," he said wearily. "I'll give it some thought. Sorry, I shouldn't be laying all this on you."

"I don't mind." For a moment their eyes met and they both recognised the longing in hers and the indifference in his.

"Kelly James?" Mower said and Val turned away, stony-faced, and started the car.

The girl was sitting on her hospital bed in a dressing gown kicking her heels. Her bandages were off, apart from the cast on her arm, and her hair was restored to something like normal, though she had brushed it firmly forward to hide her bruises. Her face lit up when the two police officers came into the ward although Val guessed that it was simply a reaction to the possible relief of her evident boredom.

"D'you know there's no telly in here?" she said, swinging her legs back up onto her bed and arranging herself against the piled up pillows as if about to hold court. Val glanced into the other cubicles where most of the patients appeared to be asleep.

"I suppose most people are too sick to want it," she said. "You look better anyway."

Kelly fingered the fading bruises down her neck and shoulder.

"Nurse says they'll disappear in a week or so," she said. "God, I'll be glad to get out of here. I can't do me make-up or nothing. And my hair's a sight."

"Kelly, last time we spoke to you, we asked you if you saw Gary again that Saturday night and you said you didn't. Are you still quite sure about that? He didn't come back to the club and pick you up again?"

Kelly gazed back at the two police officers with a sweet smile and wide blue eyes, which neither Mower nor Val Ridley fully believed were as full of innocence as they seemed.

"No, I told you. I didn't see nobody I knew after I left the club. I never saw who it were who hit me. It were dark and they came up behind me, didn't they? I never saw them."

"And you don't remember what happened after that?"

"I can't remember owt," the girl said, returning to her former truculence.

"Is your mother coming to take you home tomorrow?" Val asked, changing tack. "Or will it be Carl?" She could not be sure but she thought the girl's expression changed for a second at the mention of her mother's boyfriend.

"You know you don't need to go home, don't you?" Val went on vehemently. "If there's anything happening there that's worrying you, Social Services will take care of you."

"Go into care, you mean?" Kelly said blandly. "Nah, Gary'll look after me."

"It's not legal for you and Gary to be sleeping together, Kelly. You know that. You're underage and Gary's very likely to be charged. He can get into a lot of trouble."

"You wouldn't," Kelly said scornfully.

"It's not down to us," Val said. "D'you not want to go home?"

The girl glanced away and did not reply.

"Has Carl been hitting you, Kelly?" Val persisted, determined to break through the girl's apparent complacency. "You don't have to put up with that."

"No, it's my mum he hits," Kelly said dimissively. "I told you,

I'm all right. He won't touch me." And with that they had to be content.

Kevin Mower was hardly aware of where DC Val Ridley was driving him next. All his attention was focussed on the grinding pain in his stomach, which had been getting worse for weeks. It kept him awake at night and when he eventually slept he was tormented by those vivid unreal dreams in which anything and nothing seemed possible. His world had crashed into the dust on the day Rita Desai had died and he could not see how anything approaching a normal life could ever be restored.

There was no-one to whom he could even begin to describe the grief that had overtaken him when he saw Rita lying dead that bright summer afternoon. Michael Thackeray, he guessed, knew exactly what he was going through but Michael Thackeray was not a man who inspired confidences and apart from the conventional expressions of regret they had not discussed Mower's loss. He had decided at the very beginning to bury himself in work but now, weeks later, he had come to the realisation that there was no escape there. And still the rage inside him grew and seemed to be fanning the fire in his guts.

He got out of the car in a daze when Val Ridley parked in the shadow of Priestley House and followed her up the concrete staircase to the flat Kelly James shared with her mother and her mother's boyfriend. Hegerty came to the door, unshaven and bleary-eyed in jeans and a vest, still carrying the can of lager he had evidently been drinking.

"Yeah?" he said. Val glanced at Mower but when he made no attempt to speak she took charge again, as she had done all afternoon.

"We need to talk to you about Kelly," she said. "Can we come in?" It was not a question that expected a negative response.

"Lorraine's not here. She's at work," Hegerty prevaricated.

"It's not Lorraine we want to see. It's you," Val said, moving firmly through the door so that Hegerty had to step backwards to let her in. She glanced over her shoulder to make sure that Mower was following. A television set was switched on to the afternoon's racing in the living room and the small table in front of the sofa was littered with lager cans and betting slips and an overflowing ashtray. Hegerty threw himself back onto the sofa where he had evidently been lying and flicked the TV sound off with a remote control. He was a well-built man, who looked as if he worked out. Val wondered where he found the money to keep himself in shape.

"I were watching summat," he said, his expression surly. "What is it you want?"

"We just want you to go over that Saturday night with us again," Val said.

"We told you," Hegerty said. "There's nowt else to tell. Kelly went out with her mates. We went out later. We got back about two, went to bed, woke up when you lot started hammering t'bloody door down next morning."

"Neither you nor Lorraine thought it was necessary to check that Kelly was home?"

"We was pissed," Hegerty said. "Normal like, Lorraine might have poked her head round t'bedroom door, but she didn't that night. She were out of it. I had to put her to bed, didn't I?"

"Did you?" Val said very quietly. "Pretty much unconscious, was she, by the time you got her to bed?"

Hegerty hesitated for a moment.

"Pretty much," he said eventually.

"So she really wasn't in a fit state to know what Kelly or you were doing was she?"

"What the fuck do you mean?" Hegerty asked, pulling his feet off the sofa and sitting very straight, his eyes alert now.

"I mean she wasn't sober enough to check whether Kelly was in?"

"That's what I said, didn't I?"

"So she wouldn't know whether or not you were in either, would she?" Val said.

"What's that supposed to mean? Course she knew. I came in with her, I went to bed with her, didn't I?" Hegerty's eyes flickered from his interrogator to Mower, who had sat down on a chair close to the door, and back again. "Oh, I'm sure you did – eventually. But Lorraine's not likely to know what time that was, is she? Did you go out again, Mr Hegerty?" Val asked. "Did you go out to look for Kelly when you discovered she wasn't in bed?"

"No, I fucking didn't," Hegerty said, getting to his feet and standing over Val Ridley. Behind her, she was aware that Mower had also moved.

"But Lorraine won't be able to confirm that one way or the other, will she? She was too far gone to know," Val persisted, easing herself out of her chair and backwards a step or two to stand in front of Mower.

"'Course she'll confirm it," Hegerty said. "We came in, we went to bed. What the hell are you suggesting?"

"I'm suggesting that your alibi, which everyone has taken at face value so far, doesn't really exist. Lorraine was pretty much unconscious, you said so yourself."

"She knew I was in bed with her," Hegerty said with an angry leer. "There's not many women I sleep with who don't know I'm there, sweetheart."

"We know you've been hitting Lorraine, Carl," Val shot back quickly. "Have you ever thumped Kelly as well?"

Hegerty's colour rose at that and Val wondered if she had pushed him too far. She was not sure whether she could rely on Mower for help and did not dare turn round to catch his eye.

"What the fuck did you say?" Hegerty threw back the challenge through gritted teeth. "Who told you that? I'll effing kill them."

"I can take that as a no, can I?" Val said.

"Yes, you fucking can. And that's enough fucking questions. I've told you what there is to tell. We come home, we was rat-arsed, we went to bed. We went to sleep. That's it. How were we to know that little slag was out with a fucking nig-nog? I got rid of Lorraine's half-caste brat and then I find Kelly's at it wi'another of 'em. Little whore."

Val felt rather than saw Mower explode behind her. He took two strides across the room, knocked Hegerty backwards onto the sofa and landed four or five hefty punches before he could even cry out in alarm. It took all Val Ridley's strength to pull Mower off his victim and prevent Hegerty's ineffective efforts at retaliation from becoming seriously threatening. He had been taken completely unawares by the attack and flattened by its ferocity.

"You," Val snapped at Hegerty when she had manoeuvred Mower out of the way. "You can come down to the station quietly, or I can send for back-up. I don't give a damn either way, but you've got some more questions to answer about what happened with Kelly on Saturday night. Right?" She held her mobile phone at the ready in case Hegerty chose the third option, which was what his contorted face, already red and puffy around the eyes, told her he preferred.

"I'll have you for this," Hegerty snarled in Mower's direction as he stuggled to his feet, but the sergeant had turned away, pale and drained, wrapping a handkerchief around his bruised knuckles.

"That bastard assaulted me," Hegerty said, feeling his nose carefully. "I think he's broken my fucking nose."

"Tell it to the judge," Val snapped. "I'm going to cuff you if we're taking you in the car. Any objection?"

"What's the point of objections?" Hegerty asked, submitting to the indignity of handcuffs without further complaint.

Keeping one eye on Mower and the other on Hegerty, Val escorted the two men to the car parked below. She was aware of curious eyes following their progress from windows on the long landing outside. With both men sitting silently in the back of the car, she drove carefully back down the long hill into the town centre. It was not until she had entered the main square and begun to inch her way through the traffic that Mower let out a stifled groan and she felt something slump against the back of her seat.

"The bastard's bloody collapsed," Hegerty said, with a note of triumph in his voice. "He's thrown up all over the floor, an'all. Serves him bleeding right."

Glancing over her shoulder to where Mower had slumped forward, she scowled at their prisoner.

"Shut it," she said, swinging the car sharply to the left and into the main ambulance entrance to the Bradfield Infirmary, which stood on the opposite side of the square to the police station. Parked in an ambulance bay, she pulled the back door open and helped Mower, bent double with pain, onto the pavement where a passing nurse ran to help.

"Police," Val said. "I've got a prisoner in the car I must deliver to the nick, but my colleague here's not well. He's vomiting blood. Can you deal?"

It was not until the nurse had helped Mower through the swing doors into the accident and emergency department that Val realised that she was shaking from head to foot.

"Right, you bastard," she said over her shoulder to Hegerty. "Let's get you processed. And if it turns out you've seriously damaged my colleague there, God help you." She did not seriously think that it was Hegerty's wild swings at Mower which had put him in hospital but she saw no reason to tell Hegerty that. The longer he sweated in a cell the better, as far as she was concerned.

Chapter Fourteen

Michael Thackeray stood and looked at himself in the bathroom mirror after he had finished shaving, deeply dissatisfied with what he saw. It was not the surface which displeased: he had learned to put up with the dark hair, which never looked tidy, and the deepening creases around the blue eyes were no more than he expected at his age. He was not a vain man and accepted that time would do him no favours from here on.

What disturbed him was the anxiety in his eyes and the dark shadows beneath them, the finely drawn lines around the mouth, none of which he could hide and which he knew would betray him when he kept his appointment with Superintendent Jack Longley. He had let Laura drive him back to Bradfield the previous afternoon and had then ungraciously insisted on returning to his own small flat. After ignoring the hurt in Laura's face, none of Vicki and David Mendelson's insistent and generous offers of hospitality had dented his determination to be alone. Not even the charms of their children, whom he silently adored, could move him. He needed time to think, he had told them, although what he really wanted was to hide his inner terror from Laura's probing eyes. He had been aware of three concerned pairs of eyes watching him as he walked away, but he had resolutely refused to look back.

It was more than twelve years since, as a young detective sergeant, his drinking had brought his family life crashing down around his head, snatching his son and his wife from him in one cataclysmic blow, and earning him the contempt of almost everyone he knew. Precariously dried out, he had resumed his life like a climber on the knife-edge of a mountain ridge, knowing that any day could plunge him over the precipice again. He had stayed upright, just, living one day at a time as he had been advised, his job the one certain hold he had on a perilous sort of normality.

That could be snatched away now by a beleaguered police force, which he guessed would be more interested in finding a scapegoat to appease a public horrified by the loss of a young Asian woman constable than in his personal culpability or innocence. If the worst happened, he feared that not even Laura, who had so recently brought him something approaching happiness, could save him from the demons which still lurked in the shadows of his life.

He had not dared spend last night with her. He had been too afraid his anger and despair would overwhelm them both and he would say or do something which he would bitterly regret later. But the cost of that caution had been high. His flat was cold. It looked bare and unlived in, smelled musty for lack of fresh air. The fridge was empty, the cupboards pretty well bare. Rather than go out and risk the bright beckoning doorways of the local pubs, he had ordered a take-away pizza and flung himself into bed early, to toss the night away, sleepless until dawn when he fell into an uneasy doze.

A late breakfast of coffee and stale cornflakes with canned milk left a sweet and sour taste in his mouth and an empty feeling in his gut. He dressed in a dark suit and sober tie and glanced again at the funereal figure in the mirror, the apparent solidity of which seemed unrelated to the frightened boy he knew was hiding behind the mask. He glanced at the phone but before he could decide whether or not to pick it up it rang, making him jump and curse himself for his nervousness.

"It's me," Laura said. "I'm at work. Are you OK?"

"I'm fine," Thackeray lied. "I'm sorry about last night. I needed time on my own." He glanced at his watch. "I'm going down to the nick in half an hour or so."

"Good luck, Michael." Thackeray could hear the sounds of the *Bradfield Gazette*'s busy newsroom behind Laura's measured voice. The weight of what neither of them could say hung in the air between and made him catch his breath.

"It'll be fine," he said. "I'll call you later."

"I love you," she said so quietly that he was not sure that he had really heard the words. He swallowed hard and hung up, unable to trust himself to respond.

"God help me," he said.

Superintendent Jack Longley glanced up sharply from his desk when Thackeray walked in, tension in every inch of him.

"We'll have lunch at the Clarendon," he said, getting to his feet briskly for a man of his bulk and pulling on his jacket and smoothing down what was left of his hair over his almost bald crown. "Out of the way of prying eyes."

Thackeray nodded and followed the ever-expanding figure of his boss down the stairs and straight out of the building again with a sense of relief. There was no-one at police head-quarters he felt inclined to speak to. Longley was not a man much given to small talk at the best of times and neither of them needed to say that this was not the best of times.

In the quietly discreet bar of the Clarendon Hotel, all deep leather armchairs and polished tables, still at noon almost deserted as it waited for its daily inflow of the well-heeled and sharp-suited on their way to the restaurant next door, Longley chose a secluded corner and ordered a Scotch for himself and a tonic for Thackeray from the hovering waiter without consultation or delay.

"Did you go into CID?" the superintendent asked, after the waiter had placed their glasses carefully on coasters and added a bowl of nuts. Thackeray shook his head, lighting a cigarette and drawing deeply on it.

"D'you want the bad news or the worst?" Longley did not wait for an answer. "Your lad Mower," he said, taking a swig of his Scotch that looked as if it were desperately needed. "In the nasty stuff up to his neck." Thackeray's stomach tightened as he waited for some elaboration, wondering whether this was the bad or the worst.

"I've got an official complaint on my desk that he beat the hell out of a suspect on the way to the nick yesterday. The only let-off seems to be that the suspect retaliated and has put Mower in hospital with some sort of internal bleeding, so he might get away with it. Sounds nasty, that does."

"How serious?" Thackeray asked, taking care to keep the emotion out of his voice.

"The complaint or Mower's condition? Neither of them sounds up to much to me."

"Was he on his own?" Thackeray recalled the numerous occasions he had tried to persuade Mower to take time off since the shooting. Nothing seemed to him less surprising than that the sergeant had finally cracked.

"Val Ridley was with him," Longley said. "She's gone sick today, an'all. Bloody convenient, that. I'll catch up with her when this other thing's out o'the way."

"Any other witnesses to this alleged assault?" Thackeray asked.

"Only Ridley," Longley said. "But there was plenty of evidence on Carl Hegerty's face, apparently."

"Sounds as though the place is falling apart without me," Thackeray said with unconvincing lightness.

"Aye, well, I can certainly do without your replacement," Longley said with feeling. "Right ball of fire she's turned out to be. You can call me as politically incorrect as you like, but I'm too old to start coping with a female DCI. Never mind one who seems to think she's got dibs on the chief constable's car-parking space. So let's turn our minds to getting you back in your own office *toot sweet*, shall we?"

"Haven't county got me lined up as some sort of sacrificial lamb then?" Thackeray asked.

"They may have," Longley said with a note of contempt in his voice. "But not if I've got owt to do with it. I saw our friend from HQ this morning. Dessicated sort of prick I'd not met before. But I think I sorted him out on a couple of things. I told him I was fully aware that you were planning to go up to Dale's haulage yard the day of the shooting. You'd every reason to follow that line of inquiry, and no reason to expect the sort of reception you got there. I can't see how they can squeeze neglect of duty out of that lot."

Thackeray looked at Longley, trying to hide the surprise he felt.

"You knew?" he said cautiously.

"Not the precise details of when you were going. But in principle, yes, I knew."

"I wasn't ignoring your instructions to leave it alone?" Thackeray was still far from sure that the life-line he was being thrown would bear his weight.

"What instructions?" Longley asked blandly, signalling the waiter to bring him another drink. Thackeray's glass still stood untouched in front of him as he ground out his cigarette and lit another.

"That's what you want me to say?" he said cautiously.

"That's what you've bloody well got to say unless you want to make me out a liar, you daft beggar," Longley said in a fierce whisper. "What's the matter with you, man? D'you want to go down the swanny like bloody Kevin Mower, or what?"

"Kevin knows I was disobeying instructions," Thackeray said, still not convinced. "I told him I was. And it was his girl-friend who was shot."

"Then Kevin's bloody mistaken, isn't he? Who's going to believe him if you and I say summat different? If he tries, they'll reckon it's vindictiveness and it'll have no credence, will it? Any road, I can't see Mower stabbing you in the back."

Thackeray shrugged.

"In different circumstances, maybe," he said. "With Rita dead, I just don't know."

"What about the other lad who was with you?"

"No, I said nothing to the two DCs," Thackeray said. "There was no need for them to know. It was a routine visit, after all, in spite of your reservations. None of us could have anticipated there'd be an armed man up there."

Longley scowled slightly at that, but nodded the comment through. They both knew that his reservations would not bear any closer scrutiny than Thackeray's defiance of them would. The reservations had been misplaced and Thackeray's pursuit of his own suspicions tragically justified by events. Longley drained his second Scotch and leaned back in his chair, fixing Thackeray with his shrewd pale gaze and giving him the thinnest of smiles as he glanced at his watch. It was a quarter to two.

"You'd best get back for your appointment," he said. "You're a good copper, Michael, and I want you back at your desk sharpish. You're not suspended. This disciplinary thing is just a case of going through the motions as far as I'm concerned. A necessary waste of time and public money. I've told you where you stand. It's down to you now."

Thackeray was waiting for Laura when she came out of the *Gazette* offices at four o'clock that afternoon. He looked pale and drained. He took her in his arms and kissed her and she clung to him as if he might dematerialise if she let him go.

"What happened," she said eventually when she could draw breath again.

"Nothing definite," he said. "He'll let me know within two weeks if there are to be any disciplinary proceedings. He put me through the mincer for an hour and a half, but I think, with a bit of help from Jack Longley, I might have swung it my way."

"I should bloody well think so," Laura said fiercely. "You did a brilliant job on that case. Without you there could have been more deaths." She did not need to say that her own might have been one of them. "So what now?" she asked.

"They want me to go back to Oxford and finish the course," Thackeray said. "Hopefully that will be the end of it. I'll drive myself back tonight. I haven't got the patience for the train. On top of everything else, Longley had another go at me just now for interfering in Thames Valley affairs. I'd have told him where to go but as he's just helped me out of a very nasty situation I told him I'd back off."

"You don't really mean that?" Laura said, surprised.

"I'm not sure what I mean," Thackeray said, feeling his weariness in every muscle of his body. "I don't think I'm getting anywhere with questions about the Harrisons, father or son. I'll try and see Penny Harrison tomorrow and break it to her gently. Quite apart from Longley putting the pressure on, I think I've been wasting my time there."

Laura turned away for a moment to hide her unhappiness with that. She could see that this was not a moment to push Thackeray, who looked at the end of his tether, but she was still startled to hear him give up so readily under pressure.

"Did Mower not get you any answers on Emma Capstick's car?" she asked.

"Oh Christ, you don't know about Mower, do you?" Thackeray said. "You can't have been paying attention to your crime reporter colleague today."

"I very seldom pay much attention to my crime reporter colleague," Laura said. "You know as well as I do that most of what he writes is pure fantasy."

"Yes, well, Mower's problems, unfortunately, are not," Thackeray said. He told her what Longley had told him.

"I'd like to go over and see him," he said. "Do you mind?"

"Of course not," Laura said angrily. "I'll come with you. Why on earth was he still working? Something was bound to go wrong, the state he was in."

"Because if he's learned one thing since he came to Yorkshire, it's to be as pig-headed as the rest of us," Thackeray said grimly. "I may have got myself off a hook but it looks as if he's impaled himself even more firmly on another."

They found Mower lying propped up in a hospital bed, his arm attached to a drip and his usually swarthy face grey and putty-like against the white pillows. He managed a faint smile as they came into the ward, but it was obvious to Thackeray and Laura that even that was an effort.

The business-like nurse who had let them in shook her head in warning.

"Five minutes, no more," she said. "He's a very foolish young man, your colleague. He'd ignored his ulcer so long he was lucky to come in just with severe bleeding rather than acute peritonitis. If it had burst . . ." She shrugged in a despair which was not close enough to mockery for comfort. Mower watched the three of them, his dark eyes dull with pain or drugs.

"I fucked up," he said faintly. "Sorry." Thackeray wondered just which of his problems he was apologising for.

"Just a friendly visit," he said. "I'm sure it can all be sorted when you're fit again."

"Yeah," Mower said, without conviction. "Nothing brings them back, though, does it? You've been there, done that. You must tell me about it some time."

Laura saw Thackeray go rigid as Mower blundered across unspoken boundaries that had been maintained for so long that they had all thought them immutable.

"Michael's going back to Oxford tonight," she said. "This is the only chance we had to come in together. I'll try to get in later in the week, when you're a bit better . . ."

"Don't you worry, guv," Mower said. "They won't need to sack me. After this little lot, I'm out, finished, before the job finishes me."

He turned away from his visitors deliberately and closed his eyes and it was apparent he was not going to open them again.

Laura pulled a reluctant Thackeray to the door. As they made their way down the corridor they met Val Ridley hurrying in. She looked disconcerted when she saw them.

"I thought you were off sick," Thackeray said.

"I was, sir," Val said. "But I felt a bit better this afternoon. I'll be back on duty tomorrow. I wanted to see Kevin . . ."

"To get your story straight?"

"Not exactly, sir," Val said, an obstinate expression turning her pale features as rigid as Thackeray's own.

"Don't worry, I'm not on duty," Thackeray said. "And in any case, it won't be me investigating what happened yesterday. I'd just like to think I'll have a few CID officers left when I get back from this course. It's not much to ask, is it?"

He turned on his heel and marched away down the corridor leaving the two women gazing at his retreating back.

"Oh, bugger," Val said.

"You see what you can do to talk Kevin out of his depression," Laura said curtly. "I'll deal with that one. Bloody men. They say we're the emotional ones. You have got to be joking."

Chapter Fifteen

Laura logged off her computer and made her way across the busy midday newsroom to where her colleague, Bob Baker, was hunched over his computer terminal, his fingers rattling like machine-gun fire on the keyboard. He glanced up, eyes bright beneath fashionably gelled blond hair. He stretched shirt-sleeved arms above his head and gave her a sly smile.

"What can I do for you, darling?" he asked. "A bit lonesome, are you, with your bloke away?" Laura ignored the gibe.

"Are you following up the Kelly James case today?" she asked. "I heard there was some development yesterday. Can you bring me up to speed?"

"They arrested the mother's boyfriend briefly," Baker said. "But there were no charges, and I'm reliably informed he's making a complaint about assault by one of your mates at the nick. What's that swarthy-looking detective sergeant called? Mower, is it?"

"Why did they arrest the boyfriend, then, if they hadn't enough evidence to charge him?" Laura asked, puzzled.

"You tell me, darling. You know more about the motives of coppers than I do. But I'll tell you something. You remember I did a piece on racist groups not so long ago?"

Laura nodded, recalling a series of articles, which she had felt relied more on speculation than hard fact and which had annoyed Michael Thackeray intensely.

"Carl Hegerty was one of the hangers-on up on the Heights," Baker said. "More mouth than trousers, it has to be said. But he's an unpleasant bastard. If he didn't have a go at young Kelly, I guess there's plenty of violence he has had a hand in. I expect that's why they pulled him in. He'll be one of the usual suspects."

"But what's that got to do with Kelly? She's not black."

Baker tapped the side of his nose.

"No, but her boyfriend is," he said. "Maybe our Carl wasn't too keen on that."

"How do you know that?" Laura asked, and knew as soon as she said it that the question was a mistake. Baker scowled at her.

"You've not been paying attention," he said. "Second lead, front page, Monday. Kelly's boyfriend taken in for questioning, one Gary Miller, no picture, of course, but I can tell you without fear of contradiction that Carl Hegerty would dislike our Gary on sight, especially the dreadlocks."

"Right. I missed that," Laura said. "I had a day off on Monday. But they didn't charge him either."

"Nope. If you want my honest opinion, they're floundering about on this one. The kid either knows who it was and won't tell, or it was a complete stranger, in which case they'll never find him. In the meantime, Sergeant Mower's lost his cool with Hegerty, and you can bet your life he won't let go of that in a hurry. There's only one group he hates more than blacks, and that's the police."

"Mower's seriously ill in hospital," Laura said, her anger bubbling over suddenly. "I think Hegerty may find it hard to prove an unprovoked assault. Mower's a lot more damaged than Hegerty."

"Is he now?" Baker said thoughtfully. "So it wasn't as one-sided as Hegerty's making out?"

"I'm surprised they haven't charged Hegerty with GBH or something," Laura said.

"Thanks, sweetheart," Baker said, turning back to his screen. "I'll check it out." Laura turned away to hide a satisfied smile, knowing that she had done as much as she could for Mower here. But as soon as she could decently leave the office for lunch, she drove up the steep hill to the Heights and parked outside her grandmother's house in the shadow of the flats, which loomed over the town.

Joyce Ackroyd hobbled to the door to meet her granddaughter with a welcoming smile and a sparkle in her green eyes.

"I'd almost given you up," she said, taking the Marks and Spencers bag of sandwiches out of Laura's hand and going into her tiny kitchen to put them on a plate. "Coffee?"

Laura nodded, taking a bite of the BLT she had already started in the car and carrying on her conversation with her mouth full.

"I haven't much time," she said.

"As if you ever have." Joyce's answer came back quickly but without malice. She had always been Laura's greatest supporter as she had launched herself into a career about which her parents felt at best equivocal and at worst hostile.

"You remember your friend Cathy Draper saying she'd talked to Kelly James's mother at her advice centre?"

"About her being battered by her man, what's his name? She shouldn't have told you that, you know. She's not supposed to pass on confidential information like that."

"Hegerty," Laura said. "You don't happen to know exactly where they live, do you? I want to talk to Lorraine James. Don't worry. I won't let her know how I heard about her bloke's nastier little habits."

"They're in Priestley, I think, but I don't know what number. But I do know where Lorraine works. She's down in the betting shop in that parade at the bottom of the hill. Next door to the Fairfax Arms."

"Great," Laura said. "I'll catch her away from home then. That sounds like a good idea."

Joyce looked at her granddaughter with a hint of anxiety in her eyes. After the disappointment of watching her only son grow into a man she barely recognised as her own flesh and blood, Laura, so like her in looks as well as temperament, had filled her life with an unexpected joy. But she knew that her own passionate desire for Laura's happiness was almost inversely proportionate to her ability to guarantee it.

"What are you in such a fret about, love?" she asked sharply, trying to hide her worry. Laura shrugged slightly and told her everything that had happened since she had driven back to Bradfield with Michael Thackeray.

"It's not your sergeant's place to thump him, whatever he thinks he's done," Joyce said sharply when she had finished. "I know you can't always expect the police to act like saints, but that doesn't mean you should cover up for them when they behave badly. I've seen them taking liberties in the days when they used to get away with it too easily. It's a nasty thing, a police baton. Believe me."

"And what were you doing at the time?" Laura asked mischievously. "Exercising your democratic right to lie down in the road?"

"Summat like that," Joyce admitted. "Don't you laugh, young woman. It's a right you might be glad of one day. They don't know the meaning of the word democracy, this lot."

"I wasn't exactly planning to cover up for Kevin Mower," Laura said defensively. "He got quite seriously damaged in whatever went on, you know."

"Aye, well, I dare say a lot of these things are six of one and half-a-dozen of the other," Joyce said. "So why are you wanting to see Lorraine then?"

"Just to find out exactly how violent Hegerty is, I guess."

"Dashing off on a white charger again, then?"

"I suppose," Laura said. "You should never have taught me how."

Lorraine James reluctantly agreed to take a cigarette break in the narrow alley at the back of the betting shop. She eyed Laura suspiciously through the smoke as she lit up.

"What's it to you, any road?" she asked. "I've never complained to t'police about Carl and I don't reckon to start now."

164

"Aren't you worried that he'll start on Kelly?" Laura asked. "If he'll hit one woman, he'll hit another."

"Don't be daft," Lorraine said. "He's right fond of our Kelly, is Carl."

"No problems with a teenager, then? None of the usual rows about bed-times and boyfriends? That sort of thing?"

Lorraine drew hard on her cigarette and shrugged slightly. "She does what she likes," she said, glancing away. "They all do these days, don't they?"

"And he didn't mind her having a black boyfriend?" Laura persisted.

"He didn't know she had a black boyfriend, did he?" Lorraine said sharply. "She had the bloody sense to keep that quiet, didn't she? And I certainly never told him."

"And if you had?"

Lorraine glanced away.

"I don't know, do I? After what happened with Darren I wasn't taking any chances."

"Darren?" Laura asked, puzzled.

"Darren's my lad. His dad were black an'all. I had to put him in care. He and Carl didn't get on. It were a right mess."

"So Carl wouldn't have liked history repeating itself with Kelly?"

"I've got to get back in now. You'll be getting me the sack," Lorraine said.

"Carl didn't know history was repeating itself, did he? So there's nowt to worry about there," she threw back over her shoulder as she pushed open the bookmaker's back door. But Laura suspected that the fear in her eyes told a story which was closer to the truth.

Laura spent the evening wondering whether she should pass on her suspicions to the police and if so to whom. Mower was still in hospital, "as well as can be expected", according to his ward sister, and Laura did not feel confident enough to telephone the acting DCI about whom she had heard such unnerving reports. In the end, the dilemma was solved for her by DC Val Ridley.

"There's a call for you," Vicky Mendelson said, throwing Laura the portable phone from where she sat curled up on a sofa close to her husband. When Laura realised who was on the other end of the line she took the receiver out into the garden. She was not keen to let David Mandelson, who worked for the Crown Prosecution Service, too close to her police contacts.

"I can't get Mr Thackeray on his mobile," Val said.

"He's probably still on the motorway," Laura said quietly, although there was nothing nearer than an inquisitive robin to overhear the conversation. "He went back by car and he didn't leave Bradfield till after six."

"Right," Val said. "Can you give him a message when you speak to him then? I don't want to call him from the office. It's something he asked Kevin Mower to look into for him, but I think it's a bit unofficial."

Laura listened as Val reported the result of Mower's trawl for a trace of Emma Capstick's missing car.

"So it's not been reported stolen, it's not been found abandoned? Right?" she said, gazing back at the house where the lighted French windows framed David and Vicky, arms around each other's shoulders, gazing out at the garden bathed in the last rays of the evening sun.

"I'll tell him," she said quietly. She hesitated for a moment and then told Val about her conversation with Lorraine James.

"So you think Carl knew about Gary?"

"I'm sure he did," Laura said. "You know what it's like up on the Heights. If someone's arrested the news soon gets around the estate. People won't have failed to point out just who Gary was. I don't see how he can *not* have known."

"I think you're probably right," Val said. "Are you going to write something about all this?"

"I was going to do something about battered women, but if you think it'll get in the way of your inquiries I'll hold off for now," Laura offered, glad that there was no chance her editor could hear her commit the cardinal journalistic sin of failing to file a good story. "You can fill me in later."

"It'd certainly fit in with the new DCI's agenda," Val said. "She wants a higher profile for all these domestic crimes – and she's right of course, though the lads in CID won't fall over themselves with enthusiasm when they're asked to check out who thumped who over the remote control."

"Acting DCI, I hope," Laura said sharply.

"Yeah, well, I hope so, too," Val said, and broke the connection.

"Everything OK?" David asked as Laura made her way back into the house.

"Fine," she lied, with a bright smile. "Just fine."

Thackeray had gone straight to the master's lodgings when he got back to St Frideswide's, avoiding the stream of his colleagues who had just finished dinner and were networking busily as they made their way to the narrow entrance to the buttery cellar in search of drinks. Now he stood facing Hugh Greenaway, who had evidently been working at his desk close to the open window of his study.

"Why do I get the impression that I'm being manipulated?" Thackeray asked angrily. "I go back to Bradfield and what do I find? Bloody Thames Valley police have been putting pressure on my boss to persuade me to back off. Was that your doing?"

Greenaway did not answer. He screwed the cap on his fountain pen and closed the file he had been working on.

"I spent all day yesterday going through the books with my bursar," he said. "And with Magnus Partridge's reluctant assistance, we worked out that Harrison had persuaded benefactors to donate something in the order of three

167

million pounds to the sexcentennial appeal over a period of three years or so."

Thackeray whistled quietly.

"So we are talking serious money?"

"Very serious money indeed. Much of which has already been committed to the anniversary improvement scheme."

"And how much of that did he siphon off for himself?"

Again Greenaway hesitated before he replied.

"It could be as much as a million," he said at last. "We're not sure yet."

"And you won't tell them, your generous benefactors?" Thackeray came back quickly. "You'll pretend it never happened? You'll let Harrison off the hook?"

The master's small nod of affirmation told Thackeray all he needed to know. He turned away angrily.

"Nothing's changed in twenty years, has it? In my day it was murder, now it's major fraud."

"Michael, you're exaggerating. There was never any evidence that anyone else was involved in that girl's death."

"Only the evidence of my own eyes," Thackeray said. "I was very young then and in the end I began to doubt what I'd seen. Dr Partridge was so sure, so convincing, so utterly definite. In the end, it wasn't just the coroner who was persuaded. He almost persuaded me and I'd bloody well been there, looking out of my window to see what all the shouting was about. I saw Liz Selby go over the edge of the tower, and she didn't fall and she didn't jump. She was pushed. But now we know the truth, don't we? Partridge will go to any lengths to protect this place, and so, when it comes to the crunch, will you."

"I'm sorry, Michael," Greenaway said. "My judgement is that the college's best interests are served by silence in this instance. What we are doing is in no way illegal. If we don't complain to the authorities there is effectively no crime. The benefactors don't suffer. They gave what they gave in good faith. Only the college loses. And I would just remind you that what you have been told here on a confidential basis must remain just that – confidential."

"And I would remind you of what I said before. If I have evidence of some other crime, I am duty bound to report it to the local police."

"And have you such evidence?" Greenaway asked.

"Not at the moment," Thackeray said. "But I still intend to make sure that Emma Capstick has come to no harm as a result of her liaison with Mark Harrison. Abduction – or worse – isn't a crime which St Frideswide's can simply wish away for its own convenience."

"You always were a very obstinate young man, I recall," Greenaway said lightly. "So let's hope that you are able to find Ms Capstick."

Thackeray walked across the quad to the porter's lodge, hardly aware of where he was going. His anger and disappointment choked him. But as his footfalls echoed on the flagstones under the arched gateway he was surprised to hear his name called out from the lodge itself. He turned to meet Malcolm Richards, the senior porter, standing in his lobby doorway resplendent in his dark suit and bowler hat.

"A word, Mr Thackeray, sir?"

"Mr Richards," Thackeray said, recognising in the jowly middle-aged face the features of a much younger man who had patrolled this entrance in his own time as an undergraduate. "You did well for yourself, then, getting old Peterborough's job?"

"Well enough, sir," Richards acknowledged. "But I could have done better. A little bird tells me that you're enquiring into the whereabouts of Dr Harrison. Would that be right, sir?"

"It would have been until a few minutes ago," Thackeray said, unable to conceal his bitterness. "But it seems the college doesn't feel the need to locate Dr Harrison any more."

"That's a pity, sir," Richards said. "A great pity. There's a few of us on the staff who would very much like to locate Dr Harrison."

Intrigued, Thackeray followed the porter into the lodge where he took up his station behind his broad oak counter, leaving Thackeray to lean on the other side.

"Are you going to tell me why?" he asked.

Richards pursed his lips and glanced out of the window at the shadowy quad.

"To put it bluntly, sir, a few of us was robbed."

"By Dr Harrison?"

"The very same. An investment, he called it, but when he vanished, without a word and certainly without returning our investment nor any of the profit, which was supposed to accrue, then I think it would be fair to call it robbery. Wouldn't you agree, as a policeman yourself?"

"Have you complained to the police about this?" Thackeray asked.

"No, sir, not yet, sir. Do you think that would be wise?"

"Oh, very wise," Thackeray said. "After all, in cases like this, it's only the people who make a complaint who will stand any chance of getting their money back if the culprit is found."

"Right, sir," Richards said, his lugubrious face breaking into a smile. "I had it in mind to kill him if I ever saw him again, but getting my money back would be preferable."

Thackeray turned to go, and then another thought struck him.

"Can you do me a favour?" he asked. "I brought my car down from Bradfield tonight and at the moment it's parked on double yellow lines at the mercy of your Draconian traffic wardens. Is it my imagination, or isn't there a yard at the back of the kitchens where I could park it safely?"

"By the garages, you mean, sir? I should think that can be arranged. Come with me and I'll show you exactly where you can put it next to Dr Partridge's garage. He never uses it. I

170

don't even think he can drive, to be honest with you. But it's one of the perks of the job so it never crosses his mind to give it up to someone who can."

His car safely parked in the dark cobbled yard at the back entrance to the college, Thackeray strolled back down St Giles, trying to order his whirling thoughts. A crowd of laughing young people, chattering in a language he did not recognise, spilled out of the Eagle and Child as he passed and followed him down the broad street towards the main entrance to Friddies.

Suddenly, he felt himself back in the Oxford he had known twenty years before, a part of, yet separate from the noisy crowds of undergraduates, cut off, however much he tried to conform on the rugby pitch, by his religion and his background. The tragedy was, he thought, that when he had eventually returned to try to pick up the pieces of his former life very close to the place where he had been born, he had found a sort of surly suspicion in the eyes of those who resented the fact that he had ever been away, all too similar to the suspicion that greeted him here.

He knew it should not have been like that. Others had come to this place from even more unlikely backgrounds than his own without meeting the sort of rejection he had faced at Friddies. There was something, he guessed, in his own personality, which had rubbed up those self-confident young public schoolboys the wrong way, and, in the end, dented his own self-confidence irretrievably. He had been the wrong person in the wrong college at the wrong time, he had decided years ago, after returning home to lick his wounds in private and try to make a new life for himself on his own ground. But it had never really worked.

He glanced back down St Giles before turning into the college gateway. The soft evening light cast a warm glow over the jumble of town houses and college buildings, touching the trees with gold. This must be one of the most beautiful streets in the world, he thought ruefully, and it had largely passed him by.

He was startled out of his depression by the shrill tone of his mobile phone.

"Mr Thackeray, sir?" The voice was faintly familiar, but not sufficiently so for Thackeray to place it.

"It's Sergeant Laker, sir. We met at the hospital when you came in to see Jancie McLeod?"

"Of course, sergeant," Thackeray said quickly. "Has there been some change in her condition?"

"No, it's not that, sir. She's still unconscious. Slightly better, if anything, they say. We're still keeping an eye on her, especially now it seems as if she might make it. But I thought you'd like to know about the other development, sir. They found her dog. Down by the disused railway line close to the back garden of her house."

"Dead?" Thackeray asked, although he needed no confirmation.

"Dead, sir, and thrown over the back fence into the bushes. I thought you'd like to know they're treating the case as suspicious. Not just an overdose, any more."

"Thank you, sergeant," Thackeray said, his bitter mood suddenly dispelled. In spite of Hugh Greenaway, he thought, there might still be something to be saved from the devastation Mark Harrison had created.

Chapter Sixteen

DCI Jackie Bairstow gazed at Val Ridley in disbelief.

"Gone?" she said. "Where the bloody hell has she gone to?" Val was sitting in the DCI's room looking pale and ill at ease. Any Brownie points she won for simply being female, she thought, would go straight out of the window after this cock-up.

"Her mother says she and Carl had arranged to pick her up from the hospital this afternoon. When they got there, the ward sister said that Kelly had been collected at noon. My impression was that so long as they got the bed back they weren't too bothered about when Kelly went, or who she went off with."

"Did they see who she went off with?"

"A black lad, according to the man on reception, who thankfully keeps his wits about him," Val said. "I assume it's the boyfriend."

"Right. I get the feeling we're being pissed about by someone on this case," the DCI said, getting to her feet and slipping on her jacket. "You and I are going up to those godforsaken flats to catch up with young Gary, and with Kelly's parents. Thirteen-year-old kids in need of care and protection are not simply going missing on my patch. Right?"

"Right, ma'am," Val said faintly, wondering when the patch had become Jackie Bairstow's, but following her boss down the stairs and into a car at the double. Yet for all the sound and fury the acting DCI brought to bear on the case, the two women returned to police headquarters barely an hour later no further forward in tracing Kelly James.

The Millers' flat had been locked up and silent when they had hammered on the door, and no amount of peering through the windows had suggested that the place was anything other than empty. Thwarted, DCI Bairstow had led the way up the concrete stairs to Lorraine James's flat, where they were slightly more successful. Kelly's mother let them in and waved them into the living room, where a haze of smoke drifted round the over-heated room. She lit another cigarette and slumped onto the sofa. Val Ridley noticed a reddening bruise on her forehead, not quite concealed by her hair.

"How the hell do I know where she's gone?" Lorraine said angrily. "Carl's doing his nut." Which presumably included thumping Lorraine, Val thought, although she knew the woman would not complain about that.

"Where is he?" she asked.

"Down the betting shop. Where else? I'm on a day off so he had to take his own slips, didn't he?" As Lorraine avoided the instant flash of suspicion in Val's eyes, the DC knew that there was a very logical explanation for Carl Hegerty's apparent prosperity on the dole.

"We'll catch up with him later," Jackie Bairstow said, oblivious to the undercurrents around her. "In the meantime, can you think of anywhere Kelly might have gone – either on her own or with Gary?"

Lorraine shook her head.

"I haven't a clue," she said. "Little cow. Causing all this trouble."

"Or any reason why she might have decided not to come home?" Jackie Bairstow persisted.

Lorraine offered no more than a shrug to that.

"I didn't know Carl had found out about Gary, but Kelly might've," she said. "She could have been worried about that."

"Because Gary's black?"

"No, because he's got six bloody legs," Lorraine jeered. "He's a bloody Nazi when the mood takes him is Carl. Why the hell she had to go and pick a black lad after all the trouble with our Darren I don't understand."

174

"It looks as if he treats you like a bit of a Nazi too," said Val, nodding at Lorraine's bruises.

"That's nowt to do wi' you," she snapped back.

"Did Kelly ever admit to you that she'd been raped that night? When you were visiting her in hospital. Did she let on, in a mother and daughter chat at all? It's important we know," DCI Bairstow asked.

"She said nowt to me about it," Lorraine said.

"Did she say owt about being scared of your Carl?" the DCI snapped back quickly, her accent suddenly as broad as Lorraine's.

"No, she bloody didn't."

"He's a violent fellow, one way or another," the DCI said. "What's the latest on his complaint about my sergeant? He's not going ahead with that nonsense, is he?"

Lorraine shrugged.

"He won't get anywhere any road if you lot gang up, will he?" she asked dispiritedly. "You'll all swear blind he was to blame."

"We'll put out a call for Kelly," Jackie Bairstow said, sounding a shade weary with the whole interview. "I'm not sure how much good it'll do if she's determined to stay away. But a thirteen-year-old with her arm in plaster and just out of hospital has to be a priority. Will you let us know if you hear anything, or have any ideas about where she might have gone?"

"She'll be a bloody long way off, if I know our Kelly," Lorraine said. "And she'll need to be, an'all, if I get my hands on her. Never mind what Carl might do to that lad."

DCI Bairstow stood up to go but at the door she turned back suddenly.

"There is one other thing I wanted to ask you," she said. Lorraine looked at her warily.

"When you came in the night Kelly was attacked, Carl says you were a bit the worse for wear. You went straight to bed, did you?"

"Yeah," Lorraine said. "We both did."

"You can remember that, can you? Both of you going to bed?"

"Of course, I can."

"And do you remember anything else happening that night? I mean before you woke up the next morning."

"No, I went to sleep, didn't I? Out like a light. We were pissed. You know? The way you get on a Saturday night?" Lorraine looked uneasy as she lit another cigarette.

"So you went to sleep, and I guess you slept pretty soundly?" Bairstow said casually. "So you wouldn't really know whether Carl slept as soundly as you did, would you?"

"What do you mean?" Lorraine asked.

"Just checking," the DCI said blandly. "Just making sure that nothing woke you. By the sound of it, nothing was likely to wake you, was it? Carl could have got up again – for a pee, maybe – and you wouldn't have heard him. Kelly could have come home and you'd not have known."

"He didn't get up again, did he?" Lorraine said. "He said he didn't. And Kelly didn't come home."

"Quite," Jackie Baistow said, opening the front door this time.

"We'll let you know as soon as there's any news of Kelly," she said over her shoulder. "I'm sure it won't be too long before we find her."

"Bloody hell," she said explosively to Val Ridley as they made their way back down the stained and littered staircase. "It makes you wonder why we bother, some people are so hard to help."

"Do you reckon Carl will push his complaint against Kevin?" Val asked.

"I doubt it when he realises how badly Kevin came out of the encounter, " Jackie Bairstow said dismissively. "Any way, with the defence you seem ready to put up, he'll get away with it, won't he? I hope you get some return on your investment in Mower. I wouldn't bank on it myself."

Thackeray went through the motions of attending lectures the next day, but his mind was a long way from the detail of modern management theory as applied to crime reduction. At lunchtime he strolled across the quad, intending to avoid the buffet lunch in the buttery and grab a sandwich instead at the Eagle and Child and consider whether or not to return for the afternoon's session on flattening the management pyramid, a notion that he did not think would go down too well with Jack Longley, who appeared very comfortable indeed on its existing apex. It was a grey morning, with a misty autumnal feel to it in spite of the fact that it was only just September, and he began to wish that he had brought a jacket with him from his room. He must remember to tell Laura that summer here appeared to be over before she came down again for the weekend.

As he approached the main gate he was conscious of someone overtaking him quickly, and glanced over his shoulder to find the tall figure of Cliff Gould, of the Thames Valley force, looming above him, close on his heels.

"Can I have a word?" Gould said, in a tone which Thackeray thought brooked nothing but acquiescence on his part. He shrugged.

"I was off for a quiet drink," he said, trying to keep the irritation out of his voice.

"Thought jogging was more your style," Gould said, meeting Thackeray's momentary bafflement with a cold stare.

"Oh, in the parks," Thackeray said quickly. "I didn't bother again after I fell the other morning. Decided it was more trouble than it was worth." It was obvious Gould did not believe him.

"My super asked me to have a word," Gould said, steering Thackeray through the gate and in the direction of the Lamb and Flag on the further side of St Giles. "Better make the most of the pubs. It's St Giles' Fair next week and you won't be able to get near these places." Thackeray nodded. He had heard of the annual funfair, the late descendant of the city's mediaeval country festivities, which brought a significant section of the town to a raucous standstill for a couple of days, but he had never been in Oxford at the right time to see it in operation.

"Time they stopped it," Gould said. "Brings the town to a grinding halt even more effectively than the normal traffic and attracts every pickpocket within a hundred-mile radius."

Both men had to duck as they made their way through the low doorway into the pub. Gould raised an interrogative eyebrow as he approached the bar but said nothing as Thackeray ordered his usual soft drink. They found seats in a relatively quiet corner and Thackeray waited impassively for Gould to expand on the reasons for this enforced hospitality, which he sensed Gould resented. The Thames Valley man took his time, savouring a couple of mouthfuls of his pint before he deigned to explain himself.

"It looks as though Jancie McLeod may make it after all," he said at length.

"Good," Thackeray said, not bothering to deny his interest in the girl. The sergeant at the hospital had been helpful, he thought, but had no doubt reported his presence and their conversations to his superiors, which was no more than he would have expected of one of his own officers.

"Assuming she recovers, we want her to go back to her own place," Gould said. "The connection between her and the main dealer in Cowley is apparently the best lead the drug squad have had for a long time. They want to follow it through."

"With Jancie as bait?" Thackeray said, not bothering to hide his disapproval.

"She'll be protected," Gould said.

"Like she has been so far?" Thackeray asked sceptically. "Like Tom Harrison was protected? Anyway, why are you telling me all this?"

"I've been told to pass something on in confidence about Tom Harrison," Gould said reluctantly. "When this operation's over, when the arrests are made, I've been told to tell you that there'll be further inquiries into young Harrison's death. Murder's not been ruled out. It's just been put on hold. I've been asked to reassure you about that."

Thackeray looked at his colleague without speaking for a moment, but his contempt was obvious.

"It was put on hold before the inquest, was it, when the pathologist mysteriously failed to testify about the bruising to the boy's arm?"

"It's a drug squad case. I don't know the details. The super just wanted you told that it's not closed, that you can reassure his mother about that . . ."

"And stop getting in the way?" Thackeray broke in. He felt resigned rather than angry, although he knew that Penny Harrison's reaction would not be so forgiving.

"Something like that," Gould agreed, finishing off his pint.

"You know I was mugged when I went down there, don't you?" Thackeray asked.

Gould nodded reluctantly.

"One of our lads saw it happen."

"And didn't lift a finger to help?"

"Couldn't, rather than wouldn't, is the way I heard it," Gould said defensively. "He didn't know who the hell you were but in any case he was too far away, on surveillance from a bedroom window."

"I could have been killed," Thackeray said. "Whoever hit me was not messing about."

"You took a chance, by yourself, on strange ground. If Jancie's friends are who we think they are, they don't like nosy intruders."

Thackeray put his glass down and got to his feet, controlling his anger. He spoke quietly enough not to be overheard although the passion in his voice drew a few curious glances

179

from drinkers at neighbouring tables and made Gould shift uneasily in his chair.

"Put this on the record will you, Cliff? I made some inquiries for a woman who's had a very rough time in this city. I've found out what she wanted to know: that her son's death was not an accident or suicide and that the truth, that he was murdered, was deliberately concealed by people who should be protecting the Penny Harrisons of this world, not compounding their misery. Finding out who killed the boy is your responsibility not mine – although from what you say it sounds as if you've already got a very good idea. Jancie McLeod is your responsibility too. But just remember one thing. If I don't hear pretty soon that the inquiry into Tom's death has been reopened, and that Jancie is safe and well and preferably getting some treatment, I'll write to your chief constable and to the Police Complaints Authority spelling out exactly what happened to me in Cowley and what I found out as a result. Is that clear enough for you?"

Thackeray did not go back to the college that afternoon. His interest in the course had always been minimal and had now reached vanishing point. In a thoroughly bad-tempered mood he strolled through the town, looking for some remembrance of the three youthful years he had spent here, but finding little that recalled anything pleasant. At Folly Bridge he leaned against the parapet and watched the Thames glide south on its long journey to the sea and smiled ruefully at himself.

"I must have seemed a pig-headed young prig," he thought to himself, with considerably more intuition than he had shown at the time. He recalled making his way down St Giles regularly on a Saturday evening to confession at St Aloysius where there were enough holy relics to make the three Protestant martyrs memorialised at the other end of the street shriek in protest from their pyres.

He remembered the slightly mystified amusement of his contemporaries in college as he returned from this pilgrimage, and the next morning's to Mass, amusement which turned imperceptibly to resentment as time went by and the rest of the rugby team realised that here was a man they could not remake in their own image. And above all, he wondered at the journey which toppled him from that pinnacle of boyish certainty into despair and then to his current state of chronic scepticism. He had been an outsider here, he thought, but, more damagingly, had gone home to become an outsider there too.

If he had never come to Oxford at all, he thought, the unspoken resentments, which had dogged his marriage from the very start might not have festered as they did, and he and Aileen might have found a way of living together without tearing each other apart. Perhaps.

The sun had burned away the early mist and was drawing the tourists to the waterside pub and the boat station beneath the bridge. It warmed him and he shook his head to clear it and took a deep breath of the soupy Oxford air, trying to shake off old depressions and focus on his current concerns again. He was not surprised by what Cliff Gould had told him. And that worried him. He should, he thought, have expected better of the local police. Mark Harrison's family certainly deserved better.

Turning back from the river, he made his way through the meadows to Magdalen Bridge, the only determined walker amongst the strolling holiday-makers, and back up the bustling Cowley Road to Penny Harrison's house. But there was no answer when he knocked on the door and he could see nothing through the windows, at which the curtains were tightly drawn.

Thackeray walked back to St Frideswide's in a sombre mood. The cobbles of Radcliffe Square felt unusually unaccommodating and the eyes of the great stone sculptures in

Broad Street seemed to be following him accusingly as he passed the Sheldonian Theatre where he had failed to attend to receive his degree. He was convinced that Emma Capstick was dead, yet he had no more evidence for it than her continuing silence, certainly nothing substantial enough to take to colleagues at Thames Valley already irritated by his interest in their affairs.

The traffic in St Giles was at a standstill as home-going shoppers' and workers' cars queued to make their way round the pedestrianised heart of the city, filling the air of the wide street with fumes as their engines idled. In spite of the ambitions of Lord Nuffield, mediaeval Oxford had found it impossible to adapt to the demands of the internal combustion engine and regularly ground to an asthma and heart-attack inducing gridlock.

Thackeray picked his way between the cars to the gate of Friddies. The porter, Malcolm Richards, was standing beneath the archway, his hands clasped behind his back as he surveyed the passing scene, rocking slightly from heel to toe. On the other side of the quad, Thackeray could see Magnus Partridge deep in conversation with a much younger figure silhouetted against the sun-drenched facade of the chapel. Thackeray wondered what the hell he was doing there, faced with this impregnable fortress, which in the mellow afternoon light looked as if it had not changed much for all of its six hundred years and would not change much over the next six hundred.

But something had rippled the surface calm of St Frideswide's, he concluded a moment later when Richards saluted him.

"Could I have a word, sir?" the porter asked, quietly and Thackeray did not miss the glance he cast across the quad at the senior tutor's gowned and apparently oblivious figure. Thackeray followed him into the lodge but Richards did not speak at once. He took up his stance behind the counter and stood for a moment staring down at the visitors' book in front of him.

"My little problem, sir," he said at last "It seems that it has been sorted out."

"Sorted out?" Thackeray said sharply. "How's that, then?"

"Apparently the college has a fund, sir, which can be used to assist college servants in difficulties. Goes back a long way, apparently. Like most things at Friddies, when you come to think of it."

"And who disburses this fund?" Thackeray did not disguise his scepticiam.

"Oh, the master, sir. On presentation of a case. So Dr Partridge says."

"And I suppose Dr Partridge also suggested that in all the circumstances it would not be necessary to involve the police?"

"More trouble than it's worth, sir," Richards said blandly. "All things considered."

Thackeray turned away and strode into the sunny quad. Magnus Partridge was coming towards him across the close-cut lawn dappled with shadow from the old oak. His thin face cracked into what Thackeray remembered undergraduates had to accept as the senior tutor's smile.

"Ah, Thackeray," he said. "I was hoping to catch you."

"And I you," Thackeray said but Partridge did not seem to hear him. His mind appeared to be set on a track from which there was no possibility of deviation.

"I wanted to tell you that we have had an amazing stroke of good fortune," Partridge went on. "I was just passing on the good news to young Chang, one of our postgraduates. Someone handed in a briefcase at the lodge this afternoon which upon examination turned out to belong to Dr Harrison. To my inestimable pleasure it contained some – if not all – of the research papers and disks which Chang and Miss Costello feared were misplaced when Dr Harrison departed."

"And where was this briefcase so conveniently discovered?" Thackeray asked, beginning to feel that he was being smothered in cottonwool.

"Ah, there I'm afraid I cannot enlighten you. It was handed in at the lodge by a member of the public who apparently did not leave a name. Richards was unfortunately on the telephone at the time and was not able to ascertain who the gentleman was."

"And Malcolm Richards will confirm all this, I've no doubt?"

Partridge looked at him, his eyes opaque beneath their heavy lids.

"Yes, indeed," he said. "There can be no doubt at all about that."

Chapter Seventeen

"How do you know it's blood?" the master of St Frideswide's demanded, reasonably enough.

"I've seen a lot of blood in my time," Thackeray said. "Fresh blood, dried blood, there's nothing else looks quite like it. I shall have to report it."

"Show me," Hugh Greenaway said determinedly. He was standing in the middle of his study in his shirt sleeves after answering the door to Thackeray's insistent hammering five minutes before. The look on the detective's face was enough to persuade Greenaway to let him in without protest: it was obvious that he was not bringing good news.

Greenaway pulled on his jacket and followed Thackeray in silence across the quad and up a staircase close by the chapel to the door of a set of rooms on the first floor. Thackeray unlocked the doors with a key and switched on the lights.

"Don't touch anything," he said. "This is about to become a crime scene."

"You could be mistaken, Michael," Greenaway said, without much conviction. He looked shaken and indefinably older than he had done just a week before.

"I'm not mistaken," Thackeray said flatly.

"Where did you get the keys?"

"Never mind," Thackeray said. "I got them is all you need to know."

"I should protest," Greenaway said. "You exceed your authority."

"Don't waste your breath," Thackeray said. He glanced around the study which had been Mark Harrison's. It was no different from hundreds of others in the older Oxford colleges, poorly lit from narrow windows, pride of place given to a huge desk, the walls lined with heavily laden bookshelves, the floor coverings threadbare and armchairs elderly and verging on the shabby.

"As you can see, someone has done a pretty thorough job tidying and cleaning this place up since your elusive fellow disappeared," Thackeray said. "When I first saw it I thought I was wasting my time." The room still had an occupied look, books in piles on the floor, heaps of papers and files neatly arranged on the desk alongside the telephone, the notice-board by the door with its out-of-date quota of concert and lecture details and a tutorial timetable. But for a room which had been abandoned for some months, there was a surprising absence of dust and the carpet had the vacuum cleaner tracks still visible in spite of its minimal pile.

"So what exactly have you found on your highly irregular sortie?" Greenaway asked coldly. "Murder is what you suggested. That's a very serious accusation – again. The police did examine the room when Harrison disappeared. They didn't seem to spot anything of note."

"In here," Thackeray said, leading the way into the small bathroom, which gave off to the main study area. The floor was covered with rather worn cork tiles, which had become cracked and flaky in places, particularly beneath the claw feet of what looked like an original free-standing Victorian bath.

"In a modern bathroom with lots of tiles he might have got away with it," Thackeray said. "In this place it's not so easy. You can clean a floor like this till you're blue in the face and you'll still leave some residue. Here, look, in the cracks around the feet."

Greenway peered over the crouching Thackeray's shoulder to where he moved a finger just an inch over some imperfections in the tiles, which appeared a slightly darker brown than the cork.

"That's it?" he asked, incredulously.

"I want it analysed," Thackeray said.

"Even if it is blood, Harrison could have cut himself shaving. Had an accident with a wine glass. Anything," Greenaway protested.

"Forensic will almost certainly be able to match the blood with traces Harrison has left here," Thackeray said. "There are always hairs, whatever. And his girlfriend too, if she was up here with him. In any case, we can do a thorough search of her home for traces to match. An ordinary domestic cleaner can't get rid of all the forensic signs of a person who's occupied a place for years. The blood will match Harrison's DNA. Or Emma's. Or not."

Greenaway looked at his former pupil with an angry glint in his eye.

"No-one's dead, chief inspector," he said. "There's no body. The whole college thinks it entirely reasonable that Mark Harrison and Emma Capstick left together to go wherever they have gone. Why on earth should you, or the college, or the local police, be seeking to analyse an obscure stain from Dr Harrison's bathroom floor?"

"It's blood," Thackeray said. Greenaway looked up at him in exasperation.

"Don't you think it's time you got rid of that bloody great chip on your shoulder that you've been carrying for twenty years?" he asked. "You seem quite determined to punish this college in some way for what happened when you were here. You failed to prove a murder then, so you're having another go now."

"No," Thackeray said sharply.

"It's time you stopped living in the past, Michael. Your obsessions are going to destroy you one way or another."

Thackeray looked at Greenaway for a long time before shaking his head slowly.

"This is nothing to do with the past," he said finally. "This is here and now, and that is a bloodstain, which has to be investigated."

"So what are you proposing?" Greenaway asked.

"We – or preferably, you – inform Thames Valley police of what we suspect."

"Which is?"

"I am pretty certain that Mark Harrison is alive and well and living abroad somewhere on his illicit gains," Thackeray said slowly. "He made elaborate financial arrangements to make that possible and we've no reason to believe he didn't execute his plans. Which leaves his girlfriend unaccounted for. I think he probably killed her, drove her away in her car, which is also missing, and dumped her and the car somewhere remote where no-one has found them yet, before he left the country.

"It could have happened the other way round, of course, but that seems less likely, given the brute force needed to move a body. And Mark Harrison had plenty of that, as I recall, unless he's let himself run completely to seed. Alternatively, both of them were killed, but that would assume some fairly horrific violence went on in these rooms to leave two people dead, and I can see no sign of that, to be honest."

Greenaway let out his breath in what amounted to a low groan. He looked around as if seeking somewhere to sit down but then seemed to remember Thackeray's warning and turned back to the door impatiently.

"That is an immense construction to build on one small stain, which may or may not be blood. Come back to the lodgings," he said irritably. "We need to talk about this."

"On one condition," Thackeray said. "That no-one, and I mean no-one, is allowed into this room until it's been properly examined by a forensic team. I want you to make sure you have all the keys. You personally. And guarantee the integrity of the scene."

Greenaway shrugged irritably but did not argue. He took the keys Thackeray handed him and locked the doors behind them.

"Go back to my study," he said. "I left the door open. I'll make sure there are no more keys at the porter's lodge or in the scouts' room."

"If you were an undergraduate presenting me with an essay I'd say your evidence was flimsy and your conclusion premature," Greenaway said half-an-hour later as he faced Thackeray across his desk. He looked pale and strained, Thackeray thought, and more ill at ease than he had seen him since he arrived at the college. He felt almost sorry for the master, but he was too driven by his own demons to back off now.

"Something happened here when Harrison and Emma Capstick disappeared," Thackeray said for what must have been the fifth or sixth time. "And now someone is trying to cover up and make sure there's no good reason to reopen an inquiry. Why has Harrison's briefcase conveniently turned up if not to pre-empt complaints from his research students? Why, when I suggested to Malcolm Richards that he should go to the police to complain about Harrison's dubious dealings, has a fund conveniently been found to ease his financial pain? Smooth it over. Sort it out. Cover it up. No-one is going to these lengths unless there is something seriously disreputable to hide."

Greenaway looked down for a moment at the papers on his desk before he spoke, and when he did Thackeray was hard put not to be moved by the pain in his voice and almost pleading look in his eyes.

"Unfortunately, there is something seriously disreputable to hide," he said. "Although it's not what you think."

Thackeray looked at his former tutor with a feeling of fore-boding.

"Not murder, then?"

"No, not murder," Greenaway said. "I spent another session with the bursar and Magnus Partridge this morning, and got to the bottom of Harrison's dealings at last. If I had had the

189

remotest idea what had been going on in this college before I came back from the States I think I would have got on the first plane west instead of east No way would I have volunteered to try to sort out this mess."

Greenaway got up and crossed the room to pour himself a generous Scotch, which he did not dilute with water. Kneading the glass between his hands he crossed to the window which gave onto the cloisters and gazed out at the arches where the sunshine never penetrated and rank upon rank of pale memorials to his predecessors lined the walls, just visible in the shadows. His tenure as master looked increasingly like one which would not merit memorialising, he thought, and wished himself fervently back in the crisp New England air.

"I came here as a modernising master," he said quietly, turning back to Thackeray. "That was the condition made by those who came over to Massachusetts to invite me back, and that is the only condition on which I would have accepted the appointment. In spite of what Magnus Partridge and the other antediluvians imagine, I do love this place. I always have done. It grieved me in your day that the college was unable to adjust to the necessary revolution which was going on outside, that it always had to be the last to change, that it couldn't show any sort of grace in accepting the new alongside the old. I know why Magnus wants to protect the college, although I don't approve of his methods. And now it looks as if I'll be the master who has to admit to something which this place regards as the greatest betrayal – the antithesis of everything Oxford is supposed to stand for – the dilution of the standards of excellence for which it is known throughout the world."

"But you said . . ." Thackeray hesitated, genuinely puzzled by this unexpected outpouring of emotion. "You can't be held responsible if there's a death on the premises . . ."

"But we can be held responsible if it can be proved that we have been selling our places to the highest bidder, Michael," Greenaway said.

"Ah." Thackeray's let his breath out in what was little more than a sigh, although Greenaway could not guess whether it was a sigh of regret or satisfaction.

"Harrison?" Thackeray asked.

"It came out of the blue this morning," Greenaway said, returning to his desk and picking up an airmail letter from amongst the scattered files and apparently struggling to read it in the fading light, although in fact he knew its contents by heart. "It's from a businessman in Kuala Lumpur, telling me that his son, who was expecting to start here in October, has been seriously ill, and asking me whether, as he has already paid his entrance fee, we can either hold the place until the next academic year or return his money."

"His entrance fee?"

"An interesting concept about which the college knows nothing," Greenaway said.

"And which, I presume, he paid to Mark Harrison while he was on one of his trips to the Far East?"

"Precisely. And when I tackled Partridge, he said there were at least three others, two undergraduates and one postgraduate, who to his knowledge had been recruited in a similar way, by paying Harrison thousands of pounds for the privilege. All expecting to start next term, all from wealthy and influential families."

"And that's something not even you could cover up?"

"Assuming I wished to try," Greenaway said wearily. "But over the three or four years these young people would be in college? With the fierce competition there is for places, the way the kids compare their A-level results? It would undoubtedly leak out and be all over the tabloids within weeks."

"So pay the money back and don't accept the students," Thackeray said.

"That is an option. But then the complaints will come from the Far East, from these disgruntled families who have been led to believe their children have won this glittering prize."

"Won? Even they must realise it's been bought, not won."

"I've no doubt Harrison was subtle enough to flatter to deceive, put them through some sort of entrance test, whatever . . . So you see why your determination to launch a new police inquiry at Friddies is peculiarly ill-timed?"

"I have no choice," Thackeray said. "I told you when we first spoke . . ." Greenaway waved an impatient hand.

"Next Monday more than a hundred of the college's potential benefactors will be arriving for the Feast of the Munificent Carp, as you know. An absurd occasion, but useful in this competitive world, when the future of Friddies depends on the success of our sexcentennial appeal. Magnus Partridge was quite right when he said that this is not a wealthy college. To put it bluntly, we desperately need the money as the Government cuts back on college fees. I can't let you wreck that. If you are so convinced you are right about this bloodstain, I must ask you to hold back at least until the Feast is over. I will guarantee no-one goes into Mark Harrison's room until Thames Valley police have examined it, which could be next Tuesday if you insist."

"My course finishes on Sunday," Thackeray said.

"I've already asked you to stay for the Feast"

"You're asking me to help you cover up . . ." Thackeray objected.

"Only very temporarily, Michael," Greenaway said. "For a few days." His voice was rough now although whether with anger or weariness Thackeray could not tell. "Alternatively, I could simply ask you to leave the college. Tell your chief constable that you have behaved unprofessionally, broken into a fellow's room, and are no longer welcome here."

The two men sat staring at each other like wary stags sizing each other up, and it was Thackeray who eventually glanced away from the master's unyielding gaze.

"Until after the Feast," he conceded ungraciously, getting up to go. He slipped his hand into his pocket and felt the plastic bag into which he had trickled some of the residue he had scraped from Mark Harrison's bathroom floor before he had invited the master to look at the stain. "I hold you personally responsible for that room," he said as he went out and closed the study door angrily behind him.

For the rest of the week, Thackeray went through the motions of attending his course, taking dutiful notes, which he then stacked neatly on the desk in his room, the information passing through his brain without touching the sides.

As he moved about the college he was aware of Magnus Partridge hovering on the edge of the milling groups of course members like some malevolent crow watching every move he made. Thackery avoided the evenings' social activities, conscious that his withdrawal to his room after dinner attracted comment, evidently unfavourable if the curious glances, which he met at breakfast, were any indication of his peers' disapproval.

But he cared little for the disapprobation of others when he was so expert at directing sharp knives of recrimination at himself. As he lay on his bed in the evenings smoking and desultorily turning the pages of *Our Mutual Friend*, which he had promised himself for years that he would read, he bitterly regretted acceding to Hugh Greenaway's request to delay his investigations.

All his old dislike of the college resurfaced as he glanced out of his narrow windows and watched Partridge patrolling the quadrangle below. There was a man he would take some satisfaction in charging with murder, he thought, in his wilder moments, knowing he had even less evidence for such a supposition than he did for suspecting Mark Harrison of the worst, and that the stooping, cadaverous figure of Partridge must surely be physically incapable of extinguishing the life of the strapping, rugby-playing Harrison or an energetic young woman like Emma Capstick, still less of disposing of a body. In

193

the end, he tried to shut the case, which might be no case at all, out of his mind, knowing his own judgement was almost as suspect as Hugh Greenaway had implied.

There were, in any case, other insistent problems to which his mind kept returning as he settled to sleep in the narrow, uncomfortable student bed which Laura had dismissed so preremptorily as a suitable place to make love. Laura's laughing face haunted him and he knew that he must decide soon where their future lay. He had seen the unspoken questions in her eyes the previous weekend, and knew that they would not have gone away. Perhaps Greenaway was right there too. He carried too much baggage from the past, too many guilts and resentments, and must either detach himself from them at last or, in fairness, detach himself from Laura who could not be expected to suffer indefinitely for his sins.

On the Wednesday evening he had allowed himself the luxury of calling her to finalise the arrangements for the coming weekend. Her voice had been full of life and warmth as she had described to him the new flat that she had decided to buy. But there were questions she did not ask and even at a distance of almost two hundred miles he could hear the echoes of them in her voice. Would he share it with her? He did not know the answer. Would he commit himself at last to a sensible, normal relationship? Again, he did not know and in his present state of turmoil, could not even guess when or if he would ever know. He had hung up quickly, not wanting the unspoken put into words, presenting him with choices he did not want expressed, let alone made. He was taking out his resentments on Friddies, Hugh Greenaway had suggested. How much more, then, was he taking out his resentments on Laura, whom he loved?

On the Thursday evening he hauled himself out of his depression and decided to do what he knew he should have done much sooner. He retrieved his car from the cobbled yard at the back of the college and drove the mile and a half up the Cowley Road to Penny Harrison's house.

To his surprise, the door was opened not by Penny herself but by her daughter, who let him in with only the briefest of acknowledgements.

"My mother's unwell again," she said. "I'm very worried about her."

Thackeray followed her into the tiny living-room where Penny Harrison was sitting hunched in an armchair close to the gas fire, which was turned full on. She did not look up.

"Is it going to be good for her to talk about Tom?" Thackeray quietly.

Caroline shrugged, and there was a hint of impatience in the look she threw at her mother.

"I don't think she's taking much in at all at the moment," she said. "I've asked the psychiatric nurse to come round. There's a limit to the amount of time I can spend here. I have a job to go to. Come into the kitchen. I'll make some coffee and we can talk in there."

Thackeray followed her into the small cluttered kitchen at the back of the house, and watched as she put on the kettle and spooned coffee granules into three mugs. She moved jerkily, and there was tension in the set of her head and the thin line to which she reduced what should have been an attractive mouth. She tossed her dark hair away from her face irritably. Somehow she seemed to have lost the self-assurance that had impressed Thackeray the last time they had spoken. Quickly, he told her what the local police had passed on to him about her brother's death.

"He's still just as dead, isn't he?" Caroline said bitterly. "Knowing how he died won't make much difference as far as I'm concerned, although it seems to matter to Mum."

"You'll have to decide the best moment to tell her about it," Thackeray said, passionately wanting to wash his hands of that responsibility. He knew, though, from personal experience that the how and the why of a death did matter desperately, although even the most pellucid explanations did not lessen the guilt, which could spread like a stain amongst family and friends.

"I will make sure they investigate properly," he said, but the girl just shrugged.

"I could kill my father for letting us in for all this," she said, pouring milk and pushing a sugar bowl in Thackeray's direction.

"Assuming he's not already dead," Thackeray said, wanting to shock and succeeding. Caroline looked at him appraisingly as she sipped her coffee.

"I have a confession to make," she said. "I wasn't being entirely truthful with you last time we met. I didn't want to upset my mother."

"You've heard from him?" Thackeray said, guessing immediately what this self-contained young woman had decided to keep to herself.

"Twice," Caroline said. "Once, soon after he left. I was very close to my father when I was a little girl. Adored him, in fact. I suppose it wore off when I grew old enough to recognise his selfishness and saw how he humiliated Mum, and the rest of us if it suited him. But I guess I was still more special to him than Tom. He rang me about a month after he disappeared. He wouldn't say where from but there was that timelag on the call, you know, that sort of echo you get if you're talking to the States or Australia? so I guess he was somewhere fairly far away. It was a very short call. He said he just wanted to let me know he was safe and well and that I wasn't to worry."

"And you didn't tell anyone?"

"I was going to tell my mother, but before I saw her again Tom was found dead and I didn't think it would help her to know that dad was swanning around California or somewhere while everything fell apart here. The state she was in . . ." Caroline shrugged helplessly and Thackeray guessed that

196

beneath the brittle exterior she had also struggled to deal with the damage that Harrison had inflicted on his family.

"And the second time?" Thackeray asked.

"Last week I had another call. I told him about Tom. Lost my rag, in fact, and shouted and screamed at him to get back here and help Mum . . ." She turned away suddenly to hide the tears, which overwhelmed her. Scrubbing at her eyes with a tissue, she quickly regained her composure, looking embarrassed that her facade had cracked so suddenly.

"I'm sorry," she said wearily. "It's just such a mess and I don't know how I'm going to cope."

"Did your father give you any idea where he was?"

"No, not a clue. And he certainly showed no inclination to come back."

"Given the financial irregularities he left behind, that's not very surprising," Thackeray said. "But there's one other thing I have to ask you. During either of these phone calls – and I realise it probably wasn't uppermost in your mind – did he say that he had Emma Capstick with him?"

Caroline looked at Thackeray for a moment and shuddered.

"He never mentioned her at all," she said.

"So he's got away with it again, has he?" The voice that interrupted them was like acid.

Thackeray and Caroline Harrison spun round to find Penny Harrison standing just outside the kitchen door from where she had undoubtedly heard much, if not all, of what they had been saying. Caroline went and put her arm round her mother, who was swaying slightly on her feet.

"I'm sorry," Thackeray said awkwardly. "I thought I should tell your daughter about Tom first . . ."

"I've known all along he was murdered," Penny Harrison said. "But Mark's girlfriend, his latest little tart, where's she, Mr Thackeray? Do you know that?"

"We don't," he said. "Everyone assumed she was with your husband."

Penny laughed, a shrill, manic sound, which had her daughter propelling her back into the living room and settling her down again in her chair by the fire. But now she had decided to speak, Penny Harrison was not to be stopped. She turned to fix Thackeray with gleaming eyes.

"He devastates the lives of all the women he comes into contact with," she said. "Emma wasn't the first young girl he took up with. It always ended in tears. I've always wondered if he was behind Liz Selby's suicide."

"Mark?" Thackeray said sharply. "There was never any suggestion that Liz had a relationship with Mark, was there?"

"Not what you'd call a relationship," Penny said. "But she was attacked on her staircase that week, you know? Sexually assaulted."

"Mum, " Caroline protested. "You're not suggesting Dad . . ."

"No, I didn't know," Thackeray broke in. "Nor did anyone else, as far as I'm aware. It was never mentioned at the inquest. You seriously think that was Mark?"

"I've always tried not to come to that conclusion but it's the sort of thing he'd do, isn't it? It was always when he couldn't get his own way that he turned violent. He'd shagged a couple of the other girls. Liz was probably next on the agenda and had the temerity to say no. I came later, of course. The last of his conquests in college and foolishly the one who agreed to marry him."

"Did Liz report it to the college? Did she make a complaint?" Thackeray asked, hardly believing what he was hearing.

"She told her tutor, I think, but I expect they decided to cover it up. That's what they do when things get embarrassing, isn't it? Rape, fraud, murder? What the hell? Friddies will deal with it themselves. One of these days they'll find something

198

they can't cover up and then the skeletons will come leaping out of the closets to dance round the cloisters."

"I think they just did," Thackeray said, only half to himself. Caroline Harrison looked at him with eyes full of fury.

"Bury the bastards, why don't you?" she said.

Chapter Eighteen

"If they don't want to be found they won't be and "our Jackie" can rant and rave as much as she chooses," Kevin Mower said, positioning himself carefully against his hospital pillows.

"She's thirteen, Kevin. They're not going to let it go." Val Ridley had arrived at visiting time with a bunch of grapes, which the ward sister had ungraciously thrust back into her hands as unsuitable for someone in Mower's condition.

"Milky drinks are a better bet," Mower had said wryly. "I'm going to be off the booze for a bit, too."

"God, you and the DCI both. What a team," Val said.

"Yes, well, we'll see about that," Mower offered sombrely. "What's happening with that bastard Carl Hegerty anyway? Is he sticking to his complaint?"

"As far as I know," Val said. "I've to make a statement about what happened."

Mower raised an eyebrow at that.

"And what will you be telling them?" he asked, not sure how far he had pushed Val into a corner from which she could only escape by returning blow for blow.

"What do you want me to tell them, Kevin?" she asked. "Do you care, one way or the other? Or were you kidding when you said you'd had enough? That you were leaving the job?"

Mower turned away from Val, unwilling to meet the pleading look in her eyes.

"You must tell them what you want to tell them, Val," he said. "You know what happened."

She gazed down at her rejected bag of grapes for a moment of uncomfortable silence, contemplating the stone ramparts of Mower's defences, against which she had lunged too often for her comfort or her self-respect. She shrugged and changed the subject.

"There's one line of inquiry no-one's followed up with Kelly," she said. "That's the brother, half-brother I suppose he is, the one who's in care. He might know more about his sister's activities than anyone."

"Go for it," Mower said, without much enthusiasm.

When she had left, Mower reached awkwardly into the locker beside his bed and pulled out his mobile phone. Laura Ackroyd responded quickly at the other end and he could hear the noise of the newsroom behind her.

"Will you do me a favour, Laura?" Mower asked without preamble.

"If I can," she said, without hesitation.

"I want to know more about Carl Hegerty." he said. "I'm stuck here for a bit and, anyway, no-one is going to let me near him even when I get back to work. If I get back to work. At the moment I'm got the bereavement counsellors circling round my bed like vultures now they've pinned me down in one place, so God knows when I'll escape. But I thought with your contacts on Wuthering, all the mates your grandmother's got up there too, you might be able to find out just what sort of a past that bastard's really got."

"Surely he'll be on police records if he's as bad as all that?" Laura objected.

"Not so's you'd notice, apparently," Mower said. "He seems to be on the fringe of some unpleasant political things, and given to beating up women from time to time, but you kow as well as I do that women don't report the men who thump them."

"More fool them", Laura said tartly. "I don't know, Kevin. I'd like to help but I can't imagine I'll be able to come up with anything useful. But I'll give it a go."

Laura located the door of the local branch of the England First Coalition between a betting shop and a convenience store in a parade of shops on one of Bradfield's outlying estates. The entrance was a narrow one, the door reinforced with metal plates and apart from a small spy-hole she could see no means of making her presence known.

She had taken Kevin Mower's plea for help seriously in spite of her resrvations. She had always liked Kevin, too much for Michael Thackeray's comfort on one occasion, and she was reluctant to see him wreck his career. When she had tackled Bob Baker, the crime reporter on the *Gazette*, to see whether he had any new information about Hegerty, she had drawn a blank. But her grandmother's contacts had proved more useful.

When she had called at Joyce Ackroyd's house she had found three visitors drinking tea and gossiping around the gas fire in the tiny living room. Her telephone call to Joyce seeking help had evidently galvanised her grandmother into the sort of action that had once been second nature and which she still relished when the challenge offered itself.

"This is Gary's mum, Delphine," Joyce said, her eyes sparkling with enthusiasm as she introduced a well-built and elegantly dressed black woman who nodded cheerfully at Laura. "And this is Julie from the advice centre. She works with Cathy Draper, who you met the other day." A small, pale woman with deep circles under her eyes nodded her acknowledgement. "And this is June, who's the new Labour party secretary and knows everything there is to know about these far-right groups on this side of the town." June, serious and bespectacled, clutched a sheaf of files to her T-shirt. "If anyone knows owt about your man Hegerty these ladies will know about it too," Joyce said with total conviction.

"I'd not want to be quoted in the *Gazette*," June had said cautiously.

"And what people tell me is confidential," Julie added. "You do understand, don't you?"

"I don't mind being quoted from here to Blackpool and back," Delphine said cheerfully. "The man Hegerty's a menace and it's time someone stopped him."

"Do you know where Gary and Kelly are, Mrs Miller?" Laura asked, but Gary's mother simply shrugged.

"I don't, my love," she said. "And if I did I don't suppose I'd be telling no-one. I told Gary the girl was too young for him, though I didn't reckon she was only thirteen. That was a surprise, right? But so what? I was only fifteen when I had Gary's big brother, and the others came soon after. There's nothing you can do about these things, my love, is there? She's a big bonny girl and knows what she wants."

Laura had caught her grandmother's eye and shaken her head imperceptibly. She could almost see the arguments against early motherhood forming on Joyce's lips and, although she agreed with her, she did not want anything to distract from the more urgent subject in hand.

It soon became clear that Joyce's triumvirate knew Carl Hegerty as a man of long-term and serial violence, not just involving Lorraine and, Julie alleged, possibly Kelly too, but previous girlfriends and, at some time in the past, a wife. Even more sinister was his connection to a far-right group for which he had been lucky not to have been arrested after several racist incidents in the town.

"You know there are some people you just know hate you," Delphine had said, her natural cheerfulness extinguished at the thought of Hegerty and his friends. "They don't have to say nothing, they don't have to do nothing, it's just oozing out of them, like phlegm. Hegerty's like that. I met him a few times, in the pub, in the street, though I don't think he knew about Kelly and my Gary. He didn't need to. You could just tell he thought me and my family were less than nothin' in his eyes, shouldn't be defiling the ground he walked on . . ." She stopped and looked down, as if overcome by her own eloquence.

"I don't need to know what he's done to know what he could do," she said, more slowly. "That's why I hope those kids is gone a long, long way away."

Standing now outside what she had been told was the head-quarters of Hegerty's favourite political group, Laura knocked at the door again. She did not think she had ever met what she assumed must be some sort of practising Nazi, and was not looking forward to the experience. She was aware that she was being watched by a tall Asian man with dark, deep set, impassive eyes, who had come to the entrance of the shop next door. Aware of what he must be thinking, Laura turned and told him who she was.

"Are these people ever here?" she asked. The shopkeeper shrugged.

"They come and they go," he said. "Sometimes they come and paint slogans on my windows in the night. They are terrorists. They stir up the young kids. They take care never to be around themselves when things happen. But I know. I have an alarm inside linked to the police station."

"As bad as that?"

The shopkeeper nodded sombrely.

"If I could move I would, for my wife's sake, and the children. It would be safer if we lived nearer Aysgarth Lane, and the rest of our own people. This is a white area and they don't like intruders. But the business is here. What can we do?"

He glanced up at the office windows where blinds were drawn.

"I thought there was someone there now. I saw someone go in earlier," he said. "Wait here a minute."

He went back into the shop and came back with a small spanner.

"Knock with that", he said. "So they can hear you." Laura did as she was instructed and before long they could both hear bolts being drawn on the other side of the door. The shopkeeper snatched back his spanner and dodged quickly back inside his premises and Laura wondered how one small nondescript row of shops could generate such fear.

When the door was opened she was so keyed up that she almost gasped to find herself face-to-face not with the burly thug she had expected but with a thin young man in thick-lensed spectacles who squinted at her as though, even with the optician's best efforts, he could not quite see what was in front of him.

"Yes?" he asked, his voice faintly querulous.

Laura explained who she was and reluctantly he let her through the door and waved her up the narrow flight of stairs, which eventually opened out into an office over the top of the shops on each side. The walls were papered with posters that Laura guessed would be too offensive ever to be displayed publicly, some of them decorated with German neo-Nazi swastikas, others featuring Le Pen and his French nationalists. The desks and shelves were well-stocked with expensive computers and office equipment. Whoever funded this organisation, she thought, was generous enough to keep it on the cutting edge of technology. She found the notion deeply disturbing.

The young man took his seat at the main desk, pursed his lips, steepled his hands in front of his nose and declined to give Laura his name.

"Carl Hegerty?" he said. "Why exactly did you approach us about Carl Hegerty?" He spoke precisely, with very little of the local accent in his voice.

"I was told he was one of your members," Laura said carefully.

"Then your informant was out of date," the young man said. "I am the membership secretary. Hegerty was a member briefly. But he seemed to have misunderstood our aims and objectives. We are a serious political party dedicated to extricating England from Europe and repatriating immigrants. We put up candidates at elections and hope to have a party political broadcast for the next general election. We are not a violent organisation."

"And Hegerty thought you were?"

"Hegerty and his friends are psychos," the young man said, with an expression of distaste. "They think that breaking the heads of a few immigrants is going to solve the problem. There are much more final solutions than that."

The Coalition's membership secretary met Laura's startled gaze with a bland smile and cold eyes. She did not think the words had been chosen accidentally.

"I believe Hitler thought much the same," she said. "And you know where it got him?"

"A lot of mistakes were made in those days. Hitler has been greatly misunderstood."

Laura shrugged.

"Like hell," she said, but she knew she was wasting her breath, and her sense of revulsion was so overwhelming that she could hardly sit comfortably in her chair.

"Do you have any particular reason for saying that Hegerty is violent?" she asked, forcing herself back to the reason for her visit..

"Not that I'd tell you," the young man said. "He may not be a member but his heart is in the right place."

Wearily, Laura drove back to the Heights and made her way up the steep concrete stairs to the flat Hegerty shared with Lorraine James. It was almost dusk and the lights on the staircase were out and she knew neither Kevin Mower nor Michael Thackeray would approve of her being here on her own. But she need not have worried. The landing was deserted and when she reached Hegerty's door she found it swinging open and she thought at first that there was no-one there either. She called out and when she got no reply she reached in and switched on the hall light and stepped inside. Lorraine was lying in a pool of blood just inside the living room door.

It was midnight by the time Laura left police headquarters with Val Ridley.

"Drink?" Val asked. Laura looked at her companion's pale, tense face and guessed she needed it even more than she did herself.

"It's late," she said. "Will anyone serve us? I can't invite you back. I'm staying with friends . . ."

"Come on," Val said and headed off up one of the narrow streets, which led out of the town hall square. Half way up the steep hill, she darted into a narrow alleyway where a few blue and orange bulbs around a boarded up shop-front were the only indication of life. Val opened a door, which gave into a tiny ante-room where a tall, broad-shouldered doorman in a black frock coat turned towards them belligerently. But when he recognised Val the heavy face softened into something approaching a smile.

"Oh, it's you, love," he said. "You're late."

"Just here for a quickie," Val said. She nodded at Laura. "She's my guest"

She led the way into a dimly lit bar where a black pianist was providing background music of the sort which Laura thought had gone out of fashion long before she was born.

"Very Rick's Bar," she said as they found a table and Val ordered drinks from an attentive waiter who had followed them to their table. "Does he play *As Time Goes By*?"

"I expect he would if you asked him, though his name's not Sam," Val said. "I like it here. It's relaxing after all the shit we have to put up with."

"I take it Lorraine wouldn't press charges?"

"Of course she bloody wouldn't. They never do, do they, these silly cows who fall for violent men?"

"I thought she was dead," Laura said soberly, thinking back to the moment when she had found Lorraine James and rushed to help her. She glanced at her hands and although she had washed them several times, could still feel the stickiness of blood on her fingers.

"Just dazed and badly bruised, they said at casualty," Val said. "Just the one cut over her eye, which had bled a lot."

207

"Tell me about it," Laura said. "Have they kept her in out of harm's way?"

"Nope. She wouldn't stay in overnight. Wouldn't make a statement. Zilch."

"And Hegerty?" Laura asked.

"She says Hegerty's gone. The row was over where Kelly might be hiding, but she swears she's no idea. So that's the end of that."

"What do you mean, the end of it?" Laura asked sharply.

"Well, as my new boss so succinctly puts it, we now have a case with no victim and no suspects because they've all bunked off, which is pretty well the end of the story as far as we're concerned. The DCI says she won't waste any more time on it."

"But Kelly's just a child," Laura objected.

"She'll go on the missing person's list" Val said, draining her glass and waving at the waiter for another. "No doubt she'll turn up in six months' time – on the game if she's lucky, dead if she's not." She raised her glass when the refills arrived.

"So sod them all, I say. Let's get pissed. You've not got anything better to do, have you, with the boss away?"

"Nothing better at all," Laura said. "Cheers."

Thackeray leaned on the pole of the punt and steered it towards the bank of the river where a copse came down to the water and offered a conveniently secluded point to moor the boat. He glanced at Laura who was leaning back in her seat, slim and infinitely desirable in jeans and a skinny black T-shirt, which left little to his imagination.

She had taken the train down to Oxford that morning and arrived at the college in a flurry of golden limbs and flying red hair, which took his breath away. She had sat on the narrow bed in his room hugging her knees and listening impassively as he recounted what had happened during the time she had been away. When he had finished and was staring gloomily at the threadbare carpet, she had seized his hand urgently.

"Come on," she said. "You're driving yourself crazy in this place and doing no-one any good. You've promised to wait until after the Feast, so you must wait. Now take me out and show me something worth seeing in this allegedly beautiful city."

Her enthusiasm was infectious and they had spent a contented afternoon wandering round the shady quadrangles of the ancient colleges, through Magdalen Deer Park and along the river Cherwell to the boat station.

"Right," she ordered. "I'm a tourist. You can't invite me to Oxford and not take me on a punt."

"I've never tried to steer one of those damn things," Thackeray objected, laughing in spite of himself.

"What the hell did you do when you were a student here?" Laura asked. "You can't have stayed in your room working all the time. I thought you were here in the outrageous seventies? All flares and the Sex Pistols."

"I didn't have you to share it with," Thackeray said with a lightness unusual for him.

"Just as well, as I was about nine at the time," Laura said dryly. She arranged herself on the bow seat and after a few false starts, which sent the craft veering erratically across the narrow channel of deep green water, startling the ducks, Thackeray worked out how to steer and sent them swiftly upstream. They glided beneath the trees in the University Parks and past the Victoria Arms where massed ranks of relaxed drinkers watched their progress amiably from tables on the grassy bank. Soon they were the only boat in sight as the river meandered through open fields still golden with stubble or scattered with lazy cows.

"Come ashore," he said after he had tied the painter to a low tree branch and stepped onto the bank himself. She stood up carefully, trying to keep her balance on the unstable decking.

"It's a pity we didn't bring a picnic," she said, although she knew very well that it was not food he was after. She guessed he found his college room as oppressive as she did, although he had not suggested that they stay anywhere else on this occasion. He held out his hand as she stepped across the narrow ribbon of dark water between the punt and the shore and pulled her towards him, kissing her with an anxious hunger, which disturbed her.

"This place is no good for you," she said as she allowed herself to be guided onto a patch of grass beneath the trees.

"It never was. I should never have come back," he said, slipping his hands underneath her T-shirt and confirming his supicion that she was not wearing a bra. "They got away with murder then and they'll get away with murder now if I don't do something about it."

"So do it. Nail the bastards." she murmured, lying back on the grass. "But first . . ." He did not let her finish explaining exactly what she had in mind. They made love slowly in the dappled shade of the trees and it was not until they were relaxing on their backs, with the smoke of Thackeray's cigarette drifting up to the leaves above them, that they were disturbed by laughter from another punt making its way downstream. Laura grabbed her T-shirt and covered her breasts as a gaggle of young people drifted by, giving them an ironic cheer as they passed. When they had gone she pulled the shirt over her head and zipped up her jeans, glancing up at Thackeray who had ground out his cigarette, angry at the intrusion, and was sitting watching her.

"Why did we come?" she asked. "We're a bit old for alfresco romps. We'll be getting our pictures in the *Globe* next."

"I wanted to get something right this time," he said quietly. "Everything else has fallen apart, just like the first time."

"You really have got a chip on your shoulder about this place, haven't you?"

"That's what Hugh Greenaway says. Told me to forget Friddies and get a life. He virtually accused me of being vindictive, imagining murder where none exists."

"And are you?" Laura asked, serious now. "Being vindictive, I mean?"

"I don't think so," Thackeray said. "But it's academic anyway. I've been pretty thoroughly warned off. And I'm hardly in a position to take chances."

"That's bullshit," Laura said sharply. "If you're sure . . ."

"But I'm not sure," Thackeray said bitterly. "There's damn all to go on. So let's just enjoy our weekend and go home, shall we? And let Friddies fester in its own corruption. Perhaps it's what it deserves. I certainly never want to see the place again."

They strolled reluctantly back to the college from the boat station through the leafy streets of North Oxford, golden with late afternoon sunshine. But Laura's enjoyment had been blunted by Thackeray's depression. She had never seen him so resigned to a course of action with which he was obviously deeply unhappy and she wished they could return anywhere but the college, which had so signally failed to restore his confidence after the bruising he had taken in Bradfield. But as they approached the gates Laura was aware that Thackeray's stride had quickened.

"What is it?" she asked, but then she too noticed the fire engine parked at the side of the college wall and the hoses leading in through the archway.

Thackeray strode ahead and under the arch where Malcolm Richards was standing at the door to the porters' lodge watching the activity on the other side of the quad with angry frustration in every inch of his six-foot frame.

"What is it? What's happened?" Thackeray asked, although he thought he already knew the answer.

"Seems to have been an electrical fault, sir, on staircase B. Made quite a nasty mess and unfortunately I didn't spot it until it had taken a good hold. Good job your conference has finished. There was some sort of police commander in one of those sets of rooms."

"And Dr Harrison's rooms?"

"'Fraid they're a bit of a mess, sir," the porter said. "Seat of the fire, they think. Is this young lady with you, sir?"

Thackeray nodded and turned away to meet Laura's anxious eyes. He thumped his fist against the solid oak door of the lodge and winced.

"Bastards," he said.

"Surely it was an accident?" Laura asked Richards.

"I should think so, miss," Richards said phlegmatically. "The fire officers seem to think so. No accounting for the wiring in these old buildings, they said."

Making their way across the quad to Thackeray's room, stepping carefully across the hoses and between firemen and bystanders, she took his arm.

"Let it rest until Tuesday, as you said you would," she said. "Then tell the local police everything you know and leave it to them. It's not your responsibility."

Thackeray glanced around the quad, where wreaths of acrid smoke still hung above the grass as the fire crew began to reel up its hoses, and then up at the chapel tower where the college flag hung limp against its pole in the quiet air of a golden evening.

"There are times when I'd like to raze this bloody place to the ground personally," he said. "They get away with murder."

Chapter Nineteen

Thackeray and Laura passed the rest of their weekend amicably enough exploring the city and trying out its restaurants, but there was a tension between them which Laura could not dispel. She told Thackeray about the flat she planned to buy but he did not appear to be listening with more than token interest. Dispirited, she abandoned the attempt to plan a future that included them both and gave herself up to the intense pleasures of art and food and sex.

Laura had been astonished to wake up on the Monday morning to find that the broad expanse of St Giles had been transformed overnight into a huge funfair with the stalls and rides ready and waiting to throb into action by lunchtime. Like an excited child, she dragged Thackeray round the fair for an hour as soon as it opened, returning flushed and laughing to the college clutching a massive pink teddybear and a face smeared with the raspberry residue of candyfloss.

"I've always loved fairs," she said, flinging herself onto the narrow student bed hugging the teddy to her. "I used to creep out of school with my mates when they had a little one every summer in the town. Nothing nearly as big as this, but I held the record for collecting junk prizes. In the end, I got caught creeping back in and trying to find somewhere to keep two goldfish in a plastic bag."

"The trouble with you," Thackeray said, trying to fit his bulky frame onto the bed beside her and slipping a hand round her waist. "The trouble with you is that you've never grown up."

"Perhaps I never needed to until I met you," she said, returning his kiss with interest

"Hotdogs for supper for me then, and a ride on the waltzer, while you make a pig of yourself with the glitterati,"

213

she threatened later, as she lay on the bed naked and watched him tie an unfamiliar bow tie.

"What is this Munificent Carp business anyway?" she asked.

"Oh, some mediaeval nonsense about half starved dons and a solitary carp, which suddenly began to reproduce in the fish ponds and kept them all alive until spring," Thackeray said. "A load of nonsense, but any excuse for a feast for the fellows will do in this place. The students never get a look in, of course."

"Wasn't it a mistake to stay?" she asked, more soberly. "You don't look as if you're going to enjoy it one bit."

"I want the chance to talk to Greenaway one more time," Thackeray said. "Just to see if I can persuade him to be more co-operative before I tell Thames Valley what I've uncovered." He turned to Laura and took both her hands.

"What about you?" he asked. "Can you keep yourself amused?"

"Well, on reflection, I may give the waltzer and the cage a miss," she said. "Those things used to turn me green when I was a kid, even though I couldn't bear not to give them a go. Can I use your car?"

"Of course," he said, throwing her the keys. "You know where it is."

After he had gone, she watched him cross the quad below the window, closely followed by the hurrying figure of Magnus Partridge in billowing gown, and she shivered slightly as she saw the senior tutor catch up with Thackeray and take his arm, obviously speaking animatedly as they went towards the archway that led to the cloisters and the main dining hall. Before they disappeared from view, she saw Thackeray free himself of Partridge in obvious irritation and move ahead quickly, leaving the senior tutor to wrap his gown around himself fiercely before following behind.

"I know why Michael hated this place," Laura thought as she went down the stone stairs into the quad herself and walked slowly to the small yard behind the kitchens where Thackeray's Rover was crammed alongside two others in the narrow space between the ranks of enormous rubbish bins and three garage doors which looked as if they were seldom opened. But it did not look as if she would be able to extricate the car from the narrow confines of the yard very easily.

"Damn and blast," she said after she had executed several edgy manoeuvres, which only seemed to jam the car more firmly into its narrow space. Irritably, she got out to weigh up the possibilities more closely, convinced that the only option which would enable her to swing the big car towards the gates was to open the nearest of the garage doors to give herself more clearance. She pulled at the door and found that it was firmly locked. Frustrated, she peered through the dusty window in the old-fashioned wooden door and drew a sharp breath. The light inside the garage was dim, but good enough to tell her that the car inside was a small blue Peugeot which, to judge by the thin layer of dust which covered it, had not been driven for some time. She couldn't see the registration number but she knew that the chances of it being Emma Capstick's must be very high. She pulled harder at the garage door and this time there was a sharp crack of splintering wood as the lock gave way and the door swung open on unsteady hinges.

Laura took a deep breath before venturing inside. She feared the worst and half expected to be overwhelmed by the sight and stench of a rotting corpse, but when she looked inside the car it was empty, and when she tried the boot that too swung open to reveal nothing more incriminating than an AA road atlas and a woman's waterproof jacket. Of the missing Emma Capstick, there was no other sign at all.

Laura's first thought was to rush back into the main part of the college and drag Thackeray out of the Feast to see what she had found. But as she leaned against the garage door, feeling alternately elated and horrified by what she had

215

discovered, the adrenalin drained away and she realised that there was little Thackeray or the local police would be able to do on an evening when the college was filled with eminent vistors and the quadrangles and gardens where she assumed Emma's body might be buried, were in darkness. But of one thing she was quite convinced. If Emma's car had not left St Frideswide's and had been hidden so securely for so long, then Emma herself was unlikely to have left the college either. And if Thackeray wanted to ensure that a murder inquiry was started, with or without a body, the little blue car was the key.

More soberly, she got back into the Rover, and with some more determined manoeuvring, she succeeded in reaching the gates. She got out to close the garage door on the Peugeot before edging out into the narrow lane behind the college and negotiated her way into the city's more than usually clogged traffic stream, which had been diverted to avoid the now noisily throbbing funfair in St Giles. She persisted, because there was one more thing she wanted to do in Oxford before she and Thackeray set off back to the North the next morning. After several wrong turnings, she finally found her way around the city centre and out to the main hospital on the hill.

She found Jancie McLeod in a side ward, free now of the intrusive paraphernalia of intensive care. She was surprised that there was no policeman on duty at the entrance to the ward but there was no-one at all around to challenge her as she approached down the deserted corridor. Jancie appeared from a distance to be asleep but she opened her eyes as she heard Laura open the door.

"Who are you?" she said, her voice dull. She looked deathly pale and very young against the pillows, and her eyes were full of fear. Laura told her about her connection with Thackeray.

"We're going back tomorrow," Laura said. "I just wanted to see how you were."

"I'm not sure how I am," Jancie said. "They put me in here this afternoon so I suppose I must be getting better. The doctor's been in trying to persuade me to go into rehab'."

"That sounds good to me," Laura said gently.

"I suppose," the girl said with an attempt at a shrug.

"You nearly killed yourself."

Jancie's eyes flickered away and she shook her head.

"They keep asking me what happened," she said. "But I can't remember."

"Can't, or don't want to?" Laura asked, but Jancie did not answer. If Thackeray's suspicions were accurate, Laura thought, whoever had tried to kill Jancie would not be pleased to discover her alive and, if not exactly well, fit enough to be asked questions and at least give some thought to the replies. She glanced around the small room, noticing the empty chair by the door.

"I thought the police were keeping an eye on you," she said, feeling slightly anxious.

"There's a sergeant who's usually here," Jancie said. "He's a nice guy. But I hate the detectives. Drug squad they said they were. They want me to go home and wait for Big Al to get in touch again."

Laura looked at her in horror.

"By yourself?" she asked. "They must be joking. They can't ask you to take that sort of risk."

"Bisto'll look after me," Jancie said.

"Bisto?"

"My dog," Jancie said. "Even Al's scared of him."

"I thought . . ." Laura stopped but she realised she was too late. Janice was staring at her with fierce intensity.

"Where's Bisto?" she asked. "They said he was being looked after in the police kennels."

217

"I'm not sure." Laura prevaricated but the girl was not fooled.

"He's dead, isn't he?" she whispered, her eyes filling with tears. "I knew there was something wrong. They said they couldn't bring him to see me, not even to look out of the window at him. They kept making excuses. Which of those bastards killed him then? The pigs?"

"Not the police," Laura said. "It wasn't the police, Jancie."

Suddenly, the girl swung herself out of bed and teetered into a standing position, and Laura was shocked to see the thin, scarred arms and stick-like legs revealed by the short hospital gown.

"I've got to get out of here," she said fiercely. "They've killed Bisto and they'll come for me again. I know too many things."

"That's not a good idea," Laura said. "Let me find your police sergeant. He'll get some help if you're scared."

"He wasn't here today," Jancie said. "There was a young guy but then he took a call on his mobile and disappeared. I've got to go. I can't stay here. It's not safe. They'll kill me, like they killed Tom."

Barely able to stay upright, and shivering with cold, Jancie grabbed a towelling robe from the bottom of the bed and tried to get her arms into the sleeves.

"Let me get help," Laura said but the girl pushed her away with surprising force.

"I want to get out," she said. "They can't keep me here if I don't want to stay."

"The police will look after you," Laura said, although she knew she lacked conviction on that score.

"No they fucking won't," Jancie said. "Where are they now? They're not here, are they? When you need them they're never bloody there. Look what happened to Tom with those bastards. Look what they tried to do to me. They came round that day. I could only half remember and I

218

wasn't going to tell those pigs anyway, but they came round, held me down . . ."

By this time, Jancie had pulled the robe around herself and staggered to the door and opened it. The corridor outside was still deserted and tentatively she began to make her way out of the ward, holding onto the walls as she went.

"Jancie," Laura said, despairingly. "This isn't a good idea."

"Got to get out," Jancie said desperately, taking another couple of halting steps. Reluctantly, Laura took hold of her arm and held her upright.

"I've got a car downstairs," she said, trying to hide her misgivings. "I'll take you somewhere safe."

Laura's promise was not as easy to keep as she had anticipated. One or two people had looked curiously at them as they made their way in the lift to the ground floor but seemed to accept Laura's placatory smile as sufficient justification for Jancie's state of undress. But when they came within sight of the main reception area, Laura realised that the two security guards on the reception desk were not going to let them leave without some very convincing explanation for the departure of a woman in a dressing gown. She glanced around quickly and hustled Jancie into a women's cloakroom.

"Stay here," she said, shoving the girl into a cubicle and pulling the door closed. "I'll find you something to wear."

She walked boldly out of the hospital, smiling at the bored looking security guards on reception who both sat up sharply and returned her greeting with more enthusiasm than was strictly required.

"I'll be back in a minute," she said. "I've left something in the car." What she had recalled was that Thackeray had left a trenchcoat on the back seat. The security guards smiled benignly at her as she came back into the building with it and made her way back to the cloakroom.

The coat came down to Jancie's ankles.

"Good job long is fashionable this year," Laura said cheerfully, fastening the buttons up to the girl's neck and pulling the belt tight. "Now if we go out arm-in-arm and you keep your head down we might just get away with it."

Jancie glanced down at her feet.

"No shoes," she said.

"We'll just have to hope they don't notice," Laura said with more assurance than she really felt. "I think they're there to stop intruders getting in and people taking babies out. They'll not be too bothered about two adults leaving." She wondered after she had said it how far Thackeray would class what they were doing as rational or adult behaviour. But the choice seemed to be between letting Jancie run off on her own or going with her, and that was no choice at all.

But Laura need not have worried. The security staff were fully occupied, apparently arguing with a group of three male visitors as she and Jancie made their way towards the main entrance, though as they passed the desk, Laura felt Jancie's grip on her arm tighten.

Outside the revolving doors, Jancie let her breath out in a painful gasp.

"They were there," she said.

"Who?"

"They were Big Al's blokes, back there at the desk. I told you they'd come for me. They just did."

"Come on, quick," Laura said unceremoniously and set off towards the car park at a brisk walk dragging Jancie behind her. "They obviously didn't recognise you. But I'll take you to the college. You'll be safe there."

Yet even that modest ambition did not prove too easy to accomplish as the traffic moving towards the town centre began to thicken. Huddled in the passenger seat, Jancie kept looking behind her.

"They're following us," she said urgently as Laura steered the Rover down the main road into the city at no more than

220

ten miles an hour. Laura looked in her mirror but could distinguish nothing more than a tailback of traffic, which stretched as far as she could see behind her.

"They can't be," she said, with more reassurance than she felt as she eased a little further through the congestion.

"The traffic's because of the fair, I guess," she said, as they stopped again at a diversion, which seemed to be sending them through tree-lined streets between tall Victorian mansions where few lights shone. "Do you know how I can get to the back door of St Frideswide's? It's down a little narrow street . . ."

"I dunno," Jancie said. "I don't know this part of town."

As they crawled over speed-humps and through chicanes of parked cars, Laura became increasingly anxious. She did not really believe that they were being followed but she knew that if the men Jancie was afraid of discovered from the hospital that she had gone, they might be numerous enough to start a serious hunt for the girl and the longer she and Jancie were on the streets the more vulnerable they became. At last she lost patience and veered into a parking space, causing the car behind her to hoot in outrage before it accelerated violently for a few yards to take her place in the slow-moving queue of traffic.

"Come on," Laura said. "We can get to the college more quickly by walking from here. It's straight down there, where you can see the lights from the fair."

Out of the car, the music alone was sufficient guide to take them back to St Giles where the stalls and rides were now jammed with families with over-excited children and groups of young people out for a good time. The blaring music, the piercing shrieks and squeals from the waltzer and the wall-of-death, the overpowering smell of frying onions and sickly sweet candyfloss were more than enough make Jancie's outsize coat and bare feet unremarkable in the crush. But the girl clung close to Laura, keeping one hand firmly on her arm as

221

they pushed their way through the throng from the squat shape of St Giles' church, over-shadowed by the lights of the helter-skelter towards Friddies, the facade of which was almost entirely obscured by the framework of the ghost train.

Suddenly, the pressure on Laura's arm increased.

"Over there," Jancie said. "I saw someone I know."

"Someone you don't want to know?" Laura asked, scanning the kaleidoscope of faces anxiously. Jancie nodded and clung even harder to Laura as a group of black youths steamed threateningly past through the crowd almost knocking them over.

"Did he see you?" Laura asked, pulling Jancie firmly towards the college gates. "We don't want anyone to see us going into Friddies."

"I don't know," Jancie mumbled, as she almost tripped over a small child clutching a huge silver and purple balloon, which sailed off into the night sky as he lost his grip on the string. The boy let out a howl of outrage barely audible above the thudding music from the enormous roundabout of traditional painted horses which had just begun to revolve close by. Laura pulled Jancie away from the child's irate family and, glancing over her shoulder to make sure no-one else was taking any notice of them, hustled the girl behind the back of the ghost train and safely to the door of the college, only to find the great oak gates firmly locked against them.

"Oh shit," Laura said. "I should have thought of that." She glanced up and down what was normally a quiet strip of pavement in front of the long blank college wall, its only windows high above them, and all of them as firmly closed as the gates. "Come on," she said. "We'll have to go the back way after all. They must have locked the main gates to keep the revellers out." Or maybe the potential benefactors in, she added under her breath.

Sticking close to the walls, she led Jancie back up the length of the college and round the corner into the relative quiet of a side street and from there up the lane to the second set of gates, which gave access to the back of the college, pulling the key from the pocket of her jeans as she went. The key turned painfully slowly in the huge old lock and Jancie, her back against the dark painted gates, gazed anxiously up and down the alley as Laura struggled to persuade the mechanism to turn. At last the Judas-door swung open.

"Anyone see us?" Laura asked, as she pushed Jancie ahead of her into the relative quiet of the cobbled yard. The solid bulk of the college muffled the noise of the fair here, although there was a great deal of clattering and shouting from the kitchens and Laura remembered that the Feast would still be in full swing.

"I don't think so," Jancie said, leaning against the gates again as Laura relocked them. Even in the dim light, Laura could see that the girl was shaking uncontrollably. She put an arm round her and guided her across the cobbles between the cars, and through the archway that led to the main part of the college, and then up the narrow stone staircase to Thackeray's room.

"I think you'd better have the bed," Laura said as Jancie struggled out of the over-large trenchcoat she had been enveloped in and tried to examine her bruised and dusty bare feet. "There's a bathroon through there," Laura said.

"I need a fix," the girl muttered, almost beneath her breath.

"Can't help you there," Laura said, not without some sympathy for the emaciated figure in the barely decent hospital gown who appeared to be visibly shrinking in front of her. "I don't think I can even get you a drink. The bar won't be open tonight, I don't think. Most of the conference members have gone now and they're in the middle of some mediaeval feast. The best thing I can offer you is the chance to get some sleep until it's all over and I can get hold of DCI Thackeray. He'll be able to sort everything out for you – one way or another."

"I don't want to talk to any more pigs," Jancie said dully, but she was already moving in the direction of the bed, evidently exhausted, and half fell onto it before curling into a tight foetal bundle and closing her eyes, with one arm around the shocking pink teddy bear that Laura had won at the fair. Laura pulled the bedclothes over her and tucked them around her shoulders.

"Bastards," Laura muttered to herself as she flung herself into the armchair across the room from her unexpected guest who was already snoring throatily. She was not even clear in her own mind whether she meant the drug-dealers who had reduced the girl to this pathetic wreck or the detectives who had persuaded themselves that it would be right to take advantage of her in her fragile state or both. Her overwhelming desire was to protect her from them all.

Chapter Twenty

Michael Thackeray had unwillingly shrugged himself into the academic gown he was entitled – and expected – to wear as a graduate of the university, and sipped tonic water without relish through an over-crowded and over-heated reception in the senior common room. Even above the hubbub of voices, the insistent heavy beat of the music from the fairground outside penetrated the thick walls of the anteroom outside the dining hall, throwing doubt on the wisdom of the those who had decided that the Feast must go ahead regardless of the revelries the town was engaged in just outside the college walls. But Thackeray soon realised that his hopes of talking to Hugh Greenaway again this evening were vain ones. The master was devoting himself exclusively to his more illustrious guests and when his eye caught Thackeray's his expression was blank and unfriendly.

After the company had moved into dinner, Thackeray stood behind his polished oak bench at one of the three long tables in the body of the hall, watched the master and senior fellows and guests, amongst whom Thackeray recognised at least two millionaires, process to their places at the high table. The entire company stood, heads more or less bowed, while the chaplain recited a Latin grace and he wondered sourly whether he was the only person present to question whether, if St Frideswide's could lavish hospitality on its guests on the scale of this evening's Feast, it seriously required more funds to see it into its second six hundred years.

He refused resolutely to be beguiled by the glittering glass and silver, the brooding portraits of former fellows and illustrious benefactors whose likenesses gazed down on the assembly, and the roof of dark beams and elaborate plaster-work, which here, at the very heart of the college, thankfully muffled all but an occasional reverberation of noise from outside.

Once or twice over the game soup with which the long traditional menu began, he caught Hugh Greenaway's eye briefly, but could not tell whether the sardonic glint he detected there was real or just a trick of the light from the candle-lit chandeliers, which flickered above the proceedings. He hoped it was the former but rather suspected that Greenaway had insisted on his attending the Feast simply to impress upon him one last time, amongst this distinguished, evidently wealthy and almost exclusively male company, his puny role in the affairs of the college and the distinct unlikelihood that he could affect its future in any way. It was impossible for him to tell what Greenaway was thinking from his own lowly place in the hall, although he was in far less doubt that, from time-to-time, Magnus Partridge had him fixed in a malevolent gaze from his seat at the nearer end of the high table.

Two courses further into the gargantuan meal, with the arrival of the Munificent Carp itself, a giant of a fish borne in on a specially designed silver salver carried by no fewer than four college servants in blue livery to a fanfare from the quartet, which was stationed in the gallery at the back of the hall, he knew that Greenaway's amusement was genuine. The master ritually welcomed the fish, which was sitting on its bed of vegetables and studded with truffles, with a broad smile and three low bows, before it was paraded around the hall to be greeted with bows in turn by the guests at each table and served with great ceremony, in minute portions, to everyone present.

"They import it especially from Budapest, you know," whispered Thackeray's neighbour as the ritual poem in the carp's honour was intoned by a senior fellow at high table. The elderly don had earlier confided that he was the college's wine fellow, only to be plunged into confused silence when Thackeray curtly informing him that he did not drink alcohol and so

226

had little interest in his neighbour's obsession with maintaining the high quality of the college's cellar, reputedly one of the best in Oxford.

"They can't find a carp big enough in this country," the fellow persisted, fixing Thackeray with a glittering eye. "If the legend bears any credence, they must have been considerably larger here in the fifteenth century."

Thackeray nodded grimly, wondering if he was turning into an irredeemable Roundhead, as Greenaway had predicted long ago that he might. Students these days, he recalled, had to pay fees for the privilege of attending this institution, which could so cavalierly order a fish from a thousand miles away to tease the jaded palates of these middle-aged and elderly diners who were partaking in its mediaeval rituals with such complacent respect.

As the wine glasses were filled again and a waiter made a special journey to Thackeray's place with a blue bottle of mineral water and an expression of disdain, the chatter and clatter of the meal resumed and in the narrow gallery behind him at one end of the hall, the string quartet took up its recital of early music again – not, Thackeray guessed, quite as ancient as the ceremonial the diners were sharing, but as near, perhaps, as the master of music could achieve.

They had passed around the loving cup, with a great deal more bowing, and reached the pudding, a creamy confection of almonds and rosewater, when Thackeray became aware of a sudden falling away in the crescendo of voices that had built up steadily during the meal. He glanced towards the high table and became aware that most of the diners there had their eyes fixed on a high point behind his head. The music abruptly trailed to a not very melodious halt. This time, when he caught Hugh Greenaway's eye, there was no doubt that his expression was one of alarm as he half rose to his feet and clasped a hand to his mouth in what looked suspiciously like horror.

Thackeray twisted around on the bench to see what had attracted the top table's attention. The gallery was a narrow one and the four musicians who had been playing at one end of it were now on their feet clutching their instruments as if turned to stone. At the other end of the gallery, perched precariously on the sturdy oak rail, with one arm around a supporting pillar, stood a painfully thin woman, with wild dishevelled dark hair and staring eyes, whom Thackeray recognised immediately in spite of the fact that she was stark naked.

By now the packed hall had fallen utterly silent and completely still. Not even the chink of a single spoon or fork on china broke the painful tension as Penny Harrison swayed on the narrow rail around which her bare feet appeared to curl like a monkey's.

"Murderers," she said, and her sibyllant whisper carried clearly to the high table at the other end of the room. Stone cold sober, as few others in the room were, Thackeray slid around on the bench, elbowing his startled neighbour out of the way, and stood up as quietly as he could before walking purposefully down the hall between the rows of appalled diners.

"Murdering bastards, all of you," Penny said, more loudly this time, and as one of the musicians behind her made as if to try to grab hold of her she allowed her body to swing forward, immediately above the centre table, so that she was leaning out at a forty five degree angle from the rail, held only by her grip on the upright beside her.

His mouth completely dry, and struggling for air, Thackeray reached the end of the table and looked directly up at her.

"Penny," he said quietly, his voice raw with emotion. "Let them help you down. This isn't going to do anyone any good."

For a moment, he thought she had focussed on him and taken in what he had said, but if she had heard him at all it was evidently too late. Her eyes wandered away from his again, gleaming dangerously, and raking the hall until she fixed her gaze on the high table and the master himself.

"You murdering bastard, Greenaway," Penny Harrison screamed this time before her feet seemed to lose their purchase on the oak rail and she half leapt, half fell head-first onto the cluttered dining table below with a heart-stopping crash. For a moment, there was complete silence in the hall, broken only by the faint beat of music from the fairground outside, as Penny Harrison lay face down and totally still, moaning slightly, among the shattered glass and scattered flowers of the ruined dinner table, a pool of blood spreading with appalling speed onto the white table cloth around her.

Thackeray pushed diners roughly from their seats to get close enough to take hold of her and turn her over, with one arm under her shoulders. Her head lolled helplessly to one side and the moaning ceased as all around him the guests scrambled to their feet, wiping spilt wine and almond custard from their dinner jackets and shirts as an astonished hubbub broke out all round the hall.

Thackeray was conscious of a hand on his shoulder as he felt for a pulse in Penny's neck. It was beating faintly and he laid her down again and began to remove jagged shards of glass, which had punctured her naked skin, and staunch the flow of blood on her neck and breasts with a table napkin.

"I'm a doctor," said the man in a scholar's gown who had hurried to his side. "Leave the glass. You may make it worse."

"She's alive," Thackeray said huskily, knowing it would probably be difficult to make Penny's condition worse as he watched the blood continue to pump from what he guessed was a severed artery in her upper arm. He pulled a mobile phone from his inside pocket and handed it to another bystander.

"Phone for an ambulance," he instructed curtly.

Together, he and the doctor together lifted Penny from the scatter of broken glass and spilt food on the table and laid her gently on the floor where they covered her nakedness in a clean tablecloth, which one of the college waiters had conjured up from the servery. Thackeray stepped back to leave further first aid to the doctor and as he did so he was conscious of Hugh Greenaway bulldozing his way through the melee of diners, his face a mask of scarcely concealed fury.

"How the hell did this lunatic get in here?" he asked Thackeray. "Was this anything to do with you?"

Thackeray shrugged.

"Nothing at all," he said. "You must ask your security people how she got in. I haven't seen her for days."

"This is years of work wasted," Greenaway said, distraught. "If it gets into the press . . ."

"Friddies has too many loose cannons," Thackeray interrupted, his own expression as angry as the master's. "You always did have. Maybe you always will. They tend to explode when you least expect them."

Greenaway stood for a moment gazing at Penny Harrison's white shrouded figure on the floor where the doctor was still trying to stem the flow of blood from the worst of her injuries.

"And it takes years to put the place together again," he said at last with a bitter weariness which Thackeray found still had the power to hurt. "Will you come in to see me in the morning before you leave, Michael?"

"If you think there's anything left to say," Thackeray said and turned away to leave the hall without looking back.

Laura had been dozing fitfully in the sagging armchair in Thackeray's room when she became aware of raised voices in the quadrangle outside and then the reflection of blue flashing emergency lights on the ceiling of the room. She glanced at the bed, where Jancie lay curled under the bedclothes, apparently oblivious, and then went quietly to the narrow window and looked down. She saw an ambulance and then a police car pull into the quad and roll across the sacred

230

turf to park close to the archway that led to the cloisters and the dining hall. The ambulance had taken a patient on board and pulled away before she spotted Thackeray making his way through the crowd of diners who lingered in the quad deep in animated conversation. She could see from the way he strode across the grass, taking the most direct route to his staircase, that whatever had happened at the Feast had made him very angry.

She met him at the door and put her fingers to her lips.

"We have a visitor," she said. Thackeray glanced at Jancie and groaned.

"What the hell's she doing here?" he asked.

"She was terrified," Laura said. "If I hadn't brought her here she was about to take off from the hospital on her own. Basically, she thinks she's being threatened by the drug-dealers because she knows too much and harrassed by the police because she won't help them."

"She was supposed to be under police guard."

"Well, she wasn't. Not when I went to see her, anyway. There wasn't a soul there."

"I can see I'm going to have a very interesting session with Thames Valley in the morning," Thackeray said. "I'll be very surprised if they don't charge one of us with wasting police time. Or perhaps obstructing the course of justice would suit you better?"

He crossed over to the window and looked down at the quad where Hugh Greenaway and some of his colleagues were now rounding up the scattered dinner guests and ushering them back into the cloisters towards the fellow's drawing room where he presumed some effort to rescue the evening would be made over the dessert and port. Briefly he told Laura what had happened at the Feast.

"Is she seriously hurt?" Laura asked.

"I don't know," Thackeray said. "She's lost a lot of blood. This will be one Feast they don't forget in a hurry."

231

"You've got blood on your shirt," Laura said. Irritably, Thackeray stripped off his dinner jacket and dress shirt and went into the bathroom to wash. When he came back Laura looked at him appraisingly as he pulled on a dark sweater.

"I've got some more bad news for the college, too," she said quietly, and told him about the blue Peugeot she had discovered in the lock-up garage close to where he had parked his own car so recently.

"It could be entirely innocent," Thackeray said, though Laura could see that he did not believe it.

"You made a note of the registration number of Emma Capstick's car," she reminded him.

"So I did," he said, pulling a notebook from the pocket of his jacket that he had left on the back of a chair. "Let's go and take a look, shall we?"

Laura glanced uncertainly at the sleeping girl in the bed.

"She'll be safe enough if we lock the door," Thackeray said. "I can't imagine Oxford's drug barons will come looking for her here."

Outside in the quadrangle the air was still throbbing with the noise of generators and music from the fair and they made their way in silence into the cloisters, which were slightly more sheltered from the sound. The arched walkway was fully lit tonight and from the windows above they could hear the sound of voices and the chink of glasses as the interrupted Feast continued.

Laura glanced at the memorial stones let into the paving beneath their feet.

"Are they actually buried here, these old fellows?" she asked. "Could you stick a new body in with them?" Thackeray glanced around and shrugged.

"These are just memorial stones," he said. "I don't think there are any graves down there. This is the oldest part of the college but I think in the early days they used the crypt under the chapel for burials. But not for years. Centuries, maybe."

They glanced at each other, each thinking the same thing. "You wouldn't dig up the cloisters or one of those pristine lawns if you wanted to bury a body, would you?" Laura asked, far more lightly than she felt. "It would be too obvious. But the crypt would do nicely."

"You're jumping to conclusions," Thackeray said.

"I don't think it's Penny Harrison who'll damage this college's reputation as much as her husband does in the end," Laura said, and Thackeray could only nod his agreement. If the car Laura had found turned out to be Emma Capstick's, he had little doubt that the young woman had not survived to leave Friddies at all.

They walked back through the cloisters together in silence five minutes later knowing the worst. Back in Thackeray's room, he slumped in a chair, wondering how Hugh Green-away was going to cope with the full-scale murder investigation, which he knew the local police would unleash on the college the next day as soon as he reported his now well-founded suspicions to them. In his bed, Jancie McLeod stirred uneasily but did not wake from her exhausted sleep.

Laura stood by the window gazing down at the deserted quadrangle below. Ambulance and police had long departed and the guests at the Feast were evidently still being entertained elsewhere. Eventually, Thackeray got up and went over to stand behind her, taking hold of her shoulders in an attempt to ease the tension he could see there. She leaned back against him.

"They'll blame you, won't they?" she said.

"Inevitably," he said. "It's always easier to blame the messenger. Greenaway will conveniently forget he asked me to talk to Penny Harrison and try to find Mark. The rumour mill will put it down as Thackeray's revenge."

"You're sure now Emma was murdered?"

"As sure as I am that she was Harrison's second victim," Thackeray said.

"The first being the girl who went off the top of the tower?"

"Though I don't suppose we'll ever prove that."

"I'm glad we're going home tomorrow," Laura said with a shiver. "I'm beginning to dislike this place as much as you do."

"I never want to set foot in St Frideswide's again," Thackeray said, wrapping her more tightly in his arms.

"I'm sure you'll never be invited."

For a moment they stood in silence, watching the light flicker over the ancient stones as the yellowing leaves on the old oak fluttered gently in the breeze. Laura felt the weight of the past here almost as acutely as the weight of all she wanted to say to the man who could enfold her so completely physically but balked at anything more. But even as she framed in her mind what she wanted to say, she was distracted by a movement below them.

"So where's he going in such a hurry?" she asked as a gowned figure appeared, almost scurrying from the entrance to the cloisters and across the quad. "It's Dr Partridge, isn't it? Do you think he knew what was parked in his garage?"

"I'm sure Thames Valley will want an answer to that question," Thackeray said, unable to keep a hint of satisfaction from his voice. They watched in silence as Partridge passed beneath their window and then headed across the lawn, his gown flapping around his gaunt figure.

Suddenly, Thackeray stiffened and his hands tightened on Laura's shoulders.

"He's going to the chapel," he said. "Now why the hell should he be going to the chapel at this time of night?"

"I'll bet it's not to say his prayers," Laura said. "Hadn't we better keep an eye on him?"

"I'll go," Thackeray said.

"And I'll come with you," Laura added. He looked at her for a moment and then shrugged. When Laura made up her mind it was difficult to change it, and he guessed that there was not even time to try.

The door of the chapel was ajar when they reached it but there were no lights on inside and the twilit quad barely cast a faint glow over the stone flagged antechapel, much less the narrow aisle and high wooden choir stalls of the main body of the church itself. In the dark recesses, behind pillars and Victorian monuments, the darkness was intense and the only sound was the faint creaking of ancient woodwork and the rustle of what might have been a bird disturbed in sleep or a passing bat. They stood for a moment just inside the door allowing their eyes to adjust to the gloom.

"There," Laura whispered, as another faint sound disturbed the chill, slightly musty air. On the other side of the square chamber, opposite the arch that led into the chapel proper, she had seen a faint glimmer of light, a single thread at floor level from beneath a door.

"The door to the tower is on that side," Thackeray whispered. "But I thought it was more to the left. It's difficult to remember after all this time."

"You think he could have gone up the tower?" Laura asked, with a slight shudder.

"Or down into the crypt."

"Oh, God," Laura said. "You don't think . . ."

Thackeray put a hand on her arm.

"I don't know," he said. "But I think I'm going to have to find out." He passed her his mobile phone. "Hang on to that," he said. "Just in case we need back-up. I wish to God I knew where the light switches were."

Cautiously, he led the way towards the single thread of light on the other side of the chamber, with a firm hand on Laura's arm. Their feet made no sound on the ancient stones and it was soon possible to see that the faint light came from under a studded oak door. But as Thackeray reached out to take hold of the iron handle, the door was suddenly thrust open and they found themselves face-to-face with the white-faced figure of Magnus Partridge, wild-eyed and staring, who gave an anguished shout as he lifted up the heavy suitcase he had been carrying and flung it straight at Thackeray's head. Caught unawares as the case struck him a glancing blow, Thackeray stumbled backwards, off balance for vital seconds and knocking Laura to one side. As they tried to regain their feet, Thackeray reached out an unavailing hand to grab Partridge, but he slipped through his fingers.

But before they could give chase, both of them became aware of a wafting stench of such sweet intensity that Laura swayed for a moment, thinking that she would faint. Retching, she turned away and leaned her head against the cool stones of the wall, as Thackeray slammed the old door shut again with a echoing thud.

"Is that what I think it is?" she asked, gasping for breath.

"I'm afraid so," Thackeray said, glancing down at the jumble around their feet, which he guessed were Emma Capstick's possessions that had tumbled out of the suitcase Partridge had hurled at them. "Where the hell's he gone?"

"Through that other door," Laura said faintly, pointing at the second of the two doors, now swinging open and allowing a faint trickle of light to turn the antechamber from dark to dimmest grey.

"Sweet Jesus, he's gone up the tower," Thackeray said with a groan. "Dial 999 and get some help. I'm going up after him. We don't want anyone else falling from a great height tonight."

Laura had done as she was told but now she was crouching at the top of the steep spiral staircase, which had taken all three of them in turn breathlessly past the belfry and up another storey to the door that led onto the roof of St Fridewide's tower. She had her back to the open door and in spite of the still raucous noise from the fairground outside the walls, she could just hear Thackeray and Partridge in shouted conversation.

Thackeray was perhaps six feet in front of her, standing completely still and silhouetted against the glare of the lights from St Giles's fair. When he had heard her approach up the staircase behind him, he had motioned for her to stay back, and now her eyes had adjusted to the light after the breathless climb she could see why. Magnus Partridge, gown flapping in the brisk breeze, was sitting on top of the low stone balustrade on the townward side of the tower, his legs dangling in space and only one hand maintaining his precarious balance a hundred feet above the oblivious crowds of revellers in the street below. With his shoulders hunched and his hair ruffled like feathers in the wind, he looked like a watchful vulture perched above its prey and all too likely to take off at any moment.

"Dr Partridge," Thackeray said, his voice as quiet as the racket from below allowed. "Dr Partridge, this isn't going to solve anything. Come down and we can talk about this calmly."

Partridge turned his head in Thackeray's direction briefly and laughed wildly.

"I have nothing to talk to you about, Inspector Thackeray, nothing at all." His voice was harsh and rose to a shriek as he glanced down.

"Friddies needs you to sort out this horrible mess," Thackeray said. "You owe it to the college to tell the truth now."

"You can see the truth down in the crypt," Partridge said. "You have all the evidence you were looking for when you came seeking revenge after all these years. I killed the young woman. You've found the body. The mystery's solved. There's an end to it. St Frideswide's has no more need of me. It's best if I go now."

"I don't believe you, Dr Partridge," Thackeray said urgently. "I know Mark Harrison was involved in this, just as he was involved in Liz Selby's death."

"No," Partridge said, swaying on the balustrade so violently that Laura thought the argument was over. "No, no, no, Mr Thackeray. You're wrong, just as you were wrong the first time. That was your vindictive imagination. No more. I killed Miss Capstick. She insisted on going away with Dr Harrison, and couldn't be persuaded to stay. She was determined on a scandal. He left, and she became hysterical and I struck her a single blow and she fell and hit her head on the fireplace. That was all. I did it, and I did it alone. I concealed the car, and her body, and her luggage. All hidden. Safely hidden. Until you came back."

"Come down, Dr Partridge." Thackeray's voice sounded desperate now and Laura could see that he was inching forward imperceptibly towards the senior tutor. "Come down and we can talk about this rationally."

"They should never have admitted young women to the college, you know," Partridge said, his voice rising again. "They've brought nothing but trouble. Undergraduates, wives, secretaries, none of them to be trusted, all of them harpies and whores. Nothing but trouble from the beginning to the end."

Laura suddenly realised, as she had not before, that Magnus Partridge was mad and her fear for his safety transferred itself suddenly to Thackeray.

"Michael," she said. "Keep away from him."

Whether Partridge heard her warning they never knew but he turned towards Thackeray at that moment and siezed hold of his sweater, pulling him alongside him close against the low stone balustrade, which reached barely to the height of a tall man's thighs. For a moment the two men struggled on the edge of the abyss before Thackeray broke free of Partridge's manic grip, stumbling to his knees as he was forced to abandon his attempt to pull the senior tutor back over the balustrade. He watched in despair as Partridge fell, his thin scream lost in the blaring music from the galloping horses just below. Laura rushed to the balustrade and looked down at the crowd, which was gathering around the spread-eagled body on the pavement close to a hotdog stall and all she could think was how affronted Magnus Partridge would have been to have witnessed the full banality of his own death.

For a moment, Thackeray remained kneeling with his head on the cold stone. Cautiously, Laura reached out and took his hand.

"It's over," Laura said. "You did your best."

"A rookie constable could have made a better job of talking him out of it than I did," Thackeray said.

"He wanted to do it. You couldn't have stopped him. At least he didn't take you with him," she said. Behind them they heard heavy footfalls on the stairs as the reinforcements they had summoned finally arrived.

"Here comes the cavalry," Laura said. "Come on, Michael. You got your man."

"Oh, no," Thackeray said, getting slowly to his feet. "I don't think I did that."

Thackeray and Laura walked back to St Frideswide's slowly the next morning, drained by hours of questions and statement-taking as Thames Valley's murder investigation swung into action. The decomposing body in the crypt had by now been identified as that of Emma Capstick, the bloodstain Thackeray had painstakingly preserved from Mark Harrison's now burnt-out room had been sent for analysis, the small blue Peugeot had been extricated from Magnus Partridge's lock-up garage and carried off to the police pound for forensic examination, and both of them had been dressed down by a senior Thames valley officer for concealing Jancie McLeod at Friddies.

"I told them she wasn't safe in the hospital," Laura said indignantly, as they threaded their way through the crowds of shoppers in Cornmarket.

"She's apparently agreed to go into rehab'," Thackeray said abstractedly. "I think the drug squad's more exotic plans for her have been jumped on from a great height after I made myself even more unpopular by complaining. She'll probably end up in the same hospital as Penny Harrison. Kevin Mower would say they probably deserve each other."

"That's cruel," Laura protested.

Thackeray shrugged.

"Penny Harrison's lucky to be alive," he said. "She lost a hell of a lot of blood but most of the cuts were superficial apparently. But she needs psychiatric treatment just as much as Jancie does."

"What a mess," Laura said. "Let's go home, shall we? I think I've had enough of the dreaming spires. More like nightmare towers, really."

"Not until I've seen Hugh Greenaway," Thackeray said, as they threaded their way through the shrouded stalls which filled St Giles with the silent ghosts of the raucous night before. Only a small children's roundabout, all bright coloured cars and spaceships, spun aimlessly at one end of the street, with not a child in sight. Close to the college gates, the spot where Magnus Partridge had fallen was still cordoned off with blue and white police tape and at the gate the head porter was flanked by a uniformed police officer who looked askance at them both until Malcolm Richards nodded them through with an unfriendly look in his eye.

"I get the impression they'll never welcome you back," Laura said. "I'll pack up my stuff while you go and make your farewells. I shouldn't imagine you'll be very long."

Hugh Greenaway was sitting at his desk surrounded by paper-work when the housekeeper at the Lodgings showed Thackeray into the room. He looked pale and gaunt and there was little warmth in his perfunctory hand-clasp.

"I didn't think you'd come," he said. "The damage you have done is immeasurable."

"What was it King Charles said?" Thackeray asked. "Never make a defence or an apology before you are accused? Just what is it I stand accused of, Dr Greenaway, which couldn't with more justice be laid at the door of the college itself? Uncovering the unacceptable, which Magnus Partridge claims he committed murder to conceal?"

"Claims? I thought the man confessed?" Greenaway looked genuinely surprised at Thackeray's choice of phrase.

"Oh, he confessed all right," Thackeray said. "Loyal to the last, your Dr Partridge. Loyal to the death, in fact, and I blame myself for that. I should have been able to talk him down off that roof, but I let emotion get in the way. But you and I know it was all a sham anyway, don't we?"

"I don't know what you mean, Michael," Greenaway said. "I understand that you were upset last night by what happened to Penny Harrison. That was an appalling episode. Quite appalling in the personal sense, of course, but also because of the effect it had on the celebrations. I was relieved to learn that she was not as seriously hurt as we'd at first thought."

"I'm sure you were," Thackeray said. "The number of deaths here must be becoming an embarrassment."

Greenaway got up from his desk and Thackeray suddenly realised how the overnight catastrophe had aged him. His walk had lost its jauntiness and his shoulders were uncharacteristically slumped. He waved Thackeray into an armchair and sat down himself on the other side of a coffee table.

"It wasn't easy to come back here and take over the college," he said. "I knew there would be problems, but I had no inkling that they would turn out to be anything like this, the systematic fraud, Harrison's disappearance, and now a murder, a suidice . . ."

"It won't wash, Hugh," Thackeray said, his own expression bleak. "Tell me, who was Liz Selby's tutor?"

Greenaway looked startled at this change of tack.

"Why, I was. Didn't you know?"

"No," Thackeray said. "I didn't even know she was reading history. I was preoccupied with finals that year."

241

"You're still obsessed with that death. It's ancient history now," Greenaway said irritably.

"Not so ancient, as it's turned out. Did you know she was being sexually harrassed by Mark Harrison?" Thackeray persisted. "Did she tell you that in your cosy one-to-one sessions?"

"Not that I recall," Greenaway said.

"It's not something you would forget, surely? The first female students? Surely that would be what you were all looking out for, to make sure they settled in satisfactorily? To make sure the college dinosaurs adjusted and didn't make their lives a misery?"

"She didn't tell me," Greenaway snapped. "She never mentioned harrassment, rape . . . Just what are you trying to say?"

Thackeray looked at him coldly.

"I still believe that Harrison killed her. He chased her up the tower that night and she went over the edge. Most likely pushed. When I think back to the inquest it's obvious Magnus Partridge knew. But you? That I didn't want to believe."

Greenaway shook his head and glanced away and Thackeray knew that Liz Selby had sought help from him in vain.

"You let Harrison get away with it," he said. "And because he got away with murder then, he reckoned he could get away with killing Emma Capstick as well. The blood was in his room. You saw it before someone conveniently set the place alight. I don't believe for one moment that a frail elderly man like Magnus Partridge could kill a healthy young woman like Emma Capstick with a single blow. But Harrison? The great rugger bugger? The unreconstructed philanderer? Magnus may have helped him cover up what happened, just as he – and the rest of you – covered up for him the first time, but I am absolutely sure that it was Harrison who hit her. Partridge didn't even know that she fell in the bathroom. He thought she had hit her head on the fireplace. And it must have been

Harrison who carried the body into the crypt. Partridge could not have done that alone, though the silly old fool was going to try and move her and her baggage when he thought we were getting too close. He can't have had any idea what two months do to a body. And then there's the little detail of Emma's car."

"Emma's car?" Greenaway said, as if bemused.

"Emma's car was neatly parked in a small garage at the end of a narrow yard. A skilled driver would have had difficulty reversing it into that space without scratching the paintwork. Magnus Partridge can't drive."

"Partridge confessed," Greenaway said.

"Conveniently," Thackeray said.

"The police seem to believe it."

"Only because they can't bring themselves to believe me."

"Because the rest of what you're saying is just guesswork," Greenaway objected.

"Deduction," Thackeray said flatly. "You could ask the police running the murder inquiry to check it out? They'd listen to you."

Greenaway got up and went to the window, gazing out at the quadrangle still patrolled by uniformed police officers and disfigured by parked vehicles and blue and white tape. He said nothing and as the silence lengthened Thackeray got up and walked to the door of the master's study.

"I'll be interested to see whether a call goes out through Interpol to trace Mark Harrison," he said over his shoulder as he left. "I won't hold my breath."

Chapter Twenty One

When they got back to Bradfield later that afternoon, Michael Thackeray dropped Laura at the *Gazette*, where she was overdue, and went straight to his own office. There he found DI Jackie Bairstow still in possession of his desk, nodded at her and slammed the door before striding up the stairs two at a time to see Superintendent Jack Longley.

He had driven back from Oxford too fast, furious with himself more than with Greenaway for failing to persuade anyone to pursue Emma Capstick's death any further but even more furious that he had allowed his disillusion with Greenaway to affect him so deeply. He was, he thought, far too old for hero-worship, and yet a sort of hero was what his former tutor had once been and he was surprised to discover how hard it was to let that admiration go. Almost as hard to bear as the knowledge that Mark Harrison would be allowed to prosper unmolested in whatever quiet backwater he had elected to start his life again. Harrison he wished in hell.

Laura had been largely silent on the journey back, evidently unsure of his mood.

"Let them stew," she had offered at one point. "The college, the master, the lot. They'll not hack it in the twenty-first century."

"Don't you believe it," Thackeray said. "They're survivors, every last one of them. They didn't get where they are today without perfecting the art of frustrating it all – riot, reformation, revolution, you name it, they've survived and flourished."

"The police will find Mark Harrison and bring him back," she said.

He accelerated into the fast lane with enough vehemence to ensure her silence for another twenty miles.

"No," he had said eventually and she had almost forgotten what she had said. "They won't. They won't even begin to look."

It was not until he was back at police headquarters that his frustration receded and then only because familiar faces brought familiar problems clambering over each other for attention. He knocked on Jack Longley's door with more than a little anxiety.

"I'm back," he announced rather unnecessarily when he had gained access to the sanctum.

"About bloody time," Longley said, glancing up from his paperwork. "Annoyed enough people down there, did you?"

"I suppose they've been bending your ear," Thackeray said.

"Some bloody southerner was on the blower at sparrow-fart," Longley said casually enough for Thackeray to realise with some relief that the bloody southerner had been wasting his breath. "Learn anything, did you, for all the brass we spent sending you?"

"Enough," Thackeray said shortly, although he was thinking more of what he had learned about St Frideswide's than the further shores of management theory.

"Aye, well, I'll get ma'am to pack her bags now you're back," Longley said, not bothering to hide his relief. "She's not added much to the clear-up rate or human resource management, or whatever it is they call it these days."

Thackeray allowed himself a faint smile. Longley's opinion of women officers was less than politically correct but he knew that at his age his prejudices were unlikely to be shifted. On a better day, he might have made a token protest on behalf of women officers, but today was not the day.

"How's Mower?" he asked. Longley sighed heavily.

"On the mend physically, I'm told," he said.

"And . . . ?" Thackeray ventured, with a sense of foreboding, but it was not apparently Mower's psychological well-being which concerned the superintendent.

"This complaint we've had against Mower? You're up to speed on that, are you?"

"More or less," Thackeray said.

"Aye, well, you may need to be. They've lost track of Carl Hegerty, so it'll go no further till he turns up," Longley said. "So that's something to be thankful for, I suppose. On the other hand, Val Ridley is mustard keen to track Hegerty down on account of she's convinced that it was him who attacked Kelly James."

"The one who was raped?"

"Allegedly," Longley said sourly. "That doesn't seem to be one hundred per cent certain."

"I'll talk to Val," Thackeray said. "Anything else I should know about?"

Longley gave him a long look.

"Just mind your back for a bit," he said eventually. "County are watching our every move."

"Sir," Thackeray said thoughtfully, hoping that no speed cameras had caught him that afternoon on the M1. He made his way back downstairs and opened his office door for the second time. Jackie Bairstow was packing her briefcase and obviously preparing to leave.

"I was planning to get away early tonight anyway," she said by way of less than convincing explanation. "I've left all the files in order and I expect everyone will be keen to fill you in on on-going investigations."

"No problems?" Thackeray asked.

"Not really," DI Bairstow said dismissively. "Except for Kevin Mower, of course. You need to watch him. He's like an unexploded bomb."

"I'll see what I can do to defuse him," Thackeray said.

"Disposal might be a better bet," Jackie Bairstow said briskly as she pulled on her coat. "ASAP."

In the CID office downstairs several of his detectives welcomed him back warmly enough when he made his

246

entrance, but Val Ridley, sitting at a desk in one corner of the room, watched him warily as he approached.

"Good to see you back, sir," she said cautiously.

"I've been reading the files. Carl Hegerty?" Thackeray asked. "Do we have any idea where he is?"

"The DCI said there was nothing more we could do with the case, but I spoke to Lorraine James's son – the mixed race lad who's in care – and he reckons that his sister and her boyfriend may be holed up in a caravan up beyond Arnedale where he and his father used to go fishing years ago."

"And would Carl know where that was?" Thackeray asked, seeing the anxiety in Val's eyes.

"Possibly," she said.

"In your judgement, Val, is he dangerous?"

"Oh, yes," she said. "Kevin only got his retaliation in first with that one."

"Then we'd better take a look," Thackeray said. "They may be at risk. Get hold of her mother and see if she can come with us. And I guess you'd better tell social services what we're up to, though I don't suppose they'll have any one free."

"Do they ever?" Val said.

Thackeray collected Lorraine James from her flat on the Heights, winced at the sight of her bruised face and the stitches still visible under the hairline, and settled her in the front seat of his car, with Val Ridley in the rear.

This time, with the ghost of a dead detective constable looking over his shoulder, Thackeray was taking no chances. He had arranged to meet two car-loads of uniformed officers from Arnedale at a farm that let a few dilapidated caravans parked on the banks of the river Maze during the summer months. The farmer's wife, ruddy-faced and heavily pregnant, looked at them in amazement when they arrived in force.

"They're just kids," she said. "A black lad and a white lass. She's been up here before with her brother, years back. He were coloured an'all so I reckoned maybe this lad were a relation an'all. They rented for a week but said they'd probably not be there that long. It's the end o't'season now and I reckon we'll clear the field before back-end. It's not really worth the trouble for what we can charge for them old caravans. Hardly pays to have the chemical toilets emptied."

Thackeray led the way down a rutted track to the flat meadows by the river and it soon became obvious that the rented caravan was occupied and peacefully at that. Val Ridley and Lorraine James followed close behind with the local sergeant and a couple of uniformed officers. There was a thread of smoke coming from a small fire close to the door, and the sound of rock music carried clearly on the breeze.

"It looks as though we're in time," Thackeray said to the sergeant leading the local contingent. "I may have wasted your time, I'm afraid."

He banged on the door of the van and it was opened quickly by the tall dreadlocked figure of Gary Miller.

"Oh, shit," he said and then, as he took in the scale of the force outside, he shrugged resignedly. "At least you're not bloody Carl. How did you find us, any road?"

"Not difficult," Thackeray said shortly. "You're lucky Carl didn't manage it as fast as we did. Come on, let's have you in the car, Gary. I want to talk to Kelly and her mother."

"I ain't done anything wrong," Miller said, glancing behind him to where a plaintive voice could be heard asking him to shut the door. "She's got a bad cold," the boy said. "I were going to' village to get her summat for it."

"You'd have had your work cut out. There's no shop for ten miles or more, lad," the local sergeant said, not unkindly. "Come on. Let's be having you."

Gary did not argue and Thackeray followed the two women into the caravan where they found Kelly James lying on one of the bunks, shivering even though she had huddled under a couple of blankets. When she caught sight of her mother she stared in horror at her bruised face for a moment and then turned away and buried her face close to the wall.

"Kelly, love," Lorraine said.

"Sod off," the girl said. "I've had it wi'you. I just want to be wi'Gary now."

Thackeray glanced from mother to daughter to Val Ridley, who looked as if she were about to speak. Thackeray shook his head imperceptibly.

"That's not an option, Kelly," he said harshly, addressing the back of Kelly's head. "You're too young for that. It's against the law." He was aware that both the women were watching him with something akin to shock in their eyes but he ignored them.

"If you keep on like this you'll end up in care and Gary'll end up in gaol."

For a moment, there was total silence, broken only by the sigh of the wind in the trees outside. Then Kelly turned towards them, struggling into a sitting position, panic in her eyes.

"Mu-um," she wailed. Her face was wet with tears. Val Ridley handed Lorraine a handkerchief and the girl's mother glanced anxiously at Thackeray before she sat on the edge of the bunk and wipe her daughter's eyes and nose.

"I'll teck her home," Lorraine siad. "I'll look after her . . ."

"How can you do that?" Thackeray asked. "You can't protect yourself from Hegerty. How can you protect her?"

Kelly touched her mother's face tentatively.

"You let him thump you again," she said, her voice husky but full of accusation. "Why'd you let him thump you again?"

"The same reason you let him hurt you?" Thackeray asked Kelly. "Neither of you can live without him? Is that the truth?"

"No it's fucking not," Kelly screamed, making them all jump. "I hate Carl. I hate him."

"So he did hurt you," Thackeray said. "You and your mother. How badly, Kelly? What did Carl do to you?"

249

"No, no," Lorraine said, trying to get her arms around the girl, who wriggled away to the end of the bunk where she sat hugging her knees and rocking to and fro and moaning softly.

"So what do we do then, Lorraine?" Thackeray asked more gently. "Take you both back? Charge Gary with under-age sex and let Carl carry on where he left off because no-one will make a complaint against him? Is that what you want?"

Lorraine fingered the stitches on her hairline and winced slightly, refusing to meet Thackeray's eyes. Suddenly Kelly wriggled up the bunk and took her mother's hand.

"Get rid of him, Mum," she said. "Please say you want to get rid of him. Please."

"How long would he get?" Lorraine whispered.

"For assault?" Thackeray asked impatiently. "A year, two maybe. Out in twelve months."

"It's not long, is it? I want him away for a long time."

"I can do that for you, Mum," Kelly said. "If that's what you want I can put him away for a very long time. Is that what you really really want?"

"Yes," Lorraine said and this time the girl allowed her to take her in her arms.

"Did Carl rape you, Kelly?" Val Ridley asked, glancing at Thackeray before she spoke.

"Of course he fucking did," Kelly said. "He came out looking for me that night, didn't he? An'it weren't the first time."

Lorraine groaned as her daughter buried her face in her shoulder again while Thackeray and Val Ridley exchanged a look of triumph.

"Gotcha," Val breathed.

Thackeray was back in Bradfield, well-satisfied with an afternoon's work which had seen Hegerty, who had been found skulking in woodland quite close to the caravan where Kelly James had taken refuge, charged with rape and grievous

250

bodily harm by the time Laura Ackroyd finished work that evening. He was waiting for her in the reception area of the *Gazette* and her face lit up when she saw him

"This is unexpected," she said. "You're free early."

"You should be pleased," he said. "I've just seen a cell door slam on Carl Hegerty. Lorraine and Kelly James have made statements that should put him away for a very long time. It's the first time for weeks I've felt I've got something right."

"Great," Laura said. "So where are we going to celebrate?"

"I seem to have been laying too many ghosts lately," Thackeray said. "I thought you might like to show me this flat where you're so keen to make a new start."

"It'll be a pleasure," Laura said.